Fatal
Introductions

Milford House Mysteries

edited by
JC Gatlin

MILFORD
HOUSE

an imprint of Sunbury Press, Inc.
Mechanicsburg, PA USA

MILFORD HOUSE

an imprint of Sunbury Press, Inc.
Mechanicsburg, PA USA

For information about special discounts for bulk purchases, please contact Sunbury Press Orders Dept. at (855) 338-8359 or orders@sunburypress.com.

To request one of our authors for speaking engagements or book signings, please contact Sunbury Press Publicity Dept. at publicity@sunburypress.com.

FIRST MILFORD HOUSE PRESS EDITION: June 2025

Set in Adobe Garamond Pro | Interior design by Crystal Devine | Cover by Lawrence Knorr | Edited by Debra Reynolds.

Publisher's Cataloging-in-Publication Data
Names: Gatlin, JC, et al.
Title: Fatal introductions : Milford House mysteries.
Description: First trade paperback edition. | Mechanicsburg, PA : Milford House Press, 2025.
Summary: Fatal Introductions is a collection of 20 mystery and thriller short stories written by 21 authors. With each short, you'll be introduced to the main characters featured in their own novel or series.
Identifiers: ISBN : 979-8-88819-338-9 (paperback).
Subjects: FICTION / Anthologies (multiple authors) | FICTION / Mystery & Detective / General | FICTION / Mystery & Detective / Historical.

Designed in the USA
0 1 1 2 3 5 8 13 21 34 55

For the Love of Books!

The following mystery, suspense, thriller, and historical mystery short stories are introductions to the main characters of novels and series available at Milford House Press.

The novels referenced after each short story are available wherever fine books are sold; including online, at your favorite local bookstore, and at the publisher's website: Sunburypress.com.

CONTENTS

MYSTERY & SUSPENSE

THRILLER

HISTORICAL MYSTERY

MYSTERY & SUSPENSE

MISSING LETTERS:
A H_NGM_N Mystery

BY JC GATLIN

A scream caused Tori Younger to lower her microphone and look up, the sun in her eyes. A woman, her arms and legs flailing, plummeted to the outside patio and smashed into the hors d'oeuvres table near the pool.

Several seconds passed before Tori realized what she'd witnessed.

Dozens of hotel guests stood in silent shock. When the first shriek rang out, people scrambled in all directions. More horrified cries followed with frantic intensity.

Tori turned to her cameraman. The red light on the camera remained steady. Good, RJ was still filming. However, the portly, middle-aged man she'd been interviewing fled into the hysterical crowd heading back into the hotel.

No matter. She pointed toward the broken body lying atop the jumbo shrimp. "Get a sweeping shot of the hors d'oeuvres table, but don't focus on anything the network can't air."

RJ panned the camera across the hotel patio, where people bumped into each other, knocking down competition easels and overturning a judges' table. A few curious onlookers gawked at the jumper.

Tori tilted her head, following the *Montague's* façade all the way up its ten stories. Had the woman jumped from the roof or a lower balcony? A flash caught her eye, like a signal. Then another. Was somebody up there communicating to a person down here? She turned to the building across from the pool, then back to the quick bursts of light.

RJ tapped her shoulder and motioned as dazed hotel staff struggled to direct the crowd. "They're clearing the area."

The two moved through the thinning cluster of people. Stepping over pieces of crab cakes, stuffed mushrooms, and blood spatter, she took in the scene.

During the fall, the woman had gotten tangled in the *National Hangman Tournament* banner, and the blue and white vinyl now partially draped her upper body. A small mercy. Tufts of bloody blond hair were visible along the upper edge of the sign. Mangled legs jutted out at inhuman angles. One foot was bare, the other twisted but still covered in an ankle-high boot. Her right arm dangled over the table edge, the hand's manicured fingernails hovering above a fragmented gold watchband lying on the concrete.

Tori had never seen anything like it. In the four years she'd been covering cheerful, frivolous community events for SEBC News, her most compelling story was interviewing witnesses after the First National Bank was robbed. Now, she felt alternately repulsed and grateful. If this story got picked up nationally, maybe she'd be promoted to investigative reporter before she turned thirty.

Her thoughts were interrupted by the hotel security manager, a balding man dressed in a black suit and mirrored sunglasses, blocking the corpse. He waved his arms, urging them to move on. "Head to the parking lot," he instructed. "The police are on their way."

Sirens grew louder.

Tori didn't move. She eyed the gruesome scene a final time, willing the details into her memory.

"Ma'am . . ." The security manager's voice deepened.

Complying, Tori and RJ moved away from the body. They passed the overturned judges' table, and her heel caught a piece of paper. She bent her leg to remove the trash.

The security manager yelled, "Not telling you again."

Tori shouted back, "We're going, we're going," and followed RJ through the gate. In the parking lot, she studied the discarded customer satisfaction card that had caught on her shoe. On the back, a handwritten note requested "Meet me in Room 902."

* * *

Tori reported on location in front of the *Grand Montague Hotel* as police corralled guests and Hangman tournament players onto the circle drive. After she completed the segment and lowered her mic, she flagged RJ to cut.

"We need a better spot." He lifted the camera off his shoulder and squinted. "The sun's causing a lens flare."

She'd just started working with this cameraman, a guy in his early twenties who still wore T-shirts and cargo shorts, compared to her on-air-proper dark blue jacket and skirt and perfectly coifed auburn hair. But, despite his age and relaxed professionalism, he'd proven dependable, even in high-stress situations.

And a dead body qualified as one.

A young man called out from the hotel entrance and jogged toward them by the curb. "Police are moving all press to the east parking lot." He had an incredibly tanned face, an expensive haircut, and a perfectly tailored suit. When they acknowledged him, he grinned with equally impossibly-white teeth. "You got that RJ, you fugly scrub?"

"And there he is." RJ's head bobbed over the side of his camera, and he chortled. "Creed. My least favorite *kept man* on the planet."

The fellow flipped RJ the bird and addressed Tori. "Other news stations are setting up."

"Creed, Creed, Creed," Tori said playfully. She would never call him a gigolo, but the guy had scored financial security in the considerably older Kathleen Montague, the eccentric millionaire who had restored and reopened the hotel. Now he could be their ace card. "Can't you sneak us inside? If we could report from the roof—"

"The roof?" Creed flinched and brought his hands to his chest like he'd been shot. "No way."

"How about I get you on air? After this suicide, the *Montague* needs your thousand-watt smile." Tori stroked his ego. "You're dashing, and the camera loves you."

He pointed toward the east building. "Sorry. It's out of my hands."

RJ set down his camera. "Don't make me bring up NOLA?"

"New Orleans?" Creed thought a moment. Tori watched the two men communicate in their indecipherable bro-code language.

RJ draped an arm around his buddy's shoulder. "You owe me. Remember?"

Creed slipped a white passkey to RJ, exposing pale skin around his wrist. "This'll get you into the delivery entrance. Take the service elevator up to the roof." He winked. "But now we're even."

Tori thanked him as RJ picked up his camera. They rounded the side of the hotel and used the passkey to enter a door marked "Deliveries Only." The hallway through the kitchen took them to a service elevator.

As the elevator passed the fifth floor, then the sixth, Tori asked, "What happened in New Orleans?"

"What didn't happen?" RJ smirked.

Tori shrugged and changed the subject. "I saw someone on the roof."

"Wait a second." His expression stilled and grew serious. "You mean after the jumper . . ."

"Right after," Tori clarified. "At least, I think I saw someone. There were these flashes, several of them, like a signal." The elevator came to a stop.

On the rooftop, cops walked among the ventilation units and HVAC systems. An officer by a satellite dish warned the pair that this vicinity was off-limits.

"It's okay." A large man stood at the short wall along the roof's edge. "Let 'em through."

Tori placed the bearded man in his sixties as the recently retired Police Chief Lansing.

"No filming though," he added.

RJ lowered his camera, and they crossed the flat rooftop. He nudged her. "You know the chief of police?"

"We go way back. I covered his retirement party last week." She shook Chief Lansing's hand. "I wanted to get you on-air during the tournament, but you disappeared on me."

He nodded. "I was helping secure the area until my old team got here. They still kinda follow my lead, you know."

Tori peeked over the perimeter wall. The view of the patio and pool below made her head spin. A flicker of apprehension coursed through her. "Was it suicide?"

Chief Lansing smoothed the hair on his chin. "Too early in the investigation."

"Do you have any idea who the jumper was? Off the record, of course."

"Not yet." His left eyebrow rose a fraction. "Not like they're telling me much."

Tori gazed down again, and this time was able to focus. An M.E. team was bagging the body and positioning a gurney. Next to her, RJ had his camera aimed at the activity below.

When the chief didn't object, she continued. "Was the woman's boot up here? Or her purse?"

"No. Personally, I don't see her jumping from the roof," he said. "How would a guest even have access?"

The elevator doors opened, and a tall, birdlike woman stepped out. As she walked, large silver and gold bracelets on her arms clanged and glinted in the sunlight. Tori recalled seeing the wealthy Kathleen Montague in photos but had never met her.

Kathleen must have recognized them too. "What are you people doing up here?"

RJ lowered his camera.

"I'm Tori Younger, with SEBC News," Tori started. "I was covering the National Hangman Championship when—"

"I know who you are," Kathleen spat. "My question was what, not who."

"We were—"

"I want you to explain how you obtained access to the roof," Kathleen interrupted.

Tori and RJ exchanged a look. Neither of them wanted to throw his buddy under the bus.

Kathleen's stare drilled into them. "Creed gave you access, didn't he?"

"We got up here on our own accord," Tori insisted. "Creed wasn't involved."

Kathleen angrily hustled the duo to the elevator and glared at them until the doors shut.

Inside the car, RJ muttered under his breath. "I can't believe Creed married that old bat. I hope the boat is worth it." He reached for the elevator panel, but Tori stopped him.

"Lansing doesn't think the woman jumped from the roof."

"Okay, Clickbait," RJ teased. "I'll bite."

"She may have taken the big leap from Room 902." Tori showed him the customer satisfaction card. "I think she dropped this when she fell."

He read the note on the back. "You took this from the patio?"

"It's not like it's the suicide note." She pressed the button for floor nine.

At Room 902, RJ used the passkey. Inside, bedcovers and pillows lay scattered on the floor. The bedside table lamp was overturned. Water ran in the bathroom. The balcony doors were open wide, and the drapes billowed in the breeze.

RJ whistled.

"Don't touch anything," she cautioned.

He lifted his camera and filmed the room. She stepped onto the balcony. A patio chair was toppled. The missing boot lay discarded next to a large bronze bracelet.

"I'd better call Chief Lansing."

Police officers were in the room within minutes, Lansing still with them.

Kathleen and Creed filed in after. Her face tightened with hostility. "What are you still doing here?"

Lansing nodded. "I'm afraid Ms. Montague is right. You'll need to wait in the lobby."

"We're leaving," Tori said as RJ stopped filming. She observed the nightstand and the desk, searching for the missing purse. She noted the lamp again. How was it not broken in the struggle? She turned to Lansing. "We didn't touch anything, and it's pretty clear that woman didn't commit suicide."

The chief gazed at the disorder, then at Kathleen. "Who checked into this room?"

"I'd have to refer to our records." Kathleen lifted a questioning eyebrow to Creed.

"The guest's name was Jeri Riddle," came a voice by the door.

The hotel security manager, wearing his dark sunglasses inside, leaned against the doorframe, watching. "And she has been identified as the woman on the patio."

Creed gasped, stuttering. "J-Jeri?" He choked on the name, brushing past Kathleen, his eyes wide, mouth trembling. "Are you sure?"

Kathleen's posture grew rigid and resentful. "Jeri Riddle? That whore is back?"

Creed stumbled backward to the edge of the bed; his head lowered.

Kathleen turned her back to him. "You told me that was over."

A detective entered, addressing the room. "Everybody who ain't a cop, out . . . and that includes you, Lansing."

As the others took the service elevator, Tori and RJ were alone in the main elevator. "Something is bugging me." Her eyes darkened. "Did that room feel staged to you?"

He held the camera between them. "I don't know. Looked like a couple of MMA fighters went a few rounds."

"But the perfectly placed boot," Tori continued. "The overturned but unbroken lamp. Something isn't right. It all seems too—"

"—messy?"

"—flawless." She contemplated the note written on the back of the customer satisfaction card. "Did you ever read *Who Smoked the Trophy Husband?* It's a true crime about an older, wealthy socialite who murdered her young husband for cheating on her. What if, in this case, the elderly wife murdered the cheating trophy husband's girlfriend?"

"You think Creed is a trophy husband?"

"Not my point . . . but I might, if I was an elderly millionaire," she said. "I would forever be on the defensive before some young hardbody stole him away."

They found the lobby busy with police activity. Officers taped off the patio and pool area as the M.E. team wheeled out the black body bag.

"The thing that bothers *me* about the room is . . ." RJ muttered as he filmed the action. "Why are the Men in Black investigating?"

"Come again?"

"The dude in the black suit and sunglasses lurking in the corner." RJ panned the camera. "Looks like a Men In Black agent hunting aliens from a Will Smith movie."

"That's hotel security," she explained. "Not Will Smith."

"Either way, Not-Will-Smith is way suspicious."

As if on cue, Tori spotted the hotel security manager in the crowd. "Don't look now, but Not-Will-Smith just made us." She patted RJ's arm.

He lowered the camera.

The hotel security manager rushed them with Kathleen in tow.

"You're still filming?" Kathleen wagged a finger, rattling the chunky gold bracelets on her arm. "Must I have security remove you? Or perhaps I should call the mayor, whom I know personally."

"No need to bother the mayor." RJ returned the camera straps to his shoulder.

Tori planted her feet. "What were you doing during the Hangman Tournament?"

Kathleen raised a penciled eyebrow. "Excuse me?"

Tori pressed. "Where exactly were you when your husband's mistress fell to her death?"

"I'm done with this conversation." Kathleen huffed and nodded to her security manager. "Handle this."

Before Not-Will Smith could react, Tori inclined her head in surrender, and she and RJ headed out. "I take it she really wants us gone."

"Like a musty smell," RJ said, pushing through the revolving doors.

Outside, the police kept onlookers jammed behind barricades. Officers interviewed witnesses. News vans and reporters filled the parking lot.

RJ stood beside Tori, also taking in the media. "WGBTV-News. ABC-Action News. MSNBC . . ."

". . . they're all here," Tori finished, realizing she actually *was* in the middle of a national story. "We go back on air in a few minutes. What do we know about the victim?"

RJ pulled out his phone and began typing. "Let's see what we can dig up."

"Wait a sec." Tori pointed to the lobby where Creed was lugging two suitcases and golf clubs through the crowd. He plopped them down by the center fountain. Irons and drivers spilled from the bag. Tori smiled. "Let's talk to your buddy about his girl on the side."

RJ's mouth twisted with exasperation. "No way he's giving us an interview."

"It never hurts to ask." Tori marched back through the revolving doors.

RJ chased after her. "He just lost his girlfriend, and probably his boat. You know Kathleen is on the phone with a divorce attorney."

"Then we'll tread lightly." She headed for the center fountain.

Balancing the camera with one arm, he reached for her with the other. "He's one of my oldest friends. What are you going to say?"

"Let's find out." She broke free of his grip and called to Creed. When he lifted his chin, she softened her voice. "Have you ever read *Who Smoked the Trophy Husband?*"

Creed gave her a blank stare as he sat on the edge of the fountain beside his suitcases and golf clubs.

RJ set down his camera. "She's calling you a trophy husband, but don't take it personally. What she means is, do you think your cougar of a wife killed your girlfriend?"

So much for treading lightly.

"We think Kathleen may have intercepted a note from Jeri." Tori handed Creed the customer satisfaction card.

"What is this?" He scanned the card and handed it back. "Ain't Jeri's handwriting."

Tori's jaw clenched. "We just assumed—"

"I don't know who wrote that, but it wasn't Jeri." Annoyance colored Creed's face. "And why would she check into a room? We never got together at the hotel."

RJ sat beside his buddy. "What can you tell us about her?"

Creed didn't answer right away. "Well . . . she was hot. And sweet."

Typical male. "So is barbeque sauce," Tori grumbled.

"Was she rich?" RJ asked off-handedly as he typed on his phone.

"Nope. Flat broke." Creed ran a nervous hand through his hair. "But she was coming into significant coin, and she was gonna buy me a truck. And replace my *Richard Mille*." He raised his hand, showing off the pale skin where his watch used to be. "She kept saying as soon as she scored, we're gonna run away to Bermuda."

"Do you know what she was doing at the hotel?" Tori watched the yellow police tape ripple outside on the patio. "Was she participating in the tournament?"

"She just showed up." Creed stared back at them with equal confusion. "She thought I invited her, so I told her to stay outta sight till the tournament was over."

RJ didn't look up from his phone. "You ever run a background check?"

Creed shrugged. "Why would I?"

"Because she was recently paroled." RJ showed Creed his screen. "Search her name, and the first thing that comes up is a mug shot."

Creed's mouth fell open. "Huh?"

He reminded Tori of a wounded animal. "You really didn't know?"

Creed's frown deepened. He shoved his hands into his pockets and bowed his head. "I never really got past her, you know, hotness."

Tori took the phone from RJ and scanned the search results. "She spent two years in prison for a bank heist." She looked back at Creed. "Did Kathleen know?"

Kathleen herself answered, making Tori jump. "I knew all about that tramp's history. And I warned you to stay away from her."

Not-Will Smith stood beside Kathleen, his arms crossed, shaking his head.

Kathleen pressed her lips together, probably doing her best to hold her temper. "I'm sure the gold digger had a plot to bilk me out of more money."

The security manager gripped Creed's arm and forced him to his feet. "All right, pretty boy, the free ride is over."

"Don't think you're getting your mitts on my fortune either." Each word came out of Kathleen's mouth spaced, almost inflectionless. "The prenup stands."

RJ picked up his camera as Creed slid his nine-iron back into the bag.

Tori told them to put everything down. She turned to Kathleen. "You never answered my question. What were you doing during the Hangman Tournament?"

Kathleen waved a dismissive hand. Her heavy bracelets glinted in the bright lobby lights. "Exactly what are you implying?"

"Let me put it another way," Tori said. "Who booked Room 902? I doubt Jeri made the reservation."

A detective joined them. "Those are some excellent questions we'd like answered as well." He held up an evidence bag to reveal the large bronze bracelet. "Does this belong to you, Ms. Montague?"

Kathleen's razor-sharp eyebrows shot up. "My third husband gave me that bracelet for our anniversary." She reached, but the detective held the bag from her grasp. "Where'd you find it?"

The detective gave her a suspicious squint. "In Room 902."

Another officer emerged behind the check-in counters, waving a clutch purse in an evidence bag. "We found this in Ms. Montague's office. Jeri Riddle's driver's license is inside."

The detective cuffed Kathleen's hands behind her back. "We're placing you under arrest for suspicion of murder."

"This is ludicrous." Kathleen's thin lips pulled back in a snarl. "Wait until my attorneys get done with you. I'll sue for unlawful arrest."

Chief Lansing stood in the background among the police officers. He gave Tori a subtle smile, a quiet thank you for her assistance. She turned to RJ, who was already filming Kathleen being hauled outside.

Satisfied with her scoop, Tori counted down to their live, on-location coverage.

* * *

At a quarter to midnight, Tori curled up on her couch, surrounded by bookcases filled with true crime books. She swiped through news clips on her tablet. Reports of the murder appeared on every streaming service, but only Tori managed an interview with retired Police Chief Lansing. And only Tori broke the news about the victim's criminal record. Still, her pride dulled with a sense of unease.

Jeri Riddle's incarceration lingered in Tori's mind. She felt like she was playing in that Hangman Tournament but hadn't solved the word. A crucial letter was still missing. The wealthy hotel owner, with everything to lose, pushing the broke, convicted felon off a balcony just didn't spell M-U-R-D-E-R.

She called RJ, and his sleepy face filled her tablet screen. "Okay Spoiler Alert," he said. "Lay it on me."

"Creed said Jeri was coming into *significant coin*." On the screen, Tori opened the hotel footage RJ had taken. "He had to be referring to the bank heist. That money was never recovered."

"He didn't know about the bank heist or Jeri's prison stint." RJ yawned, sounding impatient.

"Then who did?" Tori swiped through random clips of the tournament. She noticed Not-Will-Smith among the crowd, watching. "Could someone else have known and been blackmailing her?"

"Only if she already dug up the loot."

"Exactly." She brought up another clip: Creed in the lobby, talking to a guest. She zoomed in on his hand and hit pause. "What if Jeri had already retrieved that *coin*?"

"You think Not-Will-Smith was blackmailing her about the stolen loot?" RJ asked. "He coulda reserved a room in Jeri's name. Invited her to the tournament."

"He could have . . ." Tori focused on the frozen image of Creed holding a customer satisfaction card. "But he's not the only one."

"Don't start on Cree—"

Tori talked over him. "I saw a flash on the roof after Jeri fell. At first, I thought someone was signaling . . ." She recalled Jeri's body lying atop the hors d'oeuvres table. Her limp hand hovering above a gold watchband on the concrete. The missing letter revealed itself. "Do you still have that passkey?"

He perked up. "Don't start thinking what I think you're thinking."

She shot from the couch.

RJ's face filled the screen again. "We're not going back to the *Montague*. It's the middle of the night."

"The object that was flashing is still there," she said, slipping on her shoes. "Now, call Lansing. Let him know his old police team arrested the wrong person."

* * *

At one in the morning, Tori entered the *Montague* and paused. The pool and patio were still blocked with police tape, and the lobby was quiet. Not-Will-Smith waited by the elevator doors, presumably still on duty. She didn't want him to see her. And if Creed was still in the hotel, she needed to avoid him too. For now, at least.

Tori took the back service elevator to the rooftop and made her way to the wall that bordered the roof. Her hair blew in the night breeze. The city lights barely illuminated her path.

Leaning over the wall, she willed herself not to look down at the patio ten stories below. A narrow ledge, a foot below her, ran between decorative supports. She shooed away pigeons and stretched. Her hand scraped along the rough finish until her fingers brushed something solid. Something smooth. She grasped the object and righted herself.

In her palm was a gold watch face missing its wristband. An engraving on the back read: *Thank you for 30 years. Happy retirement.*

"Did you find what you were looking for?"

Tori spun around. She closed her fist around the watch. "I did."

Chief Lansing stood motionless several feet away.

Tori took a breath. "You pushed Jeri off the roof, not the balcony."

Lansing's smile was almost disarming. "I was up here hunting for that Rolex when you found me earlier." His blue eyes turned ice cold for a split second then calmed. "I was hoping you were going to tell me that you found evidence implicating Kathryn's boy toy or her security manager."

"To be honest, I was hoping that too." Tori slipped the watch into her pocket and removed the customer satisfaction card. Her hand trembled. "Earlier, you said you left the tournament to help secure the area. You'd already disappeared when I looked for you for an interview." She raised the card. "And this well-placed note was intended to lead the investigative detectives to the staged crime scene in Room 902."

Lansing made a tssk, tssk sound under his breath. "When I saw you had it, I figured you'd grab the headline and run. *Jealous wealthy hotel owner murders philandering husband's girlfriend.* Thus, diverting suspicion away from me."

"Suspicion for which crime though?" Tori forced confidence in her voice. "Murdering Jeri? Or your involvement in her bank heist? That money was never recovered. I suspect you know where the stash is hidden, don't you?"

He stepped nearer, closing the space between them. "Jeri contacted me as soon as she was paroled. Said she had evidence that the D.A. would find interesting. So, I invited her here, to her boyfriend's hotel, booked her a room with cash, and staged her untimely demise." He took another step closer. "I couldn't have her ruining my retirement."

Tori stumbled backward, bumping into the perimeter wall. She glanced over her shoulder. The height made her dizzy. The card blew out of her hand.

Lansing's disarming smile disintegrated. "I can't allow *you* to ruin my plan either."

He lunged.

She lost balance, felt herself falling back.

Before she understood what happened, a heavy TV camera whizzed past her ear and Lansing let out a loud "oomph." His unconscious body slumped and rolled away. Two strong hands gripped her wrist.

RJ's scruffy face met hers. He pulled her to her feet.

Tori glanced over the wall. The camera lay in pieces ten stories below.

"You think the city will reimburse me for a new one?" RJ asked, looking over the roof's edge with her.

"The confession," she whispered, shaking her head.

"I got Lansing's little speech, and the footage is already uploaded."

"We need to call the police."

"Creed's on it," RJ said. Far away, sirens wailed. He wrapped an arm around her shoulders and, together, they limped back to the elevators. "We're gonna score beaucoup ratings in the morning."

Tori couldn't help thinking about that investigative reporter position. She pushed the lobby button. "This may be the start of a very exciting career."

RJ cringed. "But no more dead bodies, okay?"

Tori grinned as the elevator doors closed. "I can't make any promises."

Follow Tori and RJ as they solve further mysteries
in the H_NGM_N series.

———•◎ ABOUT THE AUTHOR ◎•———

JC GATLIN

JC Gatlin is a mystery-suspense author in Tampa, FL. His mystery
novel, *H_NGM_N: Murder is the Word*, won the Royal Palm Literary
Award for Best Florida Mystery of 2019 and runner-up for Best
Book of 2019. In 2021, Sunbury Press published his award-winning
mystery, *Darkness Hides*. The follow-up in the *H_NGM_N* series was
published in 2025.

Learn more about JC at www.JCGatlin.com.

Dead Man's Melody

BY SHERRY KNOWLTON

"Dinnertime, Scout," Alexa called as she opened the door to an empty deck. Surprised to see her giant English mastiff missing from his usual spot, she stepped outside.

"Scout. Where are you?" she called, wincing at the bite of cold boards on her bare soles. Through the gathering dusk, Alexa caught a glimpse of motion out toward the old growth pine forest. "Scout, is that you? Come on boy. Come," she commanded, moving to the edge of the deck.

In seconds the huge dog loped into full view, a smaller dog trailing in his wake.

"Well, this is a first," Alexa declared as the dogs bounded up to join her by the railing. Scout leaned in for a pet while his new companion circled around the mastiff to sit at her feet. Alexa extended a hand, which the dog licked then bumped with a gentle plea for a scratch. "Okay, then. I guess it's kibble for two tonight." Wondering how to track down this cutie's owner, Alexa led the way inside.

After a quick dinner of leftover Chinese, Alexa called her best friend. "Hey," she said to Melissa. "A while ago you mentioned something about using Facebook for tracking down lost dogs. Your neighbor's beagle ran away, and she found her through some site?"

"Yes. Unite-a-Pet," Melissa replied. "Oh, no. Don't tell me Scout's missing? He never wanders."

"No. Scout's right here with me. But he did disappear when he went out for his run. You know I never have to worry about him since we're surrounded by acres of woods. Today, during that short time on his own, he found a friend. A little furry black mop of a dog."

"Does this mop have a collar?"

"No collar, no ID. He looks well-cared for. I can take him to the vet to see if he's chipped. But I thought I'd try to get a head start and post on Facebook first. His owner's probably looking for him."

"Good idea. I don't know what I'd do if Ansel got lost."

"Not much chance of Ansel getting more than five feet away from you at any moment. Typical Frenchie."

"He'll be with me at the gallery tomorrow. Do you want to stop by for lunch?"

Alexa chuckled, "You mean would I like to pick up and deliver lunch for the two of us? Sounds like fun. I can fill you in on the latest from Reese. Looks like he might get home from Africa by Thanksgiving. I'm missing him more and more during these long evenings alone. How about I let you know in the morning? This unexpected dog puts a wrinkle in things."

"Sure. Just text."

"Time to make this little guy a social media star. I'll be in touch tomorrow. Thanks for the info about Unite-a-Pet." Alexa ended the call and walked to the sleeping dogs. "She patted the black furball until he opened an eye. "Wake up, boy. I need to take your picture."

Late the next morning, Alexa bundled the visitor into her ancient Land Rover Defender. As she drove her long private lane to the main road, she spoke to the attentive pup, "I can't believe we found your owner so soon. And that he lives so near the cabin. I guess social media can help sometimes."

Reaching a narrow country road, Alexa stopped to glance at the paper in her hand. Muttering aloud as she turned onto the blacktop, she read, "Left on Hemlock, then right on Brady." In five minutes, she'd located the limestone farmhouse with blue shutters which the dog's owner had described in their brief phone call.

"We're here," she told the dog. "Amazing I've never been on this road." Bringing the Land Rover to a halt in the driveway, she exited onto a gravel drive. The black dog sailed out behind her, darting to a blue side door.

Alexa followed, as a tall, thin man with a shock of white hair stepped outside. He swooped the black dog into his arms. "Yuri, I was so worried. Why did you run away to this nice lady's house? You must behave better, *pupsik*. I won't be able to let you outdoors alone anymore. And you lost your collar."

Smiling, the tall man looked at Alexa. "Thank you so much, Ms. Williams. Running away is out of character for Yuri. I'm so glad you found him. And that my cleaning lady spotted him on that lost dog page."

Charmed by the older man's formal demeanor, she replied, "Please call me Alexa. My mastiff, Scout, is the one who found," she hesitated, "Yuri?" At the gentleman's nod, she continued. "Brought him right to my cabin door. He's very well-behaved and quite affectionate."

"I could have come to your place to pick him up."

"Like I said on the phone, Mr. Karst, I'm on my way into town for Saturday lunch with a friend. So, dropping the little guy by was no trouble." She gestured at the house. "You have a beautiful home. I love old farmhouses."

"Thank you. It's been my refuge for many years. I need the quiet for my work. Would you like to come in for tea?"

Alexa looked at her watch. She had time, and this pleasant old man intrigued her. "Thank you, but I can't stay long." He led the way into a large kitchen, warmed by a gas fireplace.

"Please, sit. I'll heat the water. Is Earl Grey okay for you?" Karst gestured Alexa toward a small love seat near the hearth, then moved to a counter on the far wall.

"Sure. Earl Grey's one of my favorites," Alexa replied as she sank onto the blue toile sofa. She took in the faded print of the seating, the cheery mauve curtains, a mix of what looked like original paintings and numbered etchings on the walls. "I love the cozy feel of this room."

Karst turned to face Alexa. "My late wife is responsible for the décor. I've changed almost nothing in the years since she's been gone. I gather my memories of her to warm me by sitting in this room each day."

"I believe the things that people surround themselves with are keys to character. Seeing your house and gardens, I can tell your wife must have been a lovely woman."

"Helen," Karst's voice caught. "Yes, she was wonderful."

He brought a tray with tea pot, sugar, and two cups to the coffee table and sat in a chair opposite Alexa. "Would you pour?"

"Of course. "Alexa filled the cups and handed him one. She took a sip. "Yuri, that's an unusual name for a dog."

He scooped a spoonful of sugar into his cup. "Perhaps here in Pennsylvania. For me, it's a nod to my childhood."

"The only Yuri I'm familiar with is from *Dr. Zhivago*. I read the book and then watched the movie as a child. I so wanted to ride across the plains of a Siberian winter in a sleigh."

Karst chuckled. "I'm not from Siberia but grew up with the cold winters of that part of the world. I hate to burst your romantic image of Lara and Yuri gliding across the steppes in the snow, but cinema too often turns hard realities into idealized fantasy. That's their business."

Alexa smiled. "I notice you have a trace of accent."

"You're being kind. Decades in the states and marriage to an American—yet still I reveal my roots with every word." He shook his head.

"What a leap of courage to leave your home and travel halfway across the world to spend your life."

"Emigrating was the best choice for me. As a scientist, I had good employment here. However, I regretted the distance from my family, now all gone like my beautiful Helen."

"Are you retired?" Alexa took another sip of tea, feeling sorry for this courtly man who seemed glad for her company.

"For the most part. Although my employer recently brought me back for a project in which I have some expertise."

Karst placed his empty cup on the table. "Enough about me, *zaya*. I take it we are neighbors. What is that American expression, as the crow flies?"

"Yes. I live farther up the mountain in a cabin I bought from my parents. Someday you'll have to meet my mastiff, Scout, and boyfriend, Reese, who live with me. I work at a law firm in Carlisle. Williams, Williams, and Stewart. We practice civil law."

"Like wills? Karst asked. "I've been thinking about revising my will."

Alexa slid a business card from her pocket. She carried them in every coat and jacket. "Just give us a call. If you have certain provisions in mind, jot those down as you think of them."

Alexa rose. "Thanks for the tea, but my friend's waiting."

"I've enjoyed meeting you, Alexa. Can you stay just a few more minutes?"

Glancing at her watch, Alexa nodded.

Karst waved her back into her seat and strode over to a table strewn with books and papers. A whiteboard, covered in mathematical calculations, leaned against a nearby bookcase. Plucking a wooden stringed instrument from the corner, her host returned to his chair.

"Is that a, um, baliaka?" Alexa recognized the guitar-like instrument with the triangular base from movies.

Karst's eyes lit up. "Close, balalaika." He spoke the word slowly. "Baa La Like Ah. Since you're a Dr. Zhivago fan, I wanted to play this for you." He leaned over the exotic instrument and began to finger a tinkling melody."

Alexa cried. "Lara's Theme. Somewhere My Love." She sat back, entranced, until Karst finished the familiar tune. Alexa clapped and said, "Thank you, Mr. Karst."

"Nicholas, please. Now I know you must go. Thanks again for bringing Yuri home. I'd be lost without him. He provides me companionship and is an excellent guard dog." Winking, the old man added, "for his size."

As she left, Alexa leaned over to pat the dog on his head. "Nice to meet you, Yuri." Straightening, she grinned, "You too, Nicholas. I'm glad I could reunite you two, and I enjoyed the private concert."

Leaving the farmette, Alexa followed the driveway as it looped past a small barn and then circled back to the entrance. In the rear-view mirror, she saw Karst still holding the balalaika in his arms, Yuri at his side.

A few weeks later, Alexa went home early after an afternoon hearing in family court. Entering the cabin, she roused the snoozing Scout. "Let's go for a walk before it rains," Alexa told him and ran upstairs to change. Before long, she and the mastiff were hiking the nearby old-growth pine forest, headed toward a favorite haunt, Weaver's Pond. As usual, Scout bounded ahead to explore then trotted back to Alexa's side. Her faithful pup repeated this throughout the entire walk.

Anemic late afternoon sun filtered through the trees as they reached the pond. Alexa sank onto the fallen log she always used as a resting spot for a few minutes of forest meditation. Gazing over the water, she watched a few late autumn leaves flutter onto the calm surface.

Her thoughts drifted to Reese, still on temporary assignment for the Africa Trust in Botswana. They'd spent a few months there together, but she'd had to fly home alone, still reeling from a brush with death on a remote African plain. He'd now had to stay on much longer than expected. Whispering aloud she sighed, "I miss you, Reese."

Scout's whine startled Alexa out of her reverie.

"You're right. We're losing the light, and it's getting damp. Time to head back." She joined the dog, who loped down the trail toward the cabin.

On the walk home, Alexa's thoughts shifted. She pondered the mysterious Nicholas Karst, having prepared his will a week before. Although she hadn't learned much more about his origins, Karst had surprised her with a net worth far higher than his modest farmette suggested. Childless, he'd decided to leave much of his estate to a nephew living in France. That part of Karst's holdings was in a trust arrangement named for his deceased wife. The rest would go to organizations focused on the environment and world peace. A few days after signing the will, Karst had returned to ask her brother Graham, the managing partner at their family law office, to handle a codicil to the original document. Alexa feared Karst was dissatisfied with her services.

"No, my dear," he'd assured her. "I am a bit old-fashioned and thought this one item more suitable for your brother to arrange."

In another oddity, his will included a sealed envelope which Nicholas left with the firm—along with instructions for opening it following his death.

"Takes all kinds of clients," she laughed. Soaking in the towering evergreens around her, she continued to chatter away at Scout, "At least I don't have any bad guys chasing me through this pine forest. These past couple of months have been blissfully boring and danger free. I could get used to this."

As they emerged from the forest, Scout stopped short, fur bristling, eyes focused on the cabin. Alexa saw nothing out of order but halted beside the mastiff.

"Yap, yap, yap." A whir of black fur cleared the deck steps and raced toward them.

"Yuri? You ran away again?" The dog wore a bright blue collar with a tag that jingled as he wagged his tail at Scout, then jumped on Alexa, pawing at her legs.

"What's wrong, boy? Last time you visited, you were so laid back and calm." Yuri continued barking, nearly frantic. "Come on, let's get you both inside, and I'll call Nicholas to let him know Yuri's here."

Both dogs beelined to the water bowl in the kitchen. When they'd lapped their fill, Scout curled up on his living room bed, but Yuri ran to the door with a sharp bark.

"Okay, I'll run you home but let me call first." Alexa dialed Nicholas's cell number and got voice mail. She left a message, then peeked around the corner to see Scout fast asleep.

"Let's go, Yuri. Maybe Nicholas is out looking for you. I can't imagine he's happy you ran away again." Outside, the black dog dashed to the Land Rover with a yelp. Alexa shivered at the heavy mist which now blanketed the forest. She zipped up her jacket as she climbed into the SUV.

When they arrived, Alexa's stomach tightened. *Something was off. No house lights. Nicholas not answering his phone or returning her call. Yuri's odd behavior.* Thick fog enveloped the flatlands of the valley, and the mist had intensified to a steady drizzle. Alexa grabbed a flashlight from the glove compartment and slid from the vehicle. Scanning the property, she could see nothing of the dog's owner. Still standing by the closed driver's side door, she yelled, "Nicholas. Nicholas." A sodden tree limb to her right broke off and hit the ground with a muffled thump. Alexa gasped, trying without success to peer more than a few yards into the sodden darkness.

Maybe he's out searching? Maybe he's napping and doesn't know Yuri's gone? Alexa decided to knock on the kitchen door. She let Yuri out of the vehicle. But instead of trotting to the farmhouse, the dog raced toward the barn.

"Yuri? Come." Ignoring her, he darted through the half open barn door. Wiping at the rivulets of rain dripping into her eyes, Alexa followed. Her pace slowed as she approached the wooden building. The inside of the pitch-black barn yawned before her.

"Yap. Yap. Yap." Yuri's staccato yelping rose to a frenzied pitch.

Alexa took a deep breath and took a few tentative steps into the building, flashlight searching the interior.

"Yap. Yap. Yap."

She turned the beam toward the frantic dog and illuminated a body sprawled at the foot of the loft ladder. Yuri's little black nose snuffled at the fallen man's shock of white hair. Nicholas Karst.

Alexa rushed over. "Nicholas, can you hear me?" She sighed, anticipating the worst. She'd witnessed the utter stillness of death before. Too many times. Laying a hand on his chest, she felt no motion, no breath. Locating a wrist, she hoped for a pulse. Nothing.

"Oh, Yuri. You tried to get help, but there's nothing we can do." With tears running down her face, Alexa scooped up the little dog and trudged through the rain to get her phone and dial 911.

Drained from the shock of finding Nicholas dead and the hours of police questioning, Alexa stayed home the next day. The police had drilled her about whether she'd entered the farmhouse. When she convinced them that neither she nor Yuri had been inside that evening, they asked her to stand on the threshold of the outer door and tell them if she saw anything missing. She told the police that papers hadn't been scattered over the floor, nor the whiteboard tipped on its side during her first visit. She'd emphasized that a single brief chat over a cup of tea had given her impressions of the room, not details. So, she could be of no further help. However, Alexa felt she owed Nicholas the one kindness she could offer. She'd asked the police if she could keep the orphaned dog until a new owner could be found.

The day at home, however, wasn't providing her with much rest. Alexa's mind whirred with questions. Had Nicholas fallen from the ladder to the loft? What was in the codicil to his will and the sealed envelope? And his life, like his death, held some mystery. Was he Russian or some other Eastern European nationality? He'd dodged those questions and never clarified the scientific field that had guaranteed him a job in the United States as a new immigrant.

Still fretting the following morning, Alexa stopped by her brother Graham's office.

In a sympathetic tone, Graham asked, "Are you okay? I know you'd become fond of Nicholas Karst. And finding him dead must have been difficult."

"Yes. I liked the old guy. A fascinating character."

Graham switched to business. "We have obligations with the will. We should find out if the state police have informed his next of kin."

"Yes. That would be a nephew, in France. The primary beneficiary. The rest goes to charity."

"France, that complicates things."

"Nicholas named the firm as executor. We will have a lot to arrange. I doubt the nephew wants a farmhouse in Pennsylvania, but you never know. I have no idea what's in the codicil or the sealed envelope."

Graham smiled, "The codicil makes two bequests. He's left you some Russian instrument."

"How sweet, His balalaika." Tears leapt to Alexa's eyes.

"And his dog."

"Me? Yuri?" Alexa gulped.

"Yep, that's the one. He really wrote it more as a request. You can read the exact wording. And he's given Yuri a substantial inheritance that you'll need to administer, if you accept."

Stunned, Alexa said, "Not sure what Reese will think about two dogs. I need a little time to consider this."

"Believe me, Karst has made it well worth your while."

Alexa took a deep breath. "And the sealed letter?"

"He did say that was to be opened immediately following his death. Let's do it now. Can you find Brian to witness it? I'll get the letter from the safe."

Alexa and their partner, Brian Stewart, sat silent while Graham scanned Nicholas's letter then looked up with a baffled expression. "I've never encountered a client letter like this one." He read aloud:

Upon my death, I am instructing my attorneys to call the number at the bottom of this page. Provide the code BH2957G to the person who answers the telephone. Inform them that Nicholas Karst has died and that they need to send someone to collect my work papers.

This number belongs to a government agency in the national security sector. Depending upon the circumstances of my death, they can find working papers in my home and in my safe (to which they have the combination).

If I am under surveillance or compromised in any other way, I will hide key elements of my work. My employers will identify any missing elements. Alexa Williams can provide guidance on the location of those items. She, like I, has long been a fan of the love story of Dr. Zhivago and Lara Antipova.

"What's he talking about, Alexa?" Graham shot her a bewildered look.

"Wow," Brian babbled. "Was this old guy a spy or something?"

Alexa shook her head. "Not a spy, but some kind of top-level scientist. I knew Nicholas had a backstory, but. . . . Wait. Under surveillance? Compromised? Sounds like his death might not have been accidental."

Graham nodded. "Anything's possible with this guy. We need to call this number right now." He looked at Alexa. "And you can provide this guidance he talks about?"

Alexa pursed her lips. "We did talk about Dr Zhivago, but I'm not sure what he means. Just place the call for now."

On Saturday afternoon two weeks later, Alexa sprawled on her sofa, watching Scout and Yuri wrestle in the middle of the living room. In the chair across the room, her brother looked as exhausted as she felt. "What a circus," she moaned, scowling at the happy black dog on the floor. "And to think, you're the one who dragged us into all this."

Graham said, "I have good news. Since Kate took the kids to a birthday party, I thought I'd come out and tell you in person. The agency told me they're finishing with Nicholas's house and the investigation here in town. They're leaving Tuesday after they wrap up. They'll send a team again when we hire someone to pack up the house. So, we need to notify the feds when we get to that stage after probate. Easier that the nephew has chosen not to come here from France. I wasn't surprised. He never met his uncle even though Nicholas followed his life over the years. Although he knew the name of his uncle's trust, so there must have been some family contact along the line."

Alexa sat up. "I have mixed emotions about the feds leaving town. I spent so much time with those guys as they searched the house. While they were here, I felt safe. After all the agents' questions and warnings, anytime I'm on my own, I imagine cars following me. A strange dude came to yoga last Tuesday and that made me nervous. And I really freaked out the other night when a vehicle pulled up in front of the cabin around midnight. Probably kids looking for lovers' lane. The dogs' barking scared them away. But it sure gave me a fright."

Graham said, "You seem to be a magnet for trouble. But how would any bad guys know Nicholas left you a clue about his papers?"

She shrugged, "Yeah. Probably my imagination." After a pause, she continued. "I picked up some bits and pieces from those agents, but not enough to get the full picture. What do you think Nicholas did for the government? I know we pledged to keep this secret. But from the rest of the world. Not each other."

Alexa paused and then grew animated as she shared her theories. "I think he designed sophisticated weapons systems. And the US got him out of Russia because he was some sort of super genius willing to defect. They eventually ended up stashing him out here in the middle of nowhere. He told me he needed the quiet to do his best work. I'm sure his marriage to Helen was real. Although I doubt his name was Nicholas Karst."

Graham nodded, "We'll never know if he fell off that ladder or was pushed. They kept a tight lid on that." He grimaced. "Not to put more pressure on you, Lexie. But I heard the feds say Nicholas had completed a series of recent calculations on this secret project, but they couldn't find them. Any more thoughts on this Dr. Zhivago clue?"

Alexa shook her head. "I've wracked my brain, Graham. Nothing. Nada. Zilch. I only met Nicholas a few times while working on his will. And that first day at his home when I returned Yuri." She smiled. "Nicholas struck me as such a gentle soul that day. Not a weapons designer who lived his life as a destroyer of worlds. We hit it off. He seemed so lonely. I think talking about Dr. Zhivago brought back fond memories of his childhood in Russia." Alexa brought a hand to her chest. "I was so touched when he insisted playing "Lara's Song" on the balalaika."

"Wait. The balalaika." Alexa froze.

"What about it?" Graham asked.

"I thought he left me the instrument because of that shared moment. But I bet that's where he hid the calculations!"

"Where is it?" Graham leapt to his feet.

"At his house. I didn't want to bring it home until everything is settled with the will."

"Well, what are we waiting for?" Alexa's brother dashed across the room and grabbed his rain jacket. "Do you have the keys to the house? I'll drive."

"Right here." She swept them up from the counter and followed Graham out into another wet night.

Fifteen minutes later, Graham and Alexa sat in Nicholas Karst's kitchen waiting for the feds to come and collect the envelope they'd found taped inside the balalaika.

Alexa sighed as the anxiety she'd been living with since Nicholas's death began to lift. "I'm a little conflicted about this, you know. I'm not sure I want anyone having these high-tech weapons. But I guess I'd much rather have our government in possession of them than a foreign power. Or terrorists. Or some crackpot megalomaniac billionaire.

"Lexie, you're a true patriot," Graham razzed his little sister. "Mom and Dad would be so proud."

The headlights from a vehicle pulling into the driveway bathed the dim kitchen with long shadows.

"The feds. I'll feel better when this top-secret stuff is in the right hands," Graham said.

Alexa stood and walked to open the door; glad she'd fulfilled the trust Nicholas had placed in her. She marveled he'd based that trust on their shared love of a beautiful song.

Later that evening, a listless Alexa sat on the couch, listening to the din of heavy rain on the cabin roof and leafing through a home décor magazine. Scout slept curled in his big bed by the woodstove, Yuri snuggled beneath the mastiff's chin. When her cell trilled, Alexa grabbed the phone on its first ring. She'd been looking forward to a call from Botswana.

"Reese. I really needed to hear your voice. I've had a crazy few weeks. And, I have some news. About a little dog named Yuri . . ."

Join Alexa Williams and her English Mastiff Scout
as they encounter dangerous situations, many ripped from
today's headlines, in the Alexa Williams suspense series.

— ABOUT THE AUTHOR —
SHERRY KNOWLTON

Sherry Knowlton is the award-winning author of the Alexa Williams
suspense novels, including *Dead of Autumn, Dead of Summer, Dead
of Spring, Dead of Winter* and *Dead on the Delta* and a co-author of
the acclaimed thriller novel *American Roulette.*

Now retired from executive positions in government and health ins-
urance, Sherry lives in the mountains of Southcentral Pennsylvania,
where her Alexa Williams suspense series is set.

Learn more about Sherry at www.SherryKnowlton.com.

Murder, An Educated Guess

BY CAROLYN KLEINMAN

"If you remember anything else, be sure to call me."

Hannah Stein, an English professor at Wrightsville Community College, automatically nodded her head in assent. She wanted to help Police Detective Lawrence King, but she knew so little about the murder. Hannah told King that she had been working at her desk when a loud argument interrupted her. Angry shouts had reverberated off the walls enclosing the staircase across from her office. Next, Hannah had heard a scuffle and then a series of thuds. When she went to investigate, she found Len Talbot's body splayed on the floor at the bottom of the stairs. The hilt of a knife was protruding from his back.

Hannah's hands shook as she recalled the sight. She shivered. Her stomach ached. Not just because Talbot, the newly appointed head of the English department, had been killed. Her body was also responding to a tragedy from her past. The police would, no doubt, soon learn that Talbot's was not the first body she had discovered. Hannah had now found two. And both had tumbled down a flight of stairs.

Hannah moaned and then asked herself, "Why? Why again?"

When she was five years old, Hannah had both seen and not seen her mother's death. A pair of hands had pushed her mother down a steep flight of stairs, and her mother had fallen and landed beside Hannah in a twisted heap. Hannah had not able to attach a face or a body to those hands. Despite the fact that an identification by such a young child would have been questioned, Hannah felt she had let her mother down. The killer had not been caught.

Hannah sucked in a breath of air and tried to calm herself. King had asked her if she knew of anyone who would want to harm Len Talbot. She hoped her face had not betrayed her. Sad to say, there was a long list, and her name was on that list.

* * *

That night, Hannah and her neighbor Jodi were sitting in Hannah's kitchen. Hannah knew that Jodi, a therapist, could be relied upon for good advice, so she had invited her friend to join her for dessert. After the two had devoured large slices of cheesecake, Hannah posed a hypo-thetical problem.

Hannah said, "Let's say I have a student, a pretty girl, and she has a crush on one of the middle-aged male teachers at my college. What if the girl has been stalking this teacher and has left him numerous gifts and love notes. And what if all this blew up in her face, and, instead of the romance she expected, there was a violent encounter."

"Was this hypothetical girl raped?" Jodi asked.

"Thank goodness, no. She managed to break away and escape. But her clothes were ripped, and she was very frightened. However, now the girl the blames herself. She claims she provoked the man and got what she deserved."

"Whoa," Jodi said. "You just dropped the words 'let's say' and 'what if.' This all really happened; didn't it? Of course, you have to do some-thing to help the victim of an assault. And the girl should report what happened to the police and campus authorities."

"Yes, I know. That's not my dilemma. But . . ."

"No but. You have to stop the creep who hurt her."

"But, Jodi, he was murdered this afternoon. The man was Leonard Talbot. The same Leonard Talbot who stole the project I developed and grabbed my grant money."

"Len Talbot was murdered," Jodi said these words very slowly. She was stunned. "I only caught the last bit of the six o'clock news tonight. I remember hearing that a local teacher was killed, but I never dreamed it was someone I once dated with such disastrous results. Someone I once loved but grew to hate."

"Yes. And I found the body. There was a knife in his back."

Jodi gasped. "Really? You found the body? Hannah, are you all right?"

"It was frightening, but I'll be okay. Right now, I'm worried about my student, the girl Talbot attacked a couple of nights ago. One of her friends told me this story this morning. She's worried the girl might hurt herself. What I need to figure out, with your help, is the best way to approach this girl and convince her to get some counseling and support. She's been through so much; her Prince Charming turned into a monster, and now he's a corpse."

"Cut me another piece of that cheesecake," Jodi said. "This discussion may take a while."

Jodi was right. The two women talked for some time, and when Jodi got up to leave, Hannah added, "There's one more thing. Words were shouted before Len Talbot was killed. But I only clearly heard one. It was 'blackmail.' What am I to make of that?"

* * *

The next day, after she arrived on campus, Hannah received a long text message. There would be a morning department meeting to regroup after Talbot's murder, and she would find copies of the agenda in the tray of the English department's copier. Hannah was instructed to bring them to the meeting. She set off at a brisk pace, intent on completing her mission, and didn't realize that she was being followed. Just as she approached a secluded stand of trees on the edge of the campus, a beefy hand grabbed her arm and spun her around. She found herself facing a large man who smelled of liquor and tobacco smoke.

"You're that English teacher. Your name's Stein. Right?" he asked.

"Yes, I'm Hannah Stein. Please, let go of my arm."

"Not 'til you hear what I have to say. My name's Stevens. Bruce Stevens. And Amy's my girl. A foolish girl, but she's mine. And no one has the right to hurt her."

"I understand. I know why you're upset, Mr. Stevens. Perhaps I can help you and help Amy. But you must release my arm."

"Not 'til I'm finished. I heard it all from my girl. All about her chasing after that teacher and what he did. Amy admitted she blabbed it all to her friend. Amy shouldn't have done that. It's all shameful. And that silly friend had no right to say a word to you. We keep our family business in the family. I take care of my own."

"Mr. Stevens, Amy's friend only came to me because she thinks Amy needs help. I want to help her, too."

Spittle flew from the man's mouth as he shouted, "You still don't get it. I'm telling you to stay away from us. And keep any meddlers away from us. I handled it. There's nothing more to be done."

Abruptly, Bruce Stevens dropped Hannah's arm and stomped off. Hannah was shaken. It had been an ugly encounter. And what had Stevens meant when he said he handled it? Did he mean that he had murdered Len Talbot? Hannah sighed. Getting Amy Stevens some professional help had just become more complicated.

A short time later, Hannah reached the English department's lounge and headed towards the copier in the corner. Suddenly, Hannah was startled by a loud yelp. The sound came out of Colleen Nickels, a woman who worked in the bursar's office. Hannah noted that Colleen was clutching a stack of papers and a screw driver.

"Oh, Hannah, you scared me," Colleen said. "I didn't hear you come in."

"What are you doing here, Colleen? What's with the screwdriver?"

"Oh, I guess there's no use denying it. Hard to lie when you're staring at the damaged lock on the file cabinet behind me. I promise I'll make good on the repair. Believe me, Hannah, I had to do this."

"I don't understand."

Colleen held up the papers in her hand. "Hannah, I had to get my letters back."

Colleen collapsed onto a nearby couch. She hesitated, then uttered a few strings of words that led nowhere.

"Colleen, you're not making any sense. Please, just tell me what this is all about."

"Hannah, you know me. We may not be friends, but we're friendly. You know I'm not a bad person. It's just that good people sometimes do dumb things, right?"

"What are you trying to say?"

"I was dumb. So dumb. But you know what Len Talbot was like. He could be so charming and persistent. He was always flirting with me. The flirting was nice and writing sexy letters back and forth seemed just a little naughty and harmless. But then, it happened—we had sex. Just twice.

Believe me, it was only two times. I felt terrible and told Len I would never do that again. But he said there had to be repeat performances, or he would show my letters to my husband. I can't have that. I can't. Len said he had my letters safely locked up. I looked in his apartment and his office, but I came up empty. I just remembered that Len once mentioned he stored things here, too. I just found my letters."

"Colleen, you should go to the police and admit this before they find out themselves."

"Oh, no. We were careful. How would they find out? Please, Hannah, don't tell anyone what I told you."

"You're putting me in a terrible position, Colleen. Len was murdered. The police will dig into all aspects of his life. They'll tear apart his office. He was the new department head. They'll also check his files here and see the broken lock. Get in front of this. Talk to the police."

"I don't know. It's so risky. If this gets out, I could lose my husband, and with the scandal, I could lose my job, too. I don't know what to do."

Hannah stood by helplessly as Colleen sobbed. Unfortunately, Talbot's cruelty did not end with his death. Hannah shuddered as her thoughts circled back to what she did after she found Len Talbot's body. First, she had called 911 and campus security. Afterward, she had returned to her office. As the setting sun was bright, she had walked over to the window to lower the blind. That's when she spotted a figure running away from the building. It was Colleen Nickels. How had she forgotten that?

Hannah hustled but was late getting to her department meeting. Jay Kline was running the meeting and droned on and on. He pontificated that it was only right that he resume the duties of department head. He promised to man the helm, grab the reins, and drive them forward to greater heights. Hannah inwardly groaned. The empty clichés and mixed metaphors did little to distract her. She had weightier concerns and couldn't wait for the meeting to end. She had heard the word "blackmail" right before Talbot was killed. Did that mean Colleen Nickels had killed Len Talbot?

Sandi Price, who sat beside Hannah at the meeting, was also anxious for Jay Kline to stop talking.

"Come with me. We'll get coffee," Sandi said when Kline finally dismissed them.

Sandi looped her arm through Hannah's and guided Hannah to the cafeteria in the basement of the building. They found a table, and Hannah sat down to reserve their space. Sandi returned a few minutes later with two steaming cups.

"Okay," Sandi said, "I fixed your coffee the way you like it. Now, you tell me what you know about the murder, and I'll tell you what I heard."

Hannah smiled. Her friend did not believe in preambles. Hannah explained how she had found the body but held back from divulging more.

Sandi said, "That's not much. I guess I'm the one with all the news. I heard from a reliable source that the police may close this case soon. The murder weapon was a New Edge knife, a brand only sold in Maryland. However, one of our students, Rick Berger, was recruited to be their first Pennsylvanian sales rep last month. And many students heard Berger quarrel with Talbot. The clincher is that one of the knives from Berger's sample set is missing. The same size and shape as the one found in Len. Sounds like a slam dunk to me. What do you think?"

Hannah was quiet. She didn't know what to think.

"Oh no," Sandi said, "Jay Kline is heading our way. Sorry, friend. I hate to leave you on your own with the old windbag, but I've got a class in ten minutes and have to run. You know, Kline is weird. He never explained why Talbot took over as department head. We're talking about the same Jay Kline who clung to that position for years because he said he couldn't live without the extra money it provided. And then, after losing the job, Kline started living large and lavishly entertaining. Like I said, he's weird."

Sandi scooted out a nearby door just as Jay Kline reached Hannah's table.

"Hey, Hannah," Jay said, "Sandi left fast."

"She has a class," Hannah said.

"Of course. Anyway, I wanted to talk to you. First, thank you for picking up the copies of the agenda for the meeting today. And I want you to know that I think Talbot treated you shabbily. I want to assure you, now that I'm back in charge, that you'll get your new project and the grant money."

"Thank you, Jay. I really appreciate that."

"Good. We're back on track again. Actually, I came down to the cafeteria to meet Ed Nickels, Colleen's husband. He's been catering events on campus and catered a big anniversary gala for me last weekend. Nickels is a gourmet chef but disorganized beyond belief. I keep finding items he left behind in my kitchen. I just spotted him. I have this bag of measuring cups to return. Talk to you later, Hannah."

Hannah set down her coffee cup after Jay Kline left and thought over everything she had heard that day. Then, she called the local police station and made an appointment to see Detective Lawrence King. King was more than the arm of the law to Hannah. He had been her husband Aaron's best friend, and after Aaron died in a car accident, King had looked after Hannah and had become her friend, too. Occasionally, Lawrence would bend the rules and discuss troublesome cases with Hannah, enjoying their give and take and trusting her to be discreet.

* * *

"Had some further thoughts?" King asked when Hannah took a seat across from him in his office.

"I have a theory I thought I should share," Hannah said.

"Go on."

"I spoke to several people today and learned a few things. I think I should start with what I heard from Colleen Nickels."

King said, "I can save you some time. Mrs. Nickels came in and confessed to the murder."

"She did? She's not the one I suspect."

"Well, you're right. We ruled her out. She was in the right building at the right time, but her husband, who was bringing in trays of food, saw her in a dark hallway, right before the murder, kissing one of the gardeners. And the man corroborates that the kissing and fondling went on for some time."

"Amazing," Hannah said.

"Yes. The lady gets around. By the way, her husband is a chef and has fancy knives, same brand as the murder weapon. He confessed to the murder before his wife did. But he didn't do it either. Oh, he knew about his wife and Talbot. He was suspicious and had hired a private detective, but the timing was off. The husband was with his assistant serving food at the time of the murder. And cursing under his breath the whole time, as he had just seen his wife with the gardener. The Nickels couple confessed because each thought the other could be guilty. Strange, considering everything."

"Maybe there's hope for them yet," Hannah said.

"Not my concern," King replied. "Now, we did interview a lot of students. One let it slip that Bruce Stevens was angry with Talbot because Talbot attacked his daughter. By the way, Stevens was upset when I showed him my badge. He thought I'd come to arrest him because you had filed charges."

"We had a run-in this morning, but I'm okay. No need to go after him on my account. And I don't think he's guilty of Talbot's murder."

"You're right. After some prodding, Stevens admitted that he stopped by Talbot's office on the morning of the murder. Stevens roughed him up a bit. But nothing more. We have a witness who saw Stevens leave Talbot's office and then watched Talbot, still alive, stagger out of his office, too. Plus, we verified that Stevens was working at a site, miles away from campus, when the murder occurred."

Hannah said, "That takes care of three possibles and is in keeping with my theory. I imagine, after what I heard, that you looked at Rick Berger, too."

"So, you also know about him. We thought Berger looked good for it, but we found his missing knife, the one that was identical to the murder weapon, in his laundry. What can I say? Typical messy college kid. We discovered that Talbot was blackmailing Berger. Berger turned in a plagiarized paper, and Talbot demanded money in exchange for a passing grade. But Talbot didn't stop. Talbot kept asking for more. That led to the heated argument some students overheard. However, Berger had an alibi for the time of the murder, one he didn't give up easily. Seems his copier had run out of ink, so he was in the library making a copy of his upcoming math test. A test he stole a short time earlier. His story checked out, so we ruled him out, too. But the kid can't skate any longer. He's bound to get kicked out of this college now."

"I ruled him out, too. He doesn't have a part in my theory."

"You know, Hannah, I didn't like doing it, but I had to look at you, too. I heard you were angry when Talbot reallocated funds and you lost the program you developed. But you're a small woman, and Talbot was a big man. The placement of the knife and the force needed to put it in Talbot's back ruled you out. Still, I was amazed to discover, after I did some digging, that Talbot's body was not the first one you found."

"That's a story for another time," Hannah said. "What we have to concentrate on is the knife. How did that unusual knife end up in Len Talbot's back? Here's my explanation. I think Len Talbot blackmailed Jay Kline, who was the perennial head of the English department. I don't know what Talbot held over Jay; but it must have been significant, as Jay gave the position he cherishes to Talbot. Then, the turnabout. I think Jay found something that would guarantee Talbot would be arrested and started blackmailing Len Talbot. I have no proof, but Talbot once bragged to a friend of mine that he had rough sex with underage girls, and after hearing what he did to Amy Stevens, I believe he was capable of such despicable acts. Blackmail money would explain the sudden surge in Jay Kline's income when it should have decreased. I checked with Jay's wife. He hasn't recently inherited money, and he doesn't gamble or invest. She has no explanation for their sudden wealth."

"Interesting," King said.

"In addition, Jay and Len both had classes that ended at the same time on the floor above my office. They must have argued in the stairwell after their students left; that's when I heard the word 'blackmail.' And, ironically, it applied to both of them if my theory is correct."

"What about the knife?" King asked.

"Today, I learned that Ed Nickels catered a party at Jay Kline's home, and Nickels left things behind. I bet one of those things was a New Edge knife. It wasn't a large knife. Kline probably carried it in its sheath in a pocket, planning on returning it to Nickels. But instead, in the midst of the struggle, he plunged it into Talbot. If Kline's fingerprints are on the knife, you'll have your proof and your killer."

King replied, "We'll see. The fingerprints on the knife were smudged, but I'm hoping we have enough to make a match. I'm waiting for the results."

Detective King did not have to wait long. By the end of the day, the police were able to arrest Jay Kline and book him for murder based upon the fingerprint analysis. Kline was wobbly in the interrogation room and, eventually, broke down. His story matched Hannah's theory.

* * *

The following day, Hannah and her friend Jodi met for a celebratory lunch.

Jodi lifted her glass and said, "A toast to my clever friend. Who would've guessed that you have a secret identity? You're the modern Miss Marple."

Hannah laughed and then clinked her glass against Jodi's to complete the toast.

Learn more about Hannah Stein in *The Class Assignment Is Murder*.
Inspired by a true local crime, the novel describes how Hannah and
three of her students reexamine an old triple murder case.

❧ ABOUT THE AUTHOR ❧
CAROLYN KLEINMAN

Carolyn Kleinman is a retired English and English as a Second
Language teacher who has BS and MA degrees from the University
of Minnesota. Her first novel, *Love, Faith, and the Dented Bullet*, is
a historical fiction book that describes what happens when a WWII
Holocaust survivor meets a Mennonite farm girl in 1947. Her mystery, *The Class Assignment Is Murder*, is a fictional depiction of a real
triple murder that occurred near her home. Both novels are published by Sunbury Press. Carolyn lives in Lancaster, Pennsylvania,
with her husband Steven.

Uncovering a Con

BY SHARON MARCHISELLO

Feeling a migraine coming on, Giovanna Rogers pulled up the Excel spreadsheet for the Pecan County Spay/Neuter Clinic. The numbers didn't match what the new bank statement showed.

"Tim?" she called to her fiancé, who had just emerged from the shower. He had a towel wrapped around his waist, and his bare, muscular shoulders glistened. "When did you deposit that last donation?"

"Which one?" A lock of strawberry blond hair flopped near one blue eye as he leaned over her to stare at the computer. Tossing his head, he sent the cowlick back in place. "We got several big checks last week. You're doing great with the fundraising."

"The donation from the Electricity Co-op Employees Charitable Fund. For ten thousand dollars. I don't see it listed here." Tim had applied the sexy after-shave she loved, but at the moment, she was too bothered to notice. With the sleeve of her terrycloth bathrobe, she blotted up the drop of water he'd left on the desk.

Tim squeezed her shoulder and squinted at the spreadsheet. "It was with the grant check from PetSmart Charities. Maybe it hasn't cleared yet."

"What day did you deposit them?"

Straightening so he could adjust his towel, Tim creased his brow. "I was headed to the bank last Monday, but then they called me in for an emergency surgery. Ruth Morton's puppy got hit by a car, and I thought we might have to amputate his leg."

Giovanna winced at the thought of Ruth's sweet little Cocker Spaniel in pain. "What happened? Were you able to save Butterscotch?"

Tim nodded and tucked a strand of Giovanna's long brown hair behind her ear. "The dog is out of the woods now. His leg was broken, but I set it and inserted a pin. Butterscotch won't be able to romp and play like he used to for a while, but he'll regain the use of that leg. And hopefully, stay out of the street."

Giovanna exhaled the breath she'd been holding, grateful for her fiancé's compassionate veterinary skills. It had been the right decision to partner with him on her dream project: the spay/neuter clinic they had recently founded together. She had spent her teen years volunteering with her grandmother for an animal rescue group, where she had seen first-hand the effects of cat and dog overpopulation. The lack of convenient, low-cost clinics made it hard for their Georgia county's poorer residents to get their pets fixed. With Tim volunteering his services part-time and supervising interns from the nearby veterinary college, they were able to keep costs low and pass the savings along to pet parents and animal rescue groups.

She glanced back at the spreadsheet. "So . . . what happened with the deposit? Did you ever make it to the bank?" Tim could be absent-minded sometimes, leaving unopened mail in the backseat of his car or buried in a pile on his desk. Those big checks might still be lying in a sea of paperwork.

He rubbed his clean-shaven chin. "Jerome was on his way to the bank that morning with a stack of donations he picked up from our post office box. I gave him those two grant checks to add to the deposit."

Giovanna frowned. "The funds should be in our account by now. The last deposit posted was two weeks ago. And what's this debit for fifteen hundred dollars? To JerCo Investments?"

Tim bent over her again to inspect the displayed document. "Oh, that's the mortgage payment."

"Mortgage payment? We don't have a mortgage on the clinic." Her hand trembled, shaking the computer's mouse so the pointer danced across the screen.

He stared at her incredulously. "Don't you remember? Jerome suggested we take out a mortgage against our equity in the clinic and pull out your investment for operating expenses. He explained that emptying your personal savings account to pay cash for our building wasn't the best use of those funds."

Giovanna shook her head. "I told him I'd think about it. I never agreed to go ahead with the loan. I don't like the idea of carrying that much debt."

"Really? He said he had your approval when he asked me to sign the papers." Tim crossed the room to the dresser and slid open a drawer. "Most of our capital is tied up in that building. If we have to start buying supplies on credit, we'll be adding interest expense. Mortgage rates are at an all-time low, and Jerome got us a great deal through the investment company he owns."

Lips tight, Giovanna scrolled through the bank statement. "If we pulled our equity out of the building and took out a mortgage against it, then where's the cash?"

Tim sat on the bed to put on his socks. "It must be in the other account."

"What other account?"

He stood, picked up his trousers, and slipped one leg inside. "The money market account at JerCo Investments. Jerome says we'll earn top dollar on our operating capital. That business checking account at your grandmother's credit union pays almost no interest."

"Okay, but I wish you guys had told me about this new account." She navigated to the JerCo Investments website. "I suppose it makes sense to earn higher interest if we're maintaining a large balance. Can we write checks on it?"

"Yes, I think so." Tim zipped up his pants and grabbed a shirt from the closet.

"What's the username and password? Maybe that's where Jerome deposited those checks. We'll need to move our autopay bills there or else set up regular transfers into our checking account to cover them."

Tim picked up his wallet and rifled through it. "Must be at the office." Buttoning his shirt, he bent to kiss her goodbye. "I'll text you the login info later."

* * *

Giovanna continued examining the clinic's financial records, making notes to question Tim and Jerome about various cryptic entries and unexplained transactions. She regretted not keeping a closer eye on the books from the beginning of their venture. But after earning an accounting degree from the University of Georgia, interning at a financial services firm all through college, and working for three years as a corporate auditor, she'd grown bored with numbers. She was happy to delegate the task to Jerome so she could focus on her passion—animal rescue. She gave presentations around the county to schools, church groups, and service organizations about animal care and the importance of spaying or neutering to control the pet overpopulation crisis. Only a few of her slides depicted the financial side of their business. Her enthusiasm must have shown because donations and grants had poured in for the fledgling nonprofit clinic.

But now, her auditor's instincts had kicked in.

Tim had been her best friend since they were children. Around the time she entered college, their friendship had blossomed into romance, and, after years of exclusive dating and now, sharing a house and the dream clinic, they were planning a June wedding.

But Tim didn't have much of a head for business. Fortunately, the veterinary practice where he'd interned, and joined once he earned his Doctor of Veterinary Medicine, had hired an office manager. She took care of the accounting tasks so Tim and the other vets could focus on what they were good at: helping heal their clients' beloved pets.

That was why Jerome Haddad was such a godsend. His wife, Connie, had been Giovanna's college roommate, and the two women had stayed in touch after graduation despite moving into different careers. When Giovanna mentioned to Connie that she was quitting her corporate job to start a nonprofit spay/neuter clinic with Tim, Connie suggested they partner with Jerome, an attorney and entrepreneur with years of experience building charitable organizations.

Jerome had handled all the legal paperwork for their 501(c)(3) and license agreements, and he'd provided them with lists of potential donors from his database of nonprofit supporters. He'd also taken over the bookkeeping, leaving Giovanna and Tim free to focus on their passions.

But now Giovanna sensed she needed to be more involved in the accounting part if only to understand it well enough to explain their financial statements to potential donors. Jerome had promised to sit down with her to discuss her concerns, but so far, they hadn't been able to coordinate their schedules.

She glanced at her watch. She had to get ready for her speech at the local Rotary Club luncheon, which should result in more donations and some new volunteers for the clinic. She sent a quick text to Tim. "Did you find those login credentials for our money market account?"

Just when she thought he wasn't going to respond, his reply came: "Not yet. Headed into surgery now. Will look later."

* * *

When Giovanna returned from the Rotary Club, she sent Tim another text. "Any luck?"

No response.

She picked up the mail and shuffled through the stack of envelopes, stopping at the quarterly newsletter from her sorority. The picture on the front page made her smile; it was a candid shot of her cuddling some adorable kittens. The headline read: "Honor Student Giovanna Rogers Gives Up Corporate Career for Nonprofit World." The story below praised her animal welfare efforts, described her quest to build a low-cost spay/neuter clinic, and provided the address where philanthropic sorority sisters could send their donations. Connie must have given the information to the editor. *What a sweet friend,* Giovanna thought. No wonder donations from her old classmates had been flying in. This issue of the newsletter was over a month old; it had been sent to her old address and forwarded. The online version had come out even earlier, and Giovanna had missed seeing it.

The doorbell rang. Giovanna set aside the rest of the mail and went to answer. Her grandmother, Michelle DePalma, stood on the porch with a bouquet of fresh flowers from her garden. Her husband, Roberto, was a Master Gardener, always growing something beautiful.

"Those are gorgeous." Giovanna stepped aside to admit Michelle. "Want some tea? I just put on the kettle."

"That would be lovely, dear." Michelle headed for the cupboard and found a vase for the flowers while Giovanna prepared their tea.

As they settled on the living room couch with their cups, Michelle pulled out her phone. "I heard from my friend in Texas today, and she sent me something a little disturbing." She held the device toward her granddaughter.

Giovanna glanced at the news article her grandmother had displayed. "Local Literacy Charity Forced to Declare Bankruptcy." Not surprising. Many new businesses, including nonprofits, failed in their first few years. She hoped hers would be different. After all, she had an accounting background. She knew that "nonprofit" didn't mean "broke."

"Read it," Michelle insisted. "This sounds like your guy."

Giovanna took the phone from her grandmother and studied the article more closely. And re-read it. As the color drained from her face, a wave of nausea swept over her.

"Could it be?" Michelle put a hand on her granddaughter's shoulder.

Shaking her head, Giovanna fumbled for her phone and pressed her last contact. Voicemail. She waited for her fiancé's greeting to finish, then cried, "Tim! Call me back when you get this." After disconnecting the call, she punched in his office number.

The office manager answered. "I'm sorry, Giovanna, but Tim's still at lunch. I can have him call you when he gets back."

Her next call was to the offices of JerCo Investments. She explained she was Jerome's partner at the Pecan County Spay/Neuter Clinic and needed to set up access to their new account.

There was a pause, and then the woman returned to the line. "Ms. Rogers? Please verify your email address and I'll send you the link."

Moments later, an email from JerCo Investments popped into her inbox. Giovanna clicked on the link and set up her credentials. Then she perused the account.

She called the woman back. "This is Giovanna Rogers again. Thanks for sending me the link. But it only goes to our mortgage account. I also need access to our money market account."

The woman put her on hold. An ad for JerCo's financial services played while she waited.

"I'm sorry, ma'am, but I couldn't find any other accounts under your name."

"What? Can you check for my fiancé's name? Timothy Nelson." Maybe Jerome had set it up with her soon-to-be-married name.

"No, ma'am, I'm sorry. No Nelson either."

"Well, what names do you show on the money market account for the Pecan County Spay/Neuter Clinic?"

"Ma'am, the only account we have for that business is your mortgage."

"That's impossible! May I please speak to Jerome?"

"I'm sorry, but he's unavailable. I can give him a message if he calls in."

Seething, Giovanna couldn't remember if she thanked the woman or just hung up. She called Jerome on his cell phone.

Connie picked up on the fourth ring.

"Hi, Connie, I need to speak to Jerome right now. Can you please put him on?"

There was a long pause.

"Connie?"

"He's . . . in the bathroom. Can he call you back?"

"I'll wait."

A muffled sound suggested her friend had covered the mouthpiece, but Giovanna could make out a boarding announcement in the background. Was Connie at the airport? Connie and Jerome?

The line went dead, and when Giovanna redialed, no one answered.

"What's going on?" Michelle watched her granddaughter's face.

Giovanna made a fist. "I can't believe it. How could I have been so stupid?"

* * *

The IRS agent handed Giovanna another form to sign. "I understand you might not be able to pay the entire tax bill at once, and that's why we offer a payment plan. However, interest will accumulate on the unpaid balance every month you're in arrears."

Tim scowled. "But it wasn't our fault. Our ex-partner, Jerome Haddad, made those disallowed expenditures. He stole all our money and left the country."

The agent tsked. "It doesn't matter. His name isn't on the 501(c)(3) filing. You two are the only ones responsible."

"Isn't there anything we can do?" Giovanna sighed. "We thought we were in compliance. We've had our inspections, got our licenses . . ."

Peering over his glasses, the agent made a sound between a grunt and a chuckle. "Purchasing a luxury yacht for a 'low-cost' spay/neuter clinic is hardly compliant with IRS rules."

"But it wasn't us!" Tim slammed his fist on the table. "That jerk—"

"We have Ms. Rogers' signature on the loan agreement. With your clinic building as collateral." The agent showed them the paperwork.

Tim glared at Giovanna. "My partners are so humiliated by this scandal that they've asked me to leave the practice."

She felt as if her head would explode. "I didn't sign that document. The signature is a forgery."

"Unfortunately, there's no proof." The IRS agent turned to her with more compassion than she'd believed possible for someone in his line of work. "Look, if you believe you've been scammed, there are agencies that can help . . ."

"The Consumer Financial Protection Bureau? They said they couldn't do anything, because I don't qualify as a consumer. Law enforcement? The police can't touch Jerome because he left the country. I tried filing a lawsuit, but they can't even serve him." Shaking with anger, Giovanna showed the agent the stack of articles she'd printed. "I found out he's done this before, and no one has been able to catch him. He skips town before the charity victims know they've been scammed."

The squeamish look on the agent's face told her she was making him increasingly uncomfortable. He glanced at the clock on the wall and muttered, "Well, good luck to you, ma'am. If you have trouble making your payment deadlines, please call the office and renegotiate the timeline. Believe me, it will go much better for you in tax court."

As they walked out of the office, Tim turned on his former fiancée. "This is all your fault, you know."

"My fault?"

"You're the one who brought that man into our lives. I bet you were sleeping with him, and I was too stupid to see it."

Giovanna clenched her jaw. "You know me better than that! And besides, you agreed to take him as a partner."

"You're the accountant, and I trusted you. I'll never make that mistake again."

She stared after him. "Neither will I."

* * *

"Thanks for letting me stay with you and Roberto for a while," Giovanna told her grandmother as she hung clothes in her old bedroom closet. "Once the house sells and we get back the deposit for the reception, we can pay off the IRS."

"You're welcome to stay here as long as you want." Michelle put a hand on her granddaughter's shoulder. "Tim will cool off eventually, though, and the wedding will be back on before you know it."

"You're always the optimist." Giovanna flexed the bare fingers of her left hand.

Her grandmother sighed. Even though she must be thinking it, Michelle had not once said, "I told you so" or berated her for not doing her usual due diligence that might have uncovered Jerome's shady business dealings. She'd been too anxious to get started with the clinic and too trusting of her old roommate.

Giovanna's phone pinged with a notification. She reached for the device and glanced at the screen. "It's Connie."

Her former friend had posted a picture of herself on the deck of an ocean-going yacht named *Second Wind*.

So smug, thought Giovanna. *Wonder where they're headed with their ill-gotten gains?*

"Wow! So posh! Where are you going?" someone typed. Giovanna was glad that person had asked so she didn't have to; Connie might have gotten spooked and blocked her.

"The Galapagos Islands," Connie gushed, tacking on a couple of heart and tortoise emojis. "Jer's looking into a new business venture."

Some new scam, Giovanna thought. She looked at her grandmother. "Does your offer still stand? For a trip?"

Michelle smiled. "Of course, Honey. Getting away will do you good. Wherever you want to go. Paris? London?"

"How about the Galapagos Islands?"

Michelle cocked her head. "Roberto and I were there a few years ago, and we loved it. I'd go back in a heartbeat." She eyed her granddaughter. "You're sure? The Galapagos?"

Giovanna nodded.

"Great. I'll make the arrangements."

Giovanna smiled for the first time since her financial troubles began. *Jerome Haddad may think he's the king of conmen, but he won't get away with scamming me. I'll make sure he never does this again to anyone.*

Follow the adventures of Giovanna and Michelle on a cruise of the Galapagos in *Secrets of the Galapagos* and *Murder at Leisure Dreams—Galapagos*.

—⁃∂ ABOUT THE AUTHOR ∂⁃—

SHARON MARCHISELLO

Sharon Marchisello is the author of three mysteries published by Milford House, the fiction imprint of Sunbury Press: *Going Home* (2014), *Secrets of the Galapagos* (2019), and *Murder at Leisure Dreams–Galapagos* (2025). She also writes the DeeLo Myer Cat Rescue Mysteries from Level Best Books. Besides novels, Sharon has published short stories in anthologies and online magazines; one was a 2022 Derringer finalist. She has written travel articles, training manuals, screenplays, book reviews, and a nonfiction book.

Captain Kid & the Wizard's Gift

BY JOSEPH MAZERAC

It had rained for three weeks straight. The canals overflowed ten days ago, the tulips were under four feet of water, and the almond orchards had become mud bogs. Finally, the sun was out, but the humidity was so thick it may as well have been more rain.

To the insects, the twenty-one-day downpour meant romance. By the time there was a break in the weather, they'd reproduced so enthusiastically their swarms made it impossible to walk to the mailbox without inhaling a fly. The frogs loved it too. This was the season of prosperity foretold by their croaking moonlight songs.

The young captain wished he could be so joyful, but that was difficult to do while soaked in sweat and covered in bug bites.

He scratched his neck.

He should go back inside. He was barefoot on the porch of the cobbler's house, his favorite traveling loafers stripped of their soles on the old man's dining table. Waiting for the repair, he'd occupied the afternoon repainting the porch balusters. The color was called *Secret Garden*, which sounded luscious, but the hue drying on the humid wood could hardly be considered anything beyond drab.

Nice of the cobbler to refresh the shoes, though, for only the cost of materials. Kinder still that he provided a bed with clean sheets. But the cobbler was the nosey sort, and his wife always played matchmaker.

"Met anyone special?" she'd ask with blushing cheeks. "There's a girl at the farmer's market, seventeen years old, sturdy ankles, bushy hair, plump as a blueberry."

A downside of looking so youthful was the propensity of grown women to pair him up with teenagers.

The door squeaked open.

It was the cobbler, holding in his elderly grip a newly assembled loafer. Presenting his handiwork, he grinned. "For your inspection, sir."

The young captain took the loafer, stuffing his hand into the cavity to feel the fresh padding. "This is the same shoe?"

"Yes, indeedy, Locket & Leathers Incorporated. You can check the stamp if you don't believe me." The cobbler's smile broadened, his saddle-brown skin becoming a map of creases. Then eyeing the road, he added with heightened meaning, "The wizard is coming today. Coming for you."

"Magic-man Wistocroft?" the captain asked.

"Aye." The cobbler's smile faltered. "Said he comes to hear the frog songs, but my lady believes—and I agree with her—he's coming to give you something."

The captain withdrew his hand from the shoe. "He's not a real wizard, you know. And one of the reasons I'm staying with you is to avoid attention."

"Well, Captain Kid." The old man watched him kindly. "After doing great deeds, when folks come to give you rewards, best not make them work too hard to do it."

The captain supposed that was true. He'd risked his life in the king's experimental glass submarine, piloting the clear orb into the depths of Blackwater's bottomless trench. The mission was to survey an underwater dragon's den. He'd found the den—and the dragon within—but once the dragon spotted him, there was hardly enough time to do anything but escape. The journey wasn't completely fruitless, however. Getting away, he'd crashed into a mound of treasure, and the sub's ballast pumps sucked up some of the plunder.

Among the coins and jewelry later recovered from his holding tanks was a sapphire ring once worn by Queen Ayana during the age of *actual* wizards. Back then, Alkatan devised machines of magic and science, his brother Teritan performed experiments of lightning and earthquakes, and the wayward Valtini perfected the art of destruction. Compared to them, this Wistocroft character was little more than a juggling huckster.

The king wanted Captain Kid to go for another dive, but without a way to sneak past the sea dragon, what was the point? As for the ring, it was thought to be lost forever, so naturally people got excited when he found it.

The storm had helped him avoid accolades for weeks. Now, it seemed, recognition was unavoidable.

Two hours later, a sedan rolled up the gravel driveway. Watching from a window, the captain didn't recognize the make or model, but whatever company built the car, the candy-apple paintwork and gleaming chrome wheels were obviously customized.

Tucking in his shirt, he ambled back out to the porch. His vest was thrown over the porch swing and his white captain's cap hung on the armrest. He snatched up the vest, deciding to leave the hat where it was.

When the car shut off, a man emerged from the passenger's side. *Emerged* was the word for it because he seemed to grow out of the open car door. He was wide, thick, tall, fantastically bearded, and clothed in such an array of robes and scarves that he might've been a sultan. Also, the captain noted the shifting wind the instant the man's foot touched the driveway, now blowing out of the north with double the force of the previous gusts from the east.

Captain Kid called from the porch. "I saw a poster in Swansdale—*Come see the Wizard Wistocroft*. You dress like him, but you're three times his size."

The bearded man patted his ample belly, his thunderous voice booming across the yard. "I keep growing. Doctors say I'll be grander than the mountains in Marinack before long. But you—young as ever."

Reconsidering the hat, the captain plucked it from the armrest and twirled it onto his head. Then bounding down the steps barefoot, he noticed in the relaxing wind a sudden lack of stinging insects.

A random gust doesn't make him a wizard, the captain reminded himself.

They shook hands in the yard, Captain Kid using the opportunity to scrutinize the man up close: glinting emerald eyes, vibrant pink skin, black and silver hair, polished stones tied into the sweeping strands of his mustache. Even swollen like a balloon, he was recognizable as the traveling magician from the poster.

The captain's eyes narrowed. "Shouldn't call yourself a wizard." But before an explanation was offered, he redirected the conversation to the purpose of the visit. "If you've come for frog songs, there's a leaping frog-leg community not far from here." He pointed with his chin. "Cross the turnip field, go into the wood, and when you reach the creek, left takes you to a pond, but going the other way, there's plenty of soggy sludge-mucks. You'll be up to your armpits in bullfrogs before you know it."

Mr. Wistocroft's eyes never left Captain Kid's face. "If there's time." Then he turned to the automobile and reached inside.

His driver was a young woman, quite pretty, in a professional's sport coat and whimsical, lavender-framed glasses. Why couldn't the old ladies set him up with girls like that?

She handed the magic-man a small present wrapped in yellow-glitter paper tied with a silver bow. Before returning her hands to the wheel, she met the captain's eyes and blushed.

Maybe he should take a more proactive approach. If he walked to her side of the car and tapped the window, surely she'd roll it down for him. But right now, the ballooning, bearded figure in the robes was offering him a gift. Courtesy required the captain to receive it graciously.

He eyed the present in Wistocroft's hand. What would come in a box that size? It was a perfect little cube, too small for a coffee mug, too large for jewelry.

"Whatcha got there?" he asked.

Mr. Wistocroft's eyes glistened. At that moment, the puffy man looked like a black-bearded Father Christmas, especially with him clutching a fantastically wrapped present. "As you already know, it's a gift from the Blue King on high."

Holding the present in the palm of an open hand, he extended it to Captain Kid.

The captain sighed, taking the gift with less gratitude than he intended. He should be grateful. No doubt something special was inside.

He glanced up. "I should open it here?"

Mr. Wistocroft gazed out across the neighboring turnip field. "Open it if you like, but you'll know what it is in the moonlight." He waved a swollen hand to the forested horizon. "By frog song and water, its secret will be revealed."

"Frog song?" the captain questioned.

"And water in the moonlight," the magic-man repeated. He looked into the car, speaking to the young woman. "You wanted to ask him something?"

Gripping the steering wheel nervously, the driver leaned ever-so-slightly toward the passenger side of the car. Her green eyes were framed in lavender, and while her face was pale around the edges, everywhere else it flushed red. "Captain Kid," she said timidly, "is it true you earned a merit badge for lighting the candle in the Hall of the Forgotten? My brother said it's just a legend."

The captain reached for his vest. He needn't look down to find the patch. It was sewn to his breast pocket and had been there so long the threads were wearing thin. "I lit the candle. That part's true. It's the way people tell it that makes it a legend."

"What parts do they get wrong?" she asked.

"The part about the octopus—the size of the caverns—how cold it was."

Her eyes shined with admiration. "But you climbed the stone steps, fending off werewolves, and used a torch to light the candle. And there were ghosts, weren't there?"

"There were ghosts," the captain confirmed.

Mr. Wistocroft looked from his driver to the recipient of the royal present. "What about those werewolves?"

Captain Kid shrugged. "I had a gun with silver bullets, so . . ." As he trailed off, he eyed the driver again. "It was pleasant meeting you, miss." Then turning to Wistocroft, he reached out with a stiff right hand. "Good to finally meet you."

They shook on it, and after letting go, the magician leaned against the open car door and shrank inside.

With the delivery made, the candy-apple sedan backed out of the drive, the young woman returning the captain's smiles between back and forth looks to check the street.

When they were gone, Captain Kid turned once more to the house, finding the homeowners watching from the open door.

"What did he give you?" the lady of the house asked.

The captain showed her the present. "It's a mystery."

*   *   *

The three of them gathered at the cobbler's workstation dining table, Captain Kid sitting with the present resting on the varnished wood. He was reluctant to open it. The king of the Blue Realm was well known for giving generous gifts, but some of that generosity came with strings attached. The gift of an estate in Swansdale, for instance, might come with an expectation to take up residence and work the land. Or it could be nothing more than a handwritten note and a chocolate from the king's own chocolatier.

He jostled the package.

From across the table, the cobbler's wife watched intensely. "What do you think it is?"

"Too heavy for chocolates," Captain Kid said, which wasn't really an answer.

"One way to find out," the cobbler suggested. He'd taken his seat at the head of the table where Captain Kid's left shoe looked nearly sewn together.

The old man was right, and the captain's own apprehension would not be satisfied by delays, so working loose the ribbon, he strung it out onto the table.

"Try not to rip the paper," the woman at the table said.

The captain nodded. He had no need for secondhand wrapping, but people in these parts reused what they could. Tilting the box to look at the bottom, he saw the ends of overlapping paper, secured by a single strip of nearly invisible tape. He loosened the tape with a fingernail and then stripped it away clean.

The folds of the wrapping were already beginning to open, so with a finger, he helped it along. First, one side of the paper was unfolded. Then the other side. And when Captain Kid rested his hands upon the table-top, what he, and the cobbler, and the cobbler's inquisitive wife looked upon was a most peculiar box.

"What is it?" the cobbler asked, beating his wife to the question forming on her lips.

The box wasn't wooden, which was what the captain had expected. Instead, it was made of gritty reddish stone. Turning it over to look at every side revealed no obvious way to open it. In fact, it wasn't clear if it opened at all.

What was it then? Besides how perfectly square it was, it looked like something a farmer might plow up in a field.

The cobbler cocked an eyebrow. "This is a reward?" He reached to take the stony cube.

The captain hadn't finished his own examination, but wanting to be a gracious guest, he handed it over. As the cobbler studied it, Captain Kid remembered the magic-man's hint: by moonlight the secret would be revealed.

And something about frog songs.

With the cobbler working rough hands over the gritty stone, his wife got up for a better look.

Hovering over her husband, she poked with a finger. "Is that salt?"

The captain didn't think so, but touching his thumb to his tongue, he tasted that she was right.

Salt. Whatever could that mean?

They carried on like this for another half hour, one of them poking and prodding, another asking questions, and someone else touching the salty deposits to their tongue. All the while, the captain kept Wistocroft's cryptic instructions to himself. When it was all said and done, they'd learned nothing that wasn't clear in the first thirty seconds: the dull red box was heavy enough to be solid, and the grit on the outside was seasoned like a Saltine cracker.

Having lost interest, the lady of the house returned to her work. That day, she was pairing up all the socks in the house and mending the ones with holes in them. The cobbler, likewise, had a shoe to finish.

Meanwhile, Captain Kid sat by a window, the cube in his hand, the red coloration of the stone whispering of meaning. He listed for himself all the red rocks he could remember. *Red jasper. Granite Rose. Ruby. Rhodonite. Red agate.* None looked like his present.

The saltiness was another matter, and about that, he made no headway whatsoever.

Alas, he had to admit the solution to the puzzle would not be discovered indoors. When the cobbler finished stitching the second loafer, Captain Kid put on his refurbished shoes, stuffed the cube in a leftover grocery bag, and set off across the turnips, following the directions he'd given the so-called wizard.

Across the field was the tree line, and into the forest was a creek. Upstream, he'd find the pond with lily pads blanketing the surface. Downstream were bogs, but in either direction, there were bullfrogs aplenty. Snakes, too, and bats when the sun went down.

Arriving at the edge of the trees, he listened to the sounds of wildlife. There were footsteps in the thicket. The animal disturbing the leaves sounded as large as a deer, but such rustlings were notorious for making small animals sound large. Birds whistled observations across the treetops. Also, there was a faraway buzzing sound he couldn't identify.

Unlike the animal rustling the leaves, the buzz sounded big in a more convincing way. *A horse head hornet* was his best guess, but there were any number of stinging possibilities.

A mosquito bit his neck, and he swatted, his hand coming away with the evidence smeared across his ring finger. Bugs would drink him dry if he let them. What he wouldn't give for some of the magician's cool, insect-free wind.

The sun was going down. In another thirty minutes, it would be dark in the forest, and half an hour after that, the moon would make its first appearance.

Moonlight, frog song, water. Those were the keys to unlock the puzzle swaying in the shopping bag.

He stepped into the shadow of a river birch, webs crisscrossing the lower branches. No spider in view but its meals were bundled into webbing.

Croak.

"Ahoy," Captain Kid called to the distant frog.

Through the trees, he could faintly detect the ditch that marked the creek. He took the stone from the shopping bag, wadded the flimsy plastic sack, and stuffed it into his back pocket.

Evening was close now, the moon soon to appear, one frog already saying 'hello,' and so much moisture in the air his hands were sweating.

As he moved his hands around the stone cube, he noted his perspiration absorbing into the salty surface.

He lifted the box aloft, presenting it to all the many living things that called this forest their home. "Anyone know what to do with this?"

Crrrrrrrrr-roak. Croak-roak.

Croak-roak, another frog answered.

Before long, the conversation would be joined by so many voices, the captain wouldn't be able to hear himself think.

He proceeded to the ditch, stepping over fallen branches crawling with mushroom beetles, avoiding the holes burrowed into the soggy forest floor, and all the while flapping his free hand at flying insects.

The grass at the edge of the ditch had been trampled, deer tracks leading into the stream. On the opposite bank, the prints went up again.

The captain looked left. That way went to the pond. If he decided to go right instead, he'd be knee-high in mud before the moon came up. A mud bath adventure had a certain wild-man appeal, but he'd just gotten the shoes fixed.

"To the left," he told the failing light in the forest.

Croak, came the reply.

He followed the stream, and when he came to the flooded pond, he crouched at the water's edge. Bats were out for their evening hunt, and the captain was not the only one watching the chaotic flights. Just off the bank, in a glassy pool caught between land and lily pads, floated three small pairs of froggy eyeballs.

On the other side of the pond, one of their long-legged brethren spoke into the night. *Crrrrrr-roak. Croak-croak.*

The ones by the captain answered. *Roak-croak. Roak-croak.*

Now that they'd started, he knew they'd carry on like this until morning.

He felt restless, swatting flies, shifting his feet, edging ever closer to the waterline.

What would happen, he wondered, if he dropped the box into the shallow pool? There was no reason to do it. Yet, no good reason not to.

He'd come out here, suffered countless insect bites, muddied his new shoes, and for what? The stone was a stone was a stone.

Maybe he'd just have to ask the king about it next time he saw him. And while he thought of these things, his outstretched grip slackened on the cube.

PLUNK.

The cube splashed down, the captain laughing aloud as frogs leaped to safety.

Wiping his face with a sleeve, he saw in the rippling pool tadpoles and minnows swimming over to investigate. He swished at them with a finger, then plucked up the stone, mud and algae dripping from his hand.

"I got you all dirty," he said to his present. "The king's not gonna like that."

He lowered the stone again, splashing to wash it off. When that was done, he rocked on his heels, looking up to see the moon rising above the shadowed canopies on the other side of the pond. It wasn't a full moon but bright enough he'd be able to walk back to the house without twisting his ankle in a gopher hole.

He eyed the dripping stone. "I'm ready for my surprise."

He was talking to the stone again, but with his amusement running dry, truthfully, he was thinking about the king. Not that the king could hear him. No doubt the master of the realm was stashed securely away in a castle. What did the king do for adventure? When did he go hazarding into the night? The people who protected him would say it was too dangerous. Unfortunately, they were right.

"That's why you have me," the captain said, "to live vicariously."

Mindlessly stroking the cube with his thumb, he noticed something then. On the side that had been the muddiest, there was a slightly receding dip.

He held the cube to the light, observing a shadowed recess where, previously, all the sides had been totally flat.

Roak-roak-croak.

Croak-croak.

Roak-croak-roak.

Captain Kid scanned the pond. Not only were about a million bats out, but the three frogs had returned, bringing with them two of their buddies. One was a big fella.

"Ahoy." The captain tipped the brim of his hat.

When he glanced again at the water by his feet, a very strange sight made him stop short. Where the stone had dropped, the tadpoles and minnows were in an absolute frenzy.

Tadpoles never acted like that.

Securing the cube in both hands—and moving entirely upon impulse—he lowered the salty block. As he sank the cube below the surface of the pond, little squirming bodies bombarded him, pressing their faces between his fingers and writhing to get at the stone.

Grit poured off the rock, spreading into the water, and the floating bullfrogs lifted their slick green faces to croak into the night.

The captain could feel the stone dissolving between his hands, and when it began to crumble, he feared he'd made a terrible mistake.

Just then, emerging from the crumbling sludge, he felt a hard shape captured between his palms. He couldn't see what it was with his hands cupped—and the water was so cloudy by then—but the remnant had hard edges and a smooth, rounded top.

If this unidentified object had come from the center of the cube, it must be what he was meant to find. Swishing with his hands, he let the tadpoles and minnows fight over the melting grit until all that was left in his grasp was the hard mysterious lump.

Being cautious not to drop it, he lifted it from the water.

When something poked his palm, *A bug!* he thought at once. He must've scooped one up when he was washing off the sludge.

But then there were two more tiny pricks on the inside of his cupped hands, and whatever the hard lump was, it moved, pushing upward.

He was so startled, he nearly flung it into the forest.

What the heck was this thing?

It felt alive, but that was impossible. No way had he let the cube dissolve completely and in the process *accidentally* let a bug this size sneak into his grip. Yet, the only alternative was that this bug—this *thing*—had been encapsulated *inside* the stone. Not only that, but it traveled in Mr. Wistocroft's candy-apple car, and the king knew it was in there the whole time.

Whatever he held, it was turning a circle in his hands, and the little pinpricks felt exactly like bug-feet. Then the bug-thing pinched his palm hard enough to let him know it didn't like being held like this.

Captain Kid's heart pounded.

Croak, said a bullfrog.

Roak-croak, came the reply.

The frogs were gathering closer now. As Captain Kid stepped back from the waterline, they sang louder.

ROAK-CROAK-CROAK.

CROAK-CROAK.

CROAK-ROAK-CROAK.

The captain turned so the moonlight could shine on his hands when he opened them. He was sweating all over, his heart thumping uncontrollably, and a chill of nervousness spreading over his skin.

CROAK-CROAK-ROAK.

ROAK-CROAK.

CROAK-ROAK-CROAK.

His thumbs separated, tiny poking appendages twitching against his palm.

He opened his hand more, scared that whatever it was would jump out and be gone.

Moonlight touched the slowly opening cup of his hands, and into the silver light reached a miniscule red claw.

The frogs fell silent.

Captain Kid sank to his knees, tingles running up his arms as he stared into his hands. He could hardly believe what he saw, for nestled in his palms was a red crab no bigger than a quarter.

As the crab turned around again, another revelation astounded the captain.

This was no ordinary crustacean. Its red shell was too vibrant, and with the ridges above the stalks of the eyes, there could be no doubt: this was a *Royal Dungeness*, one of the warrior crab kings of the Red Realm!

Somebody—possibly even Mr. Wistocroft—had encased its egg in salty stone and chiseled out the cube. The captain didn't know enough about smuggling crabs to understand why anyone would do that, but whatever the reason, here it was, a baby crab that could grow without limits. As it aged, its shell would become tougher, its pincers more dangerous, and Dungeness crabs were forever loyal to whoever hatched them. Also, if the captain was right about the species, his new pet would be far smarter than even the brightest dog.

He rose to his feet, his mind opening on a world of possibilities. The king's glass submarine was great, but if they really wanted to know what was hidden in the underwater catacombs, they had to avoid that dragon.

Captain Kid lifted the crab to his face, admiring the miniature mandibles and eyes lifting so ridiculously out on stalks. Already, he was picturing a harness to mount a camera to the crab's back. He could rig the mount with coms and a transponder beacon.

"You think you could sneak past a sea dragon, little buddy?"

The crab looked up at him expectantly, its pincers making scissoring gestures at the air.

"I take that as a *yes*. But before any of that, you need a name. I'm Captain Kid, leader of future expeditions. And you are?"

Probably because of his recent isolation, only one name came to mind. *Wistocroft*. But the captain wouldn't name his crab after a magician who lied about being a wizard.

"I know," Captain Kid beamed, "I'll name you after the cobbler, a man of skill and virtue. From this day forth, and for all the days of your life, you shall be known as Joseph the crab."

All around them, frog songs echoed in the treetops, and high above, a wonderment of stars shined down. Many miles away, the king would be in his castle. Hopefully, he was busy planning more adventures.

Yet, no one could guess how important Joseph would become, not the captain, not the king, and certainly not the cobbler who lent the crab his name. But new legends would arise, recounted over campfires and whispered to little children lying down to sleep at night—tales of the captain and the crab, outsmarting a sea dragon, rescuing mermaids, and more. A day would come when they would even save the Realm itself, but that, dear friends, is a story for another time.

Croak-croak.

(The End)

Follow Captain Kid's advenure in the Castatine Chronicles.

 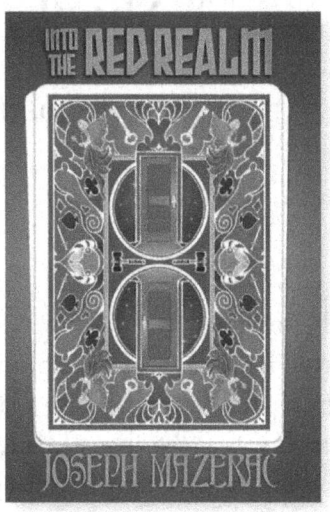

―☙ ABOUT THE AUTHOR ❧―
JOSEPH MAZERAC

Joseph Mazerac is a Royal Palm Literary Award-winner and author of the *Castatine Chronicles*. That series includes his debut novel, *Into the Attic of the World*, and continues with *Into the Red Realm*. The third book in the series is coming soon. Under the name J.M. Mazerac, he has also authored the upcoming adult fantasy novel, *Tournament of Moons*.

For more information about Joseph Mazerac and his writing, visit www.JosephMazerac.com.

A Short-Term Risk

BY JOHN L. MICEK

I'd had better days.

Marty Herman and I were pinned down in a scrapyard on Cameron Street, hunkered down behind a stack of crushed metal that had once been cars. It was a freezing cold afternoon in late January.

The wind howled down among the rows of cars, stinging my ears and making my eyes water. The sky was iron gray. There was no sun. We could hear the traffic from the street and the industrial noise from the salvage machines.

Bullets whizzed over our heads. Out of the corner of my eye, I caught a glimpse of the familiar VW insignia on one of the wrecked cars. I really did need to get my car to the garage, come to think of it. That oil change was long overdue.

Marty had that look of annoyed concentration I'd seen on his face when he struggled with software updates with his phone. He was one of the smartest and toughest cops I'd ever met. But when it came to tech, well, he'd met his match.

"Tell me you have a plan to get us out of this," I said to him.

"Of course I have a plan," Marty said, looking at me like I'd just suggested the Earth was flat.

I crouched lower behind the stack of crushed cars, wishing I'd skipped breakfast, because I could feel it churning in my stomach.

"You gonna share that with me?" More bullets. More cold wind. Things were not going well.

"Sure," Marty said, smiling grimly. "The minute I figure it out, you'll be the first to know."

* * *

And the day had started out with such promise, too.

We were headed upriver on Front Street around 7 a.m. Our running shoes slapped at the pavement, the satisfying crunch of gravel beneath us as we crossed our second mile at Division Street.

We were running a six-mile loop that started at North Street at the YMCA. We'd run along Front Street, the river moving slowly, with the chunks of ice that always clogged it at this time of year. There was a cold, hard and bright sun that gave off light, but no warmth. I knew the route without even having to think about it.

We'd run along Front Street until we ran out of sidewalk at the Jewish Community Center, just over the line at Susquehanna Township at Vaughn Street. We'd hang the right, pick one of the side streets. Maybe Green Street. Maybe Third Street, and head back into Midtown, running through the neighborhoods lined with the mid-century homes in Old Uptown that were rapidly gentrifying as more young people moved into Harrisburg, driving housing prices even higher.

"You're thinking about Lena again, aren't you?" he asked.

"Is it that obvious?" I fired back.

Marty gave me a skeptical, sideways look, the one he probably gave drunks trying to argue their way out of a DUI arrest. Even when he was running, he still looked like the Harrisburg cop he'd been for 20-odd years now.

"Yes," Marty said. "Your pace is shit. And you haven't said a word since we left the Y. I can always tell with you."

"Quite the detective," I teased him.

"I am a professional law enforcement officer, after all," he said. "No detail too small."

We crossed Division Street and kept heading north on Front Street's westbound shoulder. I could see the mountains ahead, the trees stripped bare, the wind whipping them. I knew how they felt.

* * *

"Give it up, Flynn! Give it up, Herman! Come on out. Don't be dumb about this. No one has to die today."

We heard the voices from the other side of the scrapyard. The hail of bullets had stopped, if only for a moment.

"You think they mean it?" I asked Marty, a slow smile playing at the corners of my mouth.

He grinned back at me.

"Probably not," he said. "Probably taking the time to reload."

I shook my head.

"And they seemed so sincere, too," I said. "Can't take anyone at their word these days."

The two gunmen worked for Carlo Fiore, who ran most of what passed for organized crime in Central Pennsylvania. He had an office above a red sauce restaurant in downtown Lancaster. It had been in the family for three generations. They'd been in the crime business even longer.

My mistake had been asking too many questions about the fatal ketamine overdose that had claimed the life of the youngest son of Pennsylvania's senior United States senator.

He was a Republican from the Northern Tier who'd made a fortune in tech, and then ventured into elected politics, doing so under the rich guy's standard assumption that since he was good at making apps that he'd be equally good at governing.

The gamble had worked out. He won in a landslide in a year that generally had favored Democrats.

The son, just 20, had the same alpine ski slope features, sandy brown hair, and deep blue eyes as his dad. He'd played Division One lacrosse at Duke and generally underachieved in the classroom. They'd found him dead, in a hot tub, at a house off-campus one night late in October.

The media circus had been as intense as it had been inevitable.

Naturally, no one had seen anything. There was a girlfriend, a blue-eyed girl from Columbus who swore she'd been in the next room, talking to friends and getting a drink when it happened. She came back to the sunporch where the hot tub was and saw the senator's son slumped in the water. There would be no next lacrosse season.

Marty's mistake had been saying yes when I asked him for help. He never stopped reminding me about it, either.

"You realize I only need five more years on the job before I can retire, right?" He scowled at me as he pumped another clip into his gun.

"Yeah," I said. "But you didn't want them to be five boring years, right?"

"YOU COMING OUT?" the gunnies bellowed at us across the expanse of the scrapyard. I could still hear the steady thrum of traffic from Cameron Street, and the whining of saws that cut into scrap metal.

"I'd say 'yes' but I'd hate to disappoint you," Marty bellowed back.

"YOUR FUNERAL, PAL" one of the gunnies yelled. The gunfire started again.

Marty exhaled heavily. I glared at him.

"This relationship may call for some reexamination," he said to me.

*   *   *

The dream is always the same.

I remember the last kiss, and the citrus tang of the perfume she always wore.

I remember the cloying humidity of the south Florida air, even past 9 o'clock, when I should have been in bed, in her arms, whispering small, wonderful things into her ear, instead of the harsh echoes of the argument over—over what? Who knows?—that shattered the peace between us.

I remember the sharp pain at the back of my head when they'd hit me. The explosion of a thousand stars behind my eyeballs. The instant nausea that came with it. The hard rubber of the extension cord that bit into my wrists. The copper bitterness of my own blood in my mouth.

I remember bouncing around the trunk of the Passat that we'd rented, the same one that we'd driven in days before, speeding down Interstate 75 from Sarasota, the promise of love between us, the carefree joy of the wind in her hair, the gentleness in her deep, green eyes, and the insistent pressure of her hand in mine.

It is the first time in as long as I can remember that I am purely, unapologetically happy. A lifetime of missteps, a collapsed marriage, a career meandering along uncertainly, none of it matters. The woman next to me, with her wry smile, and sense of the possible. She feels like the future.

Then the car lurches, the melody on the radio shatters. She disappears. I reach for her. But I can't find her. There is panic. And disorientation. And a deep, abiding pain. I want to cry out, but I can't.

Then I land, face first, scraping my cheek against the gravel of a parking lot. I see the cigarette butt, ringed by a woman's lipstick, just an inch or two from my right eye. The crème brûlée smell in the air that means we're somewhere around Lake Okeechobee. It's the smell that comes from the controlled burning of sugar cane.

In the glow of the sodium lights, in the empty shopping center parking lot, I look up and see the red-haired guy, holding something in his hand that reflects the lights. I hear the traffic. The flies buzz in the light. I see the circle of men around me, the guy with arms like ham hocks, the blonde surfer dude whose build was wiry but not weak.

The circle closes around me. It is suffocatingly hot.

My mouth goes dry, and my tongue is welded to the roof of my mouth. The sweat, mixed with blood, runs down into my eyes, stinging them.

I feel the barrel of the nine-millimeter pressed to my forehead. I close my eyes and wait for the end. The sense of resignation overwhelms me. I try to make peace with whatever is to come.

And then, always, I hear a woman's voice, hauntingly, shockingly familiar.

A ghostly, strawberry blonde apparition steps out of the shadows. Her beautiful, placid eyes momentarily fill with . . . regret? . . . and then they harden. I see the streaks of blood on her shirt.

Lena.

In my dream, it feels like my soul is being ripped from my body.

"Wait," she says. "He deserves to know why."

Lena.

And then I'm awake, at home, bolt upright in bed, my heart pounding through my chest, my breath comes in ragged gasps. There are tears at the corners of my eyes. I look to my right. Her space is empty. It's always empty.

Lena.

Why?

* * *

It had started to snow. On top of everything else, now it was snowing. The wind came down from the south, blowing so hard that it felt like my ears were being sliced by glass. I had not worn a hat. My gloves were starting to feel useless.

Next to me, I saw Marty frown, his mouth twisted into a grimace as he squinted against the fallen snow. Every few seconds, he'd lean above the car that gave us shelter and return fire from the two gunnies. We were at a stalemate.

And it was snowing.

"Just so you know," he said. "All of this is your fault."

I offered an expressive shrug.

"You are not the first person to tell me that," I told him. "But you also said 'yes' when I asked you for help on this."

"Next time," Marty said. "Don't ask."

Two frat kids at Duke, each the privileged sons of captains of industry whose names you'd recognize, pleaded guilty to supplying the senator's son with the ketamine that killed him. Even with the plea deal they'd struck, each was facing at least 10 years in prison.

Their lawyers had pleaded for leniency, pointing to their clients' relative youth, the absence of a criminal record, and their leadership roles on campus.

The judge in the case, an appointee by the previous White House who was not known for his sense of humor, split the difference and slapped them with five years in federal prison, followed by five years of supervised release, and fines that their children's children would probably be paying off.

That's when I got the tip that Fiore's operation basically ran the illicit drug trade down the I-95 corridor. I'd poked around some and then had a few conversations with an assistant U.S. attorney for the Middle District of Pennsylvania who I'd known for years.

With his help—documents that had conveniently fallen off the back of a truck—we were able to tie Fiore to the drugs that had killed the senator's son.

The story led The *Harrisburg Banner*'s website. And word had gotten back to me that Fiore was even less amused than the judge who'd sentenced the two frat boys.

Inevitably, the threats followed. And that's when I called Marty.

And then when I'd gotten the call about a meeting in the scrapyard, offering more evidence, he came with me.

So maybe it was my fault after all.

* * *

We kept heading north up the river, passing the Dixon University Center on our right. Off our left shoulders the river kept flowing south, to where it finally emptied into the Chesapeake Bay. We were going along good now. Our pace had quickened, and we had that easy feeling that comes when you're in the zone.

We'd passed Vaughn, headed south down Third Street, and decided to take a loop around Italian Lake. At this hour on a Saturday, there were couples and young families, pushing strollers, enjoying the winter morning, and taking in the scenery.

The sculpture in the center of the southern half of the lake (ambitiously titled "The Dance of the Eternal Spring," I'd learned at some point) was still there, the sun glinting off it. How the lake had gained its moniker was a subject of vigorous debate.

As we headed south toward Division Street a female runner, probably in her 30s, her long dark hair in a ponytail, passed us. We split to opposite sides of the path to let her through.

"Thanks, guys," she said, not even breaking her gait. But she did give me a sidelong smile.

Marty watched her leave. He looked at me. I shook my head.

"I'm not ready," I said.

"We'll see," he said.

* * *

It was getting dark. The snow was falling in thick flakes. We were freezing and running out of options.

"I recall being promised a plan," I told Marty.

"Really," he said. "You're going to throw that in my face now?"

Another expressive shrug.

"You said you'd come up with one. And that when you did, you'd let me know," I told him, pulling the collar of my peacoat higher around my face.

"What does the fact that I haven't told you anything suggest about that plan?" Marty asked me.

"I just figured you were maximizing the drama, waiting for your moment, and then exclaim 'AHA!' or 'By Jove, I've got it!' or something when inspiration struck," I said.

Beneath us, the snow had melted. Mud crept around our shoes, caking us in wet, freezing muck.

"You could have come up with a plan," he said.

"Me?"

"Yes, you," Marty said. He was huddled low, keeping a vigilant eye, making sure the two gunnies didn't sneak up on us.

"I'm but a humble scribe," I said. "You are the grizzled law enforcement veteran. This one is on you."

Marty offered me the same expressive shrug that I'd offered him.

"I got bupkes," he said.

I craned my head around the crushed car that had given us shelter. There was a path off to our left, and from there, a narrow loop lined on both sides with discarded refrigerators and other metal that, if I was guessing right, would take us behind the two gunnies.

I smiled.

"What?" Marty asked.

I smiled again.

"WHAT?" he demanded.

"By Jove, I think I've got it," I said. "Follow me."

I dropped to the ground, feeling the snow and muck seep through my clothes. We started to crawl.

"I can't believe we're doing this," I heard Marty mutter behind me.

We stayed low, taking our time, cutting a wide path through the disused appliances that were now casting long shadows in the setting sun. Around us, lights started flickering on in the scrapyard.

Ten minutes of solid crawling put us behind the two shooters. By now we were both soaked and exhausted. If I had guessed right, they were unaware that we had outflanked them.

I peered above the double stack of refrigerators that had been laid on their sides where we'd taken shelter. And that's when I saw them. They were about 10 feet ahead, with their backs to us. One of them was tall and lean with dark hair. He wore a leather jacket. His hair was slicked back. Goon central casting.

His partner was a little shorter and a little thicker. He was in a buffalo plaid winter jacket and wore a Carhartt beanie. I liked the commitment to the look.

I tapped Marty on the shoulder. He leaned up toward me. I pointed at them.

"We made it," I said.

"Great, Jack Reacher," he said. "Now what?"

I looked around. There was a beer bottle a few paces away; the dull green glass caught the light from one of the overhead sodium lights that had just blinked on.

A few feet away from that, I saw the remains of another car, and something dripped from it. I scuttled over to the bottle, grabbed it, and then scuttled over to the car. The smell was unmistakable—gasoline. Someone had forgotten to fully empty the tank. I put the bottle under the stream of the dripping gasoline.

Slowly, torturously, it began to fill.

"Sean," Marty hissed at me. "They're figuring out we're gone."

"Two seconds," I whispered back. The bottle filled halfway. I ripped a strip of cloth from my shirttail and stuffed it in the bottle. I scuttled back to Marty.

"You still smoke cigars?" I asked him.

He nodded.

"Still carry the lighter?"

"Of course," he said, fishing the Zippo out of his pocket. I grabbed it from him and lit the strip of cloth.

"You're not serious," he said, his eyes widening.

"You got a better plan?"

"No," he said.

"Okay," I said, hurling the bottle over the refrigerators at the gunnies. I heard it land. I heard the glass break. And then I heard the screams.

"Run!" I said.

And we did.

* * *

A week later I was out running—alone this time—taking the same, six-mile loop from the Midtown Y that took me upriver to Susquehanna Township.

There had been a hell of a mess at the scrapyard. It took the Harrisburg Fire Department, with an assist from neighboring Steelton, nearly the entire night to get the fire knocked down. Around a half-acre had been taken out. Miraculously, no one had been hurt.

They found the two bodies of the gunnies where they'd fallen. They were later ID'd. And Marty, ever the professional, stepped up to explain what had happened. Also miraculously, he'd only been reprimanded.

I was running down the far side of Italian Lake, heading south back toward Midtown.

I was considering what to have for lunch when I looked up and saw a woman runner coming towards me, headed north. I was ready to give her the friendly runner head nod as she passed.

She stopped when she reached me. She had dark Irish eyes. And her hair was tied back in a high ponytail. We were both bundled against the cold.

"We meet again," she said, smiling.

I smiled back at her.

"We do indeed," I said.

"I was about to do my kick here at the Lake and then head back downtown," she said. "Need company?"

I thought for a long moment. About Lena. About what had come before. About the scene at the scrapyard. And how there was never as much time as we thought there would be. I could run with her. Maybe get to know her. Ask her to lunch when we got back.

It was a short-term risk. It could be worth it.

"Absolutely," I said. "I'm Sean."

"Megan," she said.

We shook hands. And we started running.

Follow the further adventures of Sean Flynn in *Ordinary Angels*.

———❦ ABOUT THE AUTHOR ❦———
JOHN L. MICEK

John L. Micek is the author of *Ordinary Angels*, the first installment of the Sean Flynn Mysteries, published in 2019 by Sunbury Press. A Boston-based journalist, editor, author and podcast host, Micek is the politics editor for MassLive.com.

Nothing Left to Lose

BY JOHN H. TIMMERMAN

It happened just that fast.

And that surprisingly.

Joe Little Deer was, after all, not a small man. At 6' 2" and 235 pounds, his shoulders looked like a few axe handles stacked sideways. All of which didn't mean a thing when you're walking stupid. That is, with your eyes glued to the phone as you strolled out of Thomasma's Jewelry Store and turned up Main Street. It was his third trip to the store, braving the crowds of Christmas shoppers coughing and hacking and generally fouling the air. But he had decided on the diamond ring he wanted and was in and out in a hurry.

He had almost laughed when he thought about how fast the wad of C-Notes disappeared for one brilliant diamond solitaire set in 14K white gold. It was probably the enormity of this event in his personal life that made him feel a little dizzy, a little off balance. In fact, this one act had been on his mind exclusively for three or four weeks. His whole life hung on it. He could hardly worry about a little heaviness behind his eyeballs, a bit of an ache on his layered muscles.

The ring was now securely buttoned in his coat pocket, and he had just punched in Mary Shannon's number to see if he could "stop by" when he felt a weight slam against the back of his knees. And then the dizziness wasn't just there, but was overwhelming, spinning like a building imploding. Diamond-white lights stabbed his eyes and then his head slammed and bounced like a breaking egg against the icy sidewalk.

He fought against the attackers, twisting his body, trying to reclaim his balance. Hands were all over him, pressing him down. Bloody rivulets filled his eyes, turning the world an eerie rose-pink.

His nose had broken. Again. His sinuses were clogged with blood. His septum already deviated like a wandering forest trail. Joe wondered what this would do to it. He had never been what you might call handsome. His twisted and fractured nose was more eagle than human.

He felt rough hands rip open the zipper on his good leather coat, and the sudden sharp pain as a large needle plunged deep into his bicep. Then darkness rolled over him like a broad, unstoppable wave.

Little Deer had lost the strength to fight against going under. He had a vague sense of hands moving him. It felt like he was carried then shoved into a deep vault, so black no light could squeak through. For a second he panicked, thinking it was a coffin. They were going to bury him alive. Or was he alive? Then he sensed an engine starting as he was swaying on a narrow cot and someone strapped belts fastening him to the cot. A black pit swallowed him and held him fast.

He was cold. So cold. Shivering. He felt weight on him, as if he were in a freezer with frozen foods falling on him. His jaws shook. His body shook. Why was he naked in the cold? And wet. Had he wet himself?

Joe remembered the time he went sledding with his buddy Miguel. It was on his birthday, number eight. A special day, so he would have been with his best friend. He remembered this in the dark. Migi's older brother had driven them to the hills in his truck. They unloaded their home-made sleds, looked up the length of the slope they had to climb and were suddenly afraid. Ernesto climbed back into his truck, reminding them that he would pick them up in two hours, right damn here, and drove off.

Surprisingly, they were the only ones at the hill. Almost every kid around Houghton had a home-made sled, actually a steam-curved contraption like a toboggan with thin wooden rails on the bottom. A good, and well-used, sled was an heirloom, handed down through generations. Joe and Miguel both had short racing sleds, four feet long and supple as a reed. A red metal handle was affixed to the front on a pivot and an experienced rider could actually steer the rails at a breakneck pace. A kind of downhill slalom. Some sleds were ten to fourteen feet long and whole families would pile on.

The wind, coming off Superior, was icy. The slope was slick.

Within fifteen minutes, with Joe and Migi well up the slope, the temperature started dropping. It was a mean, hard cold, the kind that sucked the life out of your skin and turned your extremities numb. A gray cloud hovered over the west, moving in from Lake Superior. The frigid air was wet, a bad sign. A hard wind blew. Fresh snowfall whipped over the ground and battered the side of the hill.

Then the squall hit. In an instant a wall of snow was flung at them, so thick and hard that all visibility disappeared. Joe grabbed Migi by the arm and turned him around. He yelled into Migi's ear, "We have to go back down! Follow our footprints back."

"Let's take the sleds down," Migi shouted back.

"No. We'd slide all over the place in this wind. We have to make it to the spot to meet Ernie. Just follow me."

Clutching the sled ropes in numb fingers, they started slipping and sliding downhill, following the quickly filling boot prints.

They walked several steps too far before realizing they were at the parking lot. Sky, trees, and earth disappeared into the appalling white frenzy. The wind tugged at their scarves, stiffened their trousers with ice, pierced even the undergarments each had put on—Joe in his new leather shirt and pants Aunt Lucy had sewn for his birthday and Miguel in his flannel pajamas. Snow caked against their coats and woolen mittens.

The parking lot was vacant. Just white and blank. Joe turned slowly in a circle, peering hard into the gloom. He came to a stop. He felt Migi slip his mittened hand into his. Joe squeezed back and didn't let go.

Joe backtracked to the base of the hill. He put the two sleds together in a V shape to form a windbreak. The snow was deep here, but by kicking and pushing Joe piled it higher behind the sleds. Miguel had been watching all this woefully. His cheeks were going white, his nose sort of a gray blob like putty. Quickly Joe began burrowing into the snow pile he had created, using the snow to strengthen the sides and top until he had a snug dugout behind the sleds. He pushed Migi in, then squeezed in beside him.

They huddled together until the gray of the blizzard grew touched with darkness. Still the storm howled as all light slipped from the sky.

Joe thought of Aunt Lucy who had gifted him with a hand-sewn set of deer hide leathers for his birthday. He wore them like long underwear. No matter how well tanned, it took a while for the shirt and leggings to become supple and mold to his body. Still, they fought back the cold like nothing else.

They were both nodding off, unable to push and shove each other awake anymore, when a red whirling strobe light flashed through the snowfall. They were nearly drifted over. Joe shook himself awake, flailing violently at the drifted snow. He stood and waved his stiff arms as the State Trooper's headlights settled on him.

Joe shook uncontrollably from the terrible cold. It felt like chunks of ice were falling away from his body. Rough hands seized him. For the first time he heard sounds, but he couldn't awaken to listen to them. His kidnappers were making growling sounds, as if talking to him. He swayed in the air, like a tree toppling, then blackness engulfed him again. The darkness was heavy and damp, like the blanket you crawled under at night.

Joe and Miguel were bundled into the Trooper's back seat. He wrapped a woolen blanket around each of them. With the car's blower on high the snow and ice on their clothes began to melt. They sat in small puddles that formed on the seat. A voice came from the man in the front seat. "I found Ernesto in a ditch along the highway. He told me where to come." The heater bathed them and their eyes grew heavy. Still, they were so cold. So sleepy.

One second, he was deep in sleep, floating in blackness, the next his arms were flailing, panic driven. It had started as a small cough, then a hard one, unstopping. He was heaving for breath. It felt like an icicle had formed and hung down from the back of his throat. He could hardly swallow. In the blackness he choked and fought. Full blown panic. He was drowning. A shrill whistling sound keened through his cell. What had they done to him?

Joe tore at the weights on him, holding him down. He couldn't move his body, couldn't get air. He had to get up, out of the water and the ice and the hands pummeling him back down.

Noises in the room. Loud noises. Whistles shrieking. Another needle plunged into him, searching for an underground vein. His throat hurt.

Something sharp pierced it. He felt the slippery, hard coldness in his throat then heard a whooshing sound and it was all dark again and he knew nothing more.

Joe woke up again with no idea where he was or when it was. His eyes had stopped working. Maybe it was something they shot in his arm. He couldn't move his arms. Joe wanted to reach out, have contact with someone or something. Maybe he was floating in a cell. Or a box. He couldn't understand. No one could understand.

He was cold, as if his blood stopped pumping. The warm thing lay alongside him. It had fallen off. It had been on his chest, giving him breath. He could breathe easily now, without thinking about it. As if someone were breathing for him. The warm thing lying next to him? He suddenly realized what it was. He and Migi were lying together, arms intertwined, Migi's blue face against his chest. Breathing for him.

Migi was so asleep in the back seat of the Trooper's car that Joe couldn't rouse him. And Joe was tired. A deep-bone weariness no eight-year-old boy should ever experience. He fought to keep his eyes open. More lights strobed next to the car. That's right. Joe had heard a siren; he just thought it was the storm. The truck next to him was big and boxy, an ambulance. Someone opened the trooper's car door, reached in, and lifted Migi out. Joe watched as they carried Migi into the ambulance that once again howled back at the storm.

Then Joe was asleep, but his arms still felt the imprint of his friend's body.

Even after all these years, Joe was certain Migi had come back to warm him. He tried to speak his name but there was a thing in his throat. And he was so very sleepy. For a moment he saw light, then his eyes shuttered again.

Why? That was the question Joe awakened to. Had someone seen him purchase the engagement ring and robbed him for it? Had they deserted him here? How long? Would Mary Shannon miss him and start calling around? He remembered then. He was trying to find the button on his phone, trying to contact Mary to meet with her that afternoon. Then he grew dizzy and couldn't find the button and he thought someone knocked him down and he was falling and hit his forehead and nose on the sidewalk. He remembered blood in his throat, on his face. Was it lighter now? Maybe they were coming to let him go. Maybe to do away with him.

Would Aunt Lucy miss him? Would she be able to sense that he was lost somewhere? Aunt Lucy did have powers. She was a member of the Ojibway Council of Midewiwin, a Mide herself. Maybe she was coming to him for the Burial Ceremony. Joe wondered if he had died. Please, no. He didn't want someone to find him like this. Just toss him from the cliff into Mother Superior. Dying was dismal enough.

Thick fingers touched his eyelids, spreading them apart. The light was gray and uneven. Something shiny moved over his eyes. Joe felt a hiccup of humor. The words were in his mind. "Hey, Doc. What do you see in there? Little wheels huffing and puffing around and around? Pipes and cables? Anything you'd like to keep? Sorry, my deerskins wore out." The fingers released their pressure on his eyelids. The murmur of low voices. Joe wanted to call out, "I hear you!"

He couldn't speak. Instead, he fell asleep.

It was cool in his mouth. Cool and damp. A little curly cue thing moved over his lips and gums. Precious moisture. He tried to suck on it and it retreated. Once more with its drop of moisture. It withdrew and didn't return.

Had he dreamed it? Joe wondered if he would ever get out of this— what felt like a food freezer chilly and ice-draped. The worst thing was being alone in the dark. But he could hear voices. Not just another dream—there were voices and sounds but no words. And sometimes Joe felt that someone was with him. That he wasn't alone.

Like streams rushing together toward a waterfall, and then cascading over the lip of rock, Joe felt like that pounding water at the bottom, turning and twisting among protruding rocks. Falling down and deep. He sank under and a terrible fish rose to meet him. "So is this the end?" he asked. The orange fish turned and swam away.

Joe felt something new, a warm thing in his left hand. It was comfortable. It meant something to him. He could not say just what.

The next time he opened his eyes he saw light, and he knew it was day. His head was turned toward the window. It was not sunny, but it was day. His eyes fluttered in its brightness. He fought to keep them open. It seemed then the hardest thing he had ever done. His eyes were open.

He traced the light around the window edges. It lay brightest on the sill. He wondered if the rest of this cell he was kept in had light. His eyes tracked the periphery. He would have to turn his head. Joe remembered hands gently moving his head while he slept. He had not been afraid then. He was very afraid now. If he moved his head, if he made that effort, what or who would he see? Some monster? Someone who had kept him imprisoned in the dark?

Joe had to know. He moved. It felt like his neck muscles were creaking with the effort, as if his spine were full of rust. He kept turning his head as the corners of the room, the dim lights, came into view. He hardly recognized the person he saw—short, stocky, wrapped in a bright woolen blanket. Her gray braids disappeared under the blanket. Her eyes were gray pools.

"Hello, Joseph Little Deer. You've come back from a long journey." She held a small leather medicine pouch, brightly beaded, in her lap.

Joe tried to say her name. There was an icicle in his throat. Stiff and cold. He couldn't talk. He was too tired to feel around and remove it.

"You don't want to do that, Joe," said Aunt Lucy. "You'd probably pull your whole windpipe out." She leaned forward and pressed the red button on the control.

It was evening before they put him under again and started pulling tubes: the tracheostomy first, then the white feeding tube. They left the IV needle in his forearm. When he awakened it was morning and Mary Shannon was sitting in Aunt Lucy's chair. She bolted up when she saw his eyes flutter. Her blue eyes were bruised by tears. Her hand on his cheek was cool and safe.

Joe's speech was rusty. The words hurt, snaking past the sealed-up hole in his throat. He practiced with sounds. Mary finally rested a finger on his lips. She did the talking, telling Joe that he hadn't been kidnapped and tortured, but was hit by a ton of RSV followed by pneumonia. When he was admitted by ambulance, his temp was 105 and he was delivered straight to the stainless-steel tub for an ice pack. The fever went down but it lasted for days at a lower grade.

"How many days?" Joe croaked.

"Eleven now. But you won't be going home for a while, Joe. You lost a lot of weight, a lot of muscle. You'll be in physical therapy for a while." She smiled and the sun moved inside the room.

"Eleven?" Joe said. "I wasn't kidnapped?"

"Just by the paramedics when you decided to go down in front of Thomasma's Jewelry."

"Thoma . . . Oh, no. Mary, is my winter coat still here?"

"Relax. The paramedics went through your stuff. They found a small purple box. Does that remind you of anything? Yes? Well, we can talk about that soon. Now rest."

"Was Aunt Lucy here? I seem to remember her."

"Aunt Lucy hardly moved from here for eleven days. She told me she was guiding your spirit."

"Oh, one other thing. Could you do me a big favor? Take one of those bouquets—the one with sunflowers, I think—and set them on Miguel's grave?"

"Sure. I'll sit here a while first. You need to rest."

Follow Joe Little Deer on his next case in *Lowlife*.

—◦ ABOUT THE AUTHOR ◦—
JOHN H. TIMMERMAN

John H. Timmerman, Emeritus Professor of English at Calvin University, is the author of 26 books and 25 short stories in such leading journals as *The Texas Review, The MacGuffin, Reed Magazine, Beloit Fiction Journal,* and others. He has also published about 75 articles. Sunbury Press is the publisher of three of his books: *Lowlife, High Plains,* and *My Brother's Mountain.* The characters of Joe Little Deer, Aunt Lucy, and Mary Shannon appeared earlier in Lowlife.

A Whisper in the Dark

BY RITA WILSON

Sophie checked the Uber's license plate to make sure it matched the one on her App, as the gray SUV bearing the bright green Uber sign pulled up to the arrivals lane at Charleston Airport. The passenger window slid down, and a gray-haired man with a ruddy complexion leaned toward her from the driver's side. "Sophie?" he asked.

"Um, yes," she said, hesitating with her hand clutching the handle of her carry-on.

The Uber driver pushed open his car door without heeding the cars driving past him. He paid no attention as a taxi driver passing him swerved to avoid his door, just missing another passing car. He popped the hatch and reached for Sophie's bag, but her fingers clung to the handle.

"You wanna keep that with you?" he asked.

"Um, no, but . . ."

The driver sighed and shrugged, his palms facing upward. "You gettin' in or what?"

"Well, your, um . . ." Sophie found her voice. "The App says the vehicle is silver, but yours is gray."

"Jesus Christ Almighty!" the driver shouted, followed by another, less intense sigh. "Look, kid. Silver sounds fancier than gray. Look at my picture on your App. I promise you it's me. I'm Joe." He pointed at his chest. "Now, you gonna get in, or are you canceling? I promise I won't bite."

Sophie crawled into the back of the gray SUV, setting her bag next to her on the seat. She kept the cell phone on her lap with the Uber App open—twenty-five minutes to the address. The air conditioner was set low, and goosebumps erupted on her arms. "Excuse me," she called over the headrest in front of her. "Could you turn the air down a little?"

The driver glanced into the rearview mirror and, with a grunt, turned down the AC. "That better?" he asked.

Sophie nodded. "Yes, thank you." She took a deep breath and leaned back in the seat, beginning to unwind after the trip from Pittsburgh. She felt her shoulders relax, and turned her head to look out the window.

The driver navigated slowly through the bumper-to-bumper congestion on the highway. "Is there always this much traffic?" Sophie asked.

"This ain't nothin'," the driver replied. "You should see it at rush hour." Sophie checked her Fitbit: 10:16 a.m. Demi and Marina wouldn't be arriving until mid-afternoon. She rifled through her bag for the check-in instructions—yes, they were there.

After a few moments, they exited the highway and headed towards downtown Charleston. The greens and golds of the bordering trees soon gave way to buildings and strip malls. Sophie grimaced when she saw the complex to her right, hosting a Walmart, Sams Club, and Tanger Outlets. *This looks just like any other city*, she thought to herself, a seed of disappointment planted in her stomach.

The buzzing of the phone caught Sophie's attention, and she reached into her bag to see her cousin Demi's picture lighting up the screen. "Hey, she said. "Are you on your way to the airport?"

"We are," Demi said.

Marina, Sophie's sister, shouted into the phone, "Sopheeee! Can't wait to see you! I miss you!"

"I miss you, too. I can't believe I haven't seen you since you moved to Chicago!"

"This is going to be awesome!" Marina said. "Food, wine, shopping . . . did I say shopping?"

Sophie laughed. "Okay, let me know when you guys get to the airport. I'll be at the apartment."

"Don't just wait for us there, Sophie," Demi said. "Get out and check things out. Find us a good place for dinner!"

"Okay!" said Sophie. "Don't forget we have those ghost tour tickets for tonight." She could almost hear Demi rolling her eyes on the other side of the phone. "I see what you're doing, Demi."

Demi and Marina laughed. "Okay, see you soon, Sophie."

* * *

The Uber driver pulled onto Rutledge Avenue, where commercial buildings were replaced by small houses and sidewalks. White and pale-yellow one-story homes lined the street, many surrounded by white picket or metal fences. Tall, leafy Myrtle trees overhung the avenue, casting dappled shadows on the street. Occasional palm trees stood tall in the grassy strip between the sidewalk and the street, their large green fronds bright against the muted blue sky.

The driver turned onto Spring Street, where the foliage was sparse. The houses were taller, with double-decker porches and railings, and parked cars lined both sides of the street. The driver pulled to a stop in front of a corner storefront with *Charlestown Apothecary* stenciled on the glass door in white. Pastel pink, yellow, and blue tee shirts hung in the window, along with spider plants and flowing vines. Small cacti in ceramic pots adorned the shelf, which held pieces of chunky jewelry and handmade knickknacks of turtles and other sea creatures.

"Looks like your apartment's up there," the driver said, pointing above the store to the second story. The first floor of the building was constructed of red brick, while the second floor was pale blue painted wood. "Enjoy yourself." He handed Sophie a card. "Call if you need a ride. If my schedule works out, I'll come get you. I don't want you wandering around the city alone."

"I won't be," Sophie said. "My sister and cousin are coming in this afternoon. But thank you . . ." she glanced at the card, "Mr. Clark."

"Joe," he replied.

She got out and took a deep breath. Although the sky was clear, the air held a hint of rain, and Sophie could almost feel her hair frizzing from the humidity. She approached the brown door to the store's left, followed the directions on the keypad, and pushed open the door. A long, tall, narrow wooden staircase greeted her. *Okay*, she said to herself. She took a deep breath and dragged her suitcase up, step by step, to the top. She was met by two doors and, using the same key code, opened the door to the right.

"Oh, wow!" she said as she entered the apartment. Tall windows hung with floor-to-ceiling heavy navy-blue drapes flanked a fireplace that had been covered and painted white. Several books sat on the mantle, held in place by ornate bronze bookends. Abstract metal sculptures on either side of the books completed the mantle décor. A large copper-toned abstract cityscape hung on the wall above the fireplace. A large gray sofa and loveseat sat upon a soft oriental rug, placed in the middle of the room on the hardwood floor. The modern kitchen was to Sophie's right, the granite counters and stainless-steel refrigerator at odds with the old room, and yet somehow, working. To Sophie's left was a wide wood staircase covered with worn gray carpet. She left her suitcase on the floor and climbed the steps to investigate the apartment.

Oooh, I get first dibs on the bedroom, she thought. She surveyed the large room to the left of the stairs. It was spacious and airy, with light streaming in from the large window on the far wall. A large blue patterned rug lay on the painted wooden floor, and as she stepped on it, she realized the floor was uneven. She turned to leave the room and noticed a sign on the door that read, "This house is over 100 years old. Please treat it kindly. Any irregularities in the floor or walls are the natural progression of time and wear. The house is structurally sound."

"*Oh,*" she thought, concerned only now that the house might not be structurally sound.

She continued down the hallway, stopping to peer in at the bathroom before moving on to the bedroom to the right. Twin beds were stuffed into a small room along with a writing desk upon which sat a green-shaded accountant's lamp. A narrow window looked out over the street in front of the house. *Marina would love this room,* she thought.

The floor creaked as she entered the last room on the right, and she gasped and smiled. The double bed was covered by a white chenille blanket and flanked on either side by dark wooden nightstands upon which stood tall bronze lamps with white milk glass shades. A dark wooden door with a crystal knob opened into a large closet. A few hangers covered in a puffy pink fabric dangled from the rod. She went downstairs to retrieve her suitcase.

* * *

Sophie startled at the sound of her phone buzzing. Her eyes were heavy with the aftermath of one of those naps where you're sleepier after the nap than you were before it. She had walked down to a sandwich shop after dropping off her bags and felt drowsy as she trudged back in the midday heat. She had plopped down on the white chenille spread and fallen asleep immediately. She blinked and took a deep breath, hoping that her words would come out clearly. "Hello?"

"Sophie." It was her sister, Marina.

"Marina? Why aren't you in the air? Wait, *are* you in the air? Did you get service on the plane?' She heard a sigh at the other end of the connection.

"No, I wish," Marina said. "First they delayed our flight because of mechanical problems, and now they cancelled it."

"Oh no," Sophie moaned. "When is the next one?"

"That's the problem," Marina said. "We can't get there until tomorrow . . . I'm sorry, Sophie . . . I don't know what else to tell you . . . This sucks."

Sophie was now wide awake. "I don't know if I can return the ghost tour tickets. I'd try to exchange them for tomorrow night, but we have the dinner cruise booked." She paused and sighed. "I guess I just won't go."

"Gimme the phone," Sophie heard Demi over the speaker. "Sophie, you are going on that ghost tour. You've been talking about it for weeks, for goodness' sake! And don't tell me you don't want to go alone. You're an adult. Call an Uber and go! We'll text you when we're on our way tomorrow. And I can't wait to hear all about it . . ."

* * *

The Uber driver pulled up in front of the Vendue Hotel. Dusk was settling over the city, and the street was empty and quiet, except for the sounds of chatter that spilled out of the restaurant next to the hotel. "You're sure this is where you're supposed to meet?" the driver asked.

Sophie looked down at her phone, then at the entrance to the park across the street. "Yes," she said. "Right across from the Vendue Hotel."

"You, uh, want me to wait here with you?"

Sophie smiled at the formerly gruff Uber driver who now seemed more like a concerned uncle than a crabby stranger. "I'm fine," she said, "but thank you so much!" She got out of the car, walked over to the park entrance, and glanced at the time on her phone—7:42. The tour began at eight. She realized she was nibbling on her unpolished fingernail and quickly took it out of her mouth. She was not going to stand there and watch the next 15 minutes drag on. Behind her in the park, she heard the strains of a saxophone and decided to investigate. The Vendue Fountain sat just beyond the top of a short flight of concrete steps. A child ran with his clumsy toddler gait through the streams of water spraying from the concrete posts surrounding the center of the fountain. His mother hovered nearby along the perimeter.

Across from the fountain, a lone saxophone player blew the first notes of *Careless Whisper,* which was drowned out by a loud rumbling sound. Sophie turned to see a black mustang with a high-performance muffler rounding the corner. As the rumbling faded, the strains of the sax returned. A few stars peeked through a thin layer of gray clouds in the darkening sky. The air was humid, and Sophie felt chilly and clammy at the same time. She felt her long dark hair with her hand and realized the humidity had done a number on it. *Oh well,* she thought, *I probably look like Medusa.* She walked back down the steps to the corner where a small group had convened: a middle-aged couple, a mother and her young son, and the tour guide.

"Are you with Ghost Town Tours?" the tour guide asked.

"Yes," Sophie nodded.

"We'll be leaving in about five minutes. Just waiting on a couple others."

"Oh," Sophie said, "I had two others coming but . . ." The guide started speaking to the middle-aged couple, and Sophie turned her attention to a woman across the street who was peering up and down the street. "Are you with Ghost Town Tours?"

The woman replied, "I was waiting for someone." She looked around again and frowned. "I don't have a ticket."

"Oh!" Sophie said again. "I have an extra."

"Thank you," the young woman said, absentmindedly, as she continued to scan the street. She was a slight woman, shorter than Sophie and perhaps a few years younger. Although her skin was pale, she wore a white dress that somehow suited her. Her eyes were bright blue, and her long brown hair, equally as frizzy as Sophie's, was pulled back in a low ponytail at the nape of her neck.

The guide checked his watch and shrugged. "I guess this is it," he said. "Let's set off. My name is Gregg. I'll be taking you on a ninety-minute walk through old Charleston. Some of our pavement is a little bumpy as many of the roads are still the original stones. Watch your step. If you have any questions along the way, feel free to ask." He led them up the steps into the park.

As the clouds dissipated, a large, bright yellow-orange moon hung just over the horizon above the opposite shore of the Cooper River. The guide pointed out Fort Sumter, one of the few remaining Union hold-outs in the South in April of 1861. "After a long siege, the South Carolina Militia began firing on Fort Sumter, and a three-day battle ensued. When the Union's ammunition was depleted, they had no choice but to surrender. As they gave the Stars and Stripes a 100-gun salute while they lowered the flag, one of their cannons accidentally discharged, killing Private Daniel Hough, an Irish American immigrant." He paused. "It's said that his ghost haunts Fort Sumter. Some visitors to the fort have reported smelling the aroma of gunpowder. Others claimed to see a shadowy white image saluting the flag at dusk. This is believed to be the ghost of Daniel Hough."

Despite the warm night, Sophie felt a shiver down her spine. The man in the group whispered to his wife, "That's a load of . . ."

"Shh!" she admonished.

The young boy looked up at him. "You don't believe in ghosts?"

"Nah," the man said, shaking his head. "Just here to keep the wife happy."

The guide raised his eyebrows at the man. "I've been doing this job for years. I can assure you that ghosts are real. I've seen them. Let's move on. If you're lucky, you'll see them, too."

Sophie turned to the young woman. "I feel a little out of place. I'm glad you're here. It's nice to see someone my age." The woman smiled at her but didn't reply. Sophie continued, "I'm Sophie. What's your name?"

"I'm Hattie," she said.

"Oh, I love that!" said Sophie. "It's kind of an old-fashioned name, like Sophia."

They continued through the park and down an uneven cobblestone street, stopping at a large two-story masonry building that loomed even larger because it was built upon a high brick basement. Three arched doors were topped by windows that reflected the moonlight. "This is the Old Exchange Building," the guide began. "It was completed in 1771 by the British when they occupied Charleston. It was originally a customs house, but during the Revolutionary War, they converted the downstairs into a dungeon where they jailed American patriots. The prisoners were chained to the walls." The guide stopped and met the eyes of each member of the group. He lowered his voice. "Those who died were thrown into the marsh. Those who didn't had a worse fate—the guards let the rats loose to feed on the prisoners." The group let out a collective gasp, and the guide continued in a low voice. "People at the museum claim they can hear the mournful weeping of the prisoners."

Sophie looked at the young boy, who was now gripping his mother's hand, and at Hattie, whose face was ashen. "These are probably just made-up ghost stories," she said, but her voice was questioning. "I mean, it wouldn't be a ghost tour without scary stories, would it?"

"She's right, isn't she?" the boy asked his mother, pointing to Sophie. "They're just trying to scare us?"

"Of course," his mother answered, as her wide eyes met Sophie's.

The group continued past the Old Tavern, which the guide informed them was established in 1686 and still operated as the oldest liquor store in the country. As he began another story about corpses laid to rest on tavern tables, Sophie whispered to Hattie, "I don't want to hear this one. All this ghost stuff gives me the creeps."

"So, you do believe in ghosts?" Hattie asked.

"Well, I've never seen one," Sophie replied, "but I'm not saying they don't exist. My grandma always said she had a ghost in her house. But a friendly one. It would leave cupboard doors open and move the remote and stuff."

"Those are poltergeists, Sophie, not ghosts. You think there are friendly ghosts?" Hattie smirked. "Ghosts don't haunt because they're friendly. Listen to the stories he's telling you." She nodded at the guide. "They haunt because their deaths were unjust, and they want restitution. Or revenge. They want someone to hear them!"

"Oh!" said Sophie. She remembered the story of the ghost at her middle school—a construction worker who had been killed in an explosion.

A maintenance man reported seeing the ghost's reflection in the elevator doors, and the principal felt a hand push him when no one was there.

The guide's voice interrupted their conversation. "The building you see on the corner is St. Michael's Anglican Church." A bell tower sat atop a white building four stories high, its spire reaching into the starless night. The white church had an eerie glow against the now dark sky. "This is the church cemetery," he said, pointing behind him to the gravestones surrounded by a high wrought iron fence.

"This is the story of a young woman on her wedding day. She was set to inherit her father's estate upon her marriage. The wedding guests grew anxious when she didn't appear. A scream was heard from the sacristy, where the young bride was found dead in her wedding dress. It was suspected, but never proven, that she was poisoned by someone who had their sights set on acquiring the land. Visitors to the cemetery have seen an apparition near the gravestone." The guide paused. "Let's continue to our last stop."

The group began to follow the guide. Sophie felt chilled as her body was wrapped in a cold embrace. She turned to look behind her. "Wait," she called to the group. "Where's Hattie?"

"Who's Hattie?" the guide asked.

"The woman who was next to me," Sophie replied.

The guide raised an eyebrow and looked at the others, who glanced at each other and shrugged.

Sophie caught a movement out of the corner of her eye and quickly turned her head towards the cemetery. Brown leaves lay scattered on the ground around the tombstones. A mist descended on the graveyard, rendering the moon a bright, blurry orb. The bare trees stood sentinel over the headstones.

A slight figure in a white dress drifted through the wrought iron fencing and disappeared behind a large gray concrete marker. Sophie sprinted to the fence and looked at the headstone. It read, "Harriet Mackey, 1784–1804."

Read more about Sophie, Demi, and Marina's adventures in *When the Only Light is the Moon* as they travel through the alluring Greek countryside.

—⚬ ABOUT THE AUTHOR ⚬—
RITA WILSON

Rita Wilson is an award-winning author and artist who has been published in *Rune* and *Riverspeak* Literary Magazines, wolfmatters. org, *Voices from the Attic*, the *100 Lives Anthology*, and *Wisdom of the Crone*. Wilson earned her MFA in Creative Non-Fiction from Carlow University. She serves as Non-Fiction Editor for the *Northern Appalachia Review* and is a Co-Director of the Writing Conference of Northern Appalachia. Her memoir, *Greek Lessons*, was published in 2016, followed by a novel, *When the Only Light of the Moon*, published by Sunbury Press in May 2024.

THRILLER

A Deady Day to Leave Your Lover

BY WILLIAM BURTON MCCORMICK

Rīga, Latvia

Journalism is a difficult way to make a living.

Geoffreys slammed the guards' heads together, watched their unconscious bodies tumble down the stone stairs to the entrance of the brewery's beer cellar. He was down those steps in a flash. He found the keys to the cellar door in one guard's pocket and was inside even before the alarms sounded.

Little time now.

He flicked a switch on the climate control box. Ceiling lamps sputtered to life in the huge, warehouse-like cellar.

On either side of a narrow aisle stood towering racks of mammoth beer casks, stored on their sides and rising three barrels high, the inventory disappearing into the underground gloom. It reminded him of that last warehouse in *Raiders of the Lost Ark*.

A needle in a haystack. The last cellphone call mentioned only darkness . . .

Pain.

And beer.

Geoffreys found a crowbar propped against the first rack, began sprinting down the aisle thumping on the oak barrel lids. The resulting thuds, low, dull and far too consistent.

101

He'd need more good fortune than Laima, mythical Latvian Goddess of Luck, if he were to—

One thump produced a higher tone.

Geoffreys stopped dead in his tracks. Struck the second-row cask again with his crowbar. Yes, the sound was definitely lighter, hollower, the cask not so full of liquid . . .

One final knocking. The barrel shuddered in response.

He tore into the lid with the crowbar, had the cask open in seconds. A rich, yellow beer flowed out.

As did the soaked body of a woman, smartphone clutched in her hand.

His colleague and lover, Santa. Still breathing, thank Laima.

* * *

Far away from the terrible brewery, Santa Ezeriņa sat on a bench in Bastejkalna Park, hair and clothes still soaked with Latvian beer, a towel over her shoulders.

"I'm all sticky," she complained. "It was those crooked bankers again, Geoffreys. Trying to shut me up permanently. Keep me from reporting their crimes. Where better to store a body than the barrels in their backers' brewery? They'd let that beer age six months. Ship me out when the trail is cold."

"If it'd been a steel cask, you'd be dead. Thank Laima that Latvian brewers are old-fashioned."

"Yeah, yeah, Laima." She rubbed the towel on her head, trying to get the beer scent out of ears and hair. "When I *played* dead, Geoffreys, I never thought they'd make me part of their stock. Fortunately, they didn't quite get the barrel full after shoving me inside. Just enough to breathe and call you. Lost the cellphone when they racked it with the forklift."

"Fortunately, I came in time."

"You owed me one. A couple, really."

Her tone annoyed Geoffreys. "I don't think either of us owe each other anything."

"What about when I rescued you from the Lithuania mob twice? And that FSB stripper with the hypodermic in the garter—"

"I can't live like this. The chaos. The danger for years—"

"Years? You're not even thirty."

"And I'd like to live to see thirty, Santa. I'm sorry, it's over. We're over. I'm not doing this every week. No more adventures."

"Geoffreys—"

He walked away down the path.

She sat on the bench, emotions conflicted, confused. *What a day?*

Captured.

Barreled

Rescued.

Dumped.

Her ire rose. Who was *he* to leave her? After all the times she'd given him her scoops? Written his articles for him? Saved his life? Given two years of *her* own life to that talent-less wretch!

Santa rose to find Geoffreys, to give him a piece of her mind.

She predicted he'd head towards his apartment. Leaving the greenery of the park behind, she was quickly in Rīga's urban center, the area under renovation for the coming tourist season, scaffolding across many city buildings, artisans restoring the decorative facades Rīga was known for, mythological figures on the face of every building.

She passed a restoration artisan working on a nude figure of Laima. Geoffreys always had a fetishization for the Goddess of Luck. Most Latvians were Lutherans, but Geoffreys romanticized the pre-Christian era . . .

Well, he'd need a Goddess of Luck when she found him. Let him date Laima, take *her* to his boring family dinners . . .

Passersby stared at her.

"Yeah, yeah. I reek of beer. It was a good time, everyone! Quite the party! Wahoo!"

Santa turned a corner. A startling sight waited there.

Geoffreys was being led at gunpoint by two thugs towards a Porsche 911. A third thug sat waiting in the running car.

The Lithuanian mob!

Again!

Geoffreys resisted as they tried to force him into the car, only to be pistol-whipped by the biggest thug. Geoffreys hit the pavement. The two men lifted his body, shoved it into the cramped backseat of the Porsche.

Santa began running towards the scene.

One mobster ducked into the car, but the other noticed her approach, raised his pistol.

Thinking quickly, she snapped the gun out his hand with her beer-soaked towel, then flung it in the thug's face as she passed. While the mobster fumbled for her blindly, she leapt onto the back of the car, gripping the Porsche's rear spoiler as it sped away.

Speeding through Rīga's streets, Santa climbed over that spoiler and up the back of the car. Through the rear window she could see Geoffreys laying scrunched in the tiny backseats, clearly unconscious.

Dump me, will you.

Atop the Porsche's roof, she saw the sunroof open, the other thug emerging.

She risked freeing a hand from the car body, punched him across a granite jaw. It did nothing but hurt her hand.

Or almost nothing.

The thug position's slipped slightly at the blow, a knee falling against the driver; the wheelman instinctively swerved.

The Porsche slid to the side of the road onto the walkway, scattering pedestrians, knocking scaffolding poles free, restoration workmen and repair tarps raining down in Rīga's center.

A broken bust of the goddess Laima bounced off the hood.

Santa seized a snapped scaffolding pole from the falling debris, a torn restoration tarp hanging from it, flapping in the wind like some ancient battle flag.

She shoved the pole's end through the sunroof glass into the stomach of the thug. His screams were drowned out by the car's engine as the light went out of his eyes.

Santa slipped down onto the hood, pressing the tarp piece across the windshield, blinding the driver.

He did not slow. If anything, the car accelerated.

She glanced ahead.

The great Daugava River waited for them.

The Porsche sped off the bank. It hung a moment in the air over those slow flowing gray waters and then hit with terrible force, Santa's body skimming over the surface for meters before she sunk into the depths.

The impact scattered her wits. It took moments for Santa to recover, drifting in the current. She might not have recovered so quickly, but a glance at that Porsche sinking towards river bottom galvanized action.

Geoffreys.

She couldn't lose him.

She took a great breath and dove, following the car down into the depths. She reached it just as the Porsche hit bottom, her lungs already burning as she tried to force open the door.

The driver's lifeless face stared at her through the window, a spider-web crack marking where his skull had struck the glass.

Unable to pry the door open, she ascended to the car's top, shoved aside the other dead thug to press herself in via the sunroof. A tight fit.

Her vision was fading. Was it the darkness of the car's interior? Or was she blacking out from lack of air? Her drumming pulse, eating up oxygen.

She had no time.

Santa found a floating body in the blackness that must be Geoffreys, forced him through the roof window. Up and up, she ascended, her arm around his chest, as she kicked for the surface. Her lungs were spent, vision gone, she could only kick and hope to reach air in time.

She broke the surface, a free-flowing breeze across her face. She took several great gasps, waiting for her vision to clear. At last, she could see the riverbank, a crowd gathering at the spectacle. She paddled over, fighting the current and exhaustion, tugging Geoffreys to the bank. Gave him mouth-to-mouth as others shouted for the police.

It'd be the last time she pressed her lips to his, she promised herself.

* * *

Sitting on that same Bastejkalna Park bench past nightfall, Geoffreys rubbed a towel across his head, trying to clear the river water from his ears.

"I don't understand, Santa. You didn't take me seriously, before, did you? About ending it? That was just a mood of mine, Tigress."

"I take a death-defying ride on a Porsche top, with mob hitmen gunning at me and a plunge to the river bottom, seriously enough," said Santa standing on the park path in front of him. "It's simple, Geoffreys.

It's over. We're done. Like you, I can't live with the chaos. I'll never make twenty-nine."

"Santa, please. . . ."

Their colleague Juris drove up the path on his motor-scooter, pulling up near the bench. "What a day! Everyone in the city's talking about it. What copy you'll have! Tell me the story!"

"The story is I'm finished with Geoffreys," said Santa coldly. "No more adventures."

She left the two men wide-eyed, walking away down the park path.

"Sorry to hear it," said Juris to his friend. "She's a temperamental one, isn't she?"

Geoffreys continued to rub his head with the towel. "Laima hasn't abandoned me—yet—buddy. The goddess has a way of—"

"Oh, shut up about those old myths, will you?"

"Don't be disrespectful, Juris. If the goddess hears—"

The whirling drumming of helicopter blades caught their ears. A spotlight enveloped Santa far up the park's path. A net dropped upon her.

In seconds the whirlybird had netted Santa and was speeding away over the Rīga skyline with its struggling captive hanging below.

"Those damn bankers again!" Geoffreys sprang to his feet, threw off the towel. "Lend me your bike, Juris! Quickly!"

Juris let Geoffreys take his place. "What are you going to do?"

"Go after her, of course."

"She dumps you every week, Geoffreys. Or you dump her. Why risk your life for Santa, again?"

"I love her, Juris. And I'm an addict."

"Addict?"

"Our make-up sex is incredible."

Geoffreys gunned the engine and sped down the path in pursuit of the helicopter.

And one more fix.

Juris could only watch and wonder.

Follow the thrilling investigations of Santa Ezeriņa in *KGB BANKER*.

─◦ ABOUT THE AUTHOR ◦─
WILLIAM BURTON McCORMICK

William Burton McCormick is an Edgar, Dagger, Thriller, Shamus, Derringer, Sliver Falchion and Claymore awards finalist whose fiction regularly appears in *Ellery Queen's Mystery Magazine*, *Alfred Hitchcock's Mystery Magazine*, *The Saturday Evening Post*, *Black Mask*, *Storiaverse* and elsewhere. He is a graduate of Brown University, earned an MA in Novel Writing from the University of Manchester and was elected a Hawthornden Writing Fellow in Scotland. His novel *KGB BANKER* won Best Conspiracy Novel of the Year from BestThrillers. Com. A native of Nevada, he has lived in Russia, Ukraine, Latvia, Estonia and the United Kingdom for writing purposes.

Learn more about him at www.williamburtonmccormick.com

Harry Thursday's Private War

BY ROBERT WALTON

If Harry Thursday were to stand up straight, he'd be a good six-foot-four. He had sandy-colored hair and a pointed, slender face that ended in a squared chin. He had a nose that followed the contours of his face, straight and slender but with a queer little bend at the end where he had broken it years ago. He often had tanned, almost dark skin, and crow's feet that poked out from the outer edges of his brooding blue eyes. His hands were calloused and lean, and his arms were strong and muscular. He had the V-shaped torso of a swimmer.

His father, Alfred Thursday, had turned the family's engine die business into the successful Thursday Aeronautics and Plastics, a manufacturer of small to mid-sized airplanes whose long-time customer was, not the least, the US government. TAP boomed during WWII.

In 1958, Alfred took his only son south to the Venezuelan Amazon when Harry was only fifteen. He was searching for a new alternative to rubber for his planes. They befriended the Yeshret, a cannibal tribe who liked them both enough that the chief, Yamnuit, offered Harry his twelve-year-old daughter as a bride. Harry, naturally, accepted the bride for fear that he and his father would offend their hosts, lest they become dinner. At Alfred's request, Harry did not attempt to consummate the marriage.

Alfred had brought his new flying suit with him and tested it (against Harry's protestations) by jumping off the three-hundred-foot waterfall.

Harry and the Yeshret all waited nervously for Alfred to float into the forest, but he didn't. Harry was devastated, Yamnuit was heartbroken. Alfred fell straight down like a bag of lead *coconas* and died. Because of Thursday Aeronautics' considerable contributions to Venezuela, when word reached the Ministry of Interior of his tragic death, they renamed the waterfall Alfred Falls.

In 1966 Harry, at twenty-three, had no intention of being conscripted into military service after college; and his mother, who still owned Alfred's majority shares of the business, didn't want her son to go near Vietnam. The war was raging, and he had already graduated from UAC with a degree in Archaeology. His mother insisted he take business courses, hoping he would get a master's and come home to run the business, and so the young Thursday worked his way from summer jobs in the factory to the corporate headquarters in Bala Cynwyd and was unhappy, not because he hated business, but because he hated the structure. Archaeology was in his blood.

He took an office next to the "old man's." It had a window view of the towering city skyscrapers. The doors were solid oak, which he had replaced with frosted glass, and the brass handle he exchanged for the throttle from the first Bala 750, a twin-engine turboprop that Alfred designed in 1949.

One day, Mrs. Witts, the secretary for the executive office, knocked on his office door.

"Yes," he said. He threw his pencil down and brushed his hand through his hair, glad for the distraction.

"Harry," she said authoritatively. She had worked for Thursday Aeronautics since just after the war ended.

At five-foot-four, she was anything but timid, as her stature might suggest. She knew the business, and after Alfred died, carried the company forward, organizing the accounts and production until Uncle Ted could take control the next year. When Harry graduated from college, she gently guided him into his new position.

She stood framed by the open door, hand on the throttle, and said, "David Poole is . . ." But before she could finish her sentence, he picked the phone up and punched the outside line.

"Which line?" he asked confused.

She sighed. "He's not on the phone; he's . . ." David brushed past her, excusing himself as he did, "here to see you."

"Good day, Madame," David said cordially. "You're very kind." He bowed and waited until she closed the door behind her and turned to Harry with a broad smile. "You old fool," he said, "How the hell are you?"

Harry stood to greet him, extended his hand, and then punched him in the face with his other; not hard enough to do any damage but enough that he took a step backward, wiped his face with his hand looking for blood. At first he frowned, then, noticing there was no blood, suddenly smiled.

"That's for stealing Chris," Harry said.

David grinned and said with unwavering confidence, "You haven't changed, Harry." He walked over and added, "I can still take you on the mat."

"Maybe." They were quiet for a while, and Harry broke the uncomfortable silence and said, "I am a fool, thinking she ever liked either of us."

"Well," David said, taking a step back, "she liked one of us enough to marry me."

Harry thought about that for a second, frowned, then smiled. As Harry reached for his hand to shake again, David took a preemptory step backward, before realizing Harry's earnestness.

"She always liked you best, I guess," Harry said. "Too bad though." He paced to the window, turned, and said, "Good. Good, I'm happy for you, David." He found a pack of cigarettes on the windowsill and fished one out. David reached over and lit it for him. Harry took a long drag, exhaled, watched the smoke drift skyward, and said, "I thought you'd be in Athens getting your PhD or something."

David flopped down on the couch, "Got my master's the year after I graduated. I live in Athens now. We do. I'm vying for the Curator of the Gennadius Library. But, um, the fish aren't biting."

"Have you been there since you graduated?"

Sadly, no. I was drafted and spent two years in Saigon as a contract specialist for the Army."

"Two years? I thought the sentence was usually one," Harry said.

"I re-upped after my first tour. And you? This doesn't seem like the Harry I knew in UAC." He looked at a diploma on the wall above the small bar adjacent to the desk and squinted. "Let's see. You were one year behind me?"

"Two. I got my MA in Archaeology and have been working here summers. Now, I run the place. Go figure."

"I mean, considering your family owns the place," David said.

He joined Harry at the large picture window. During the winter months, they could see the river and points west. "Why are you here, David?"

"Do you remember when we were roommates?" He smiled, remembering the past. They met in college and had become close friends. "I felt like we'd stay young forever."

"Yes, we still are. And then reality hits, and you have the rest of your life breathing down your fucking neck. I don't want to do this for too much longer. I'm an archaeologist. It's in my blood.

"Me too, Harry. If I can secure that gig with the Gennadius, I can head up my own digs. Our digs, Harry."

Harry looked over with a grand smile. "That'd be nice."

"But first, we have a job waiting for us." That earned him a curious look. "I need to make my own money. Serious money. I don't have a real job since they kicked—er—let me go. But I did learn a valuable skill."

Harry thought he knew what his friend was getting at. He was talking about buying or selling something somewhere. "Where?"

"It's warm and beautiful. The girls are not bad either."

"Are you talking about Greece?

David chuckled. "Vietnam, Harry."

Harry shook his head and rubbed his stubbled chin. "I did everything I could to not have to go there, and now you're asking me to go there. What if they draft me when I'm over there?" He paced his office, his hands moving. "Why there, for Christ's sake?"

"It's where the money is. Believe me. I spent my time well over there. I know what we need to do. I have connections. I know people." He grinned broadly. "Things aren't going well . . ."

Harry interrupted him. "That's not what Walter Cronkite says."

David chuckled. "Well, that's because they want us to think that. The Viet Cong are wiping the mud up with our side," he paused to light a cigarette. Harry said nothing but tried to bore holes in David's head. David only smiled. "Look, I know what you're thinking. What is he going to ask me to do now? Right?

"Okay, that was college. You were careless. If Bussey hadn't already been suspicious that things were going missing, you'd have been in the clear. I told you how I stole things from the cafeteria. I didn't tell you to do it yourself. Besides, you made out all right."

"Made out?" Harry finally said after a long pause. "He was going to turn me over to the cops. My mother would have killed me."

"You talked yourself out of it."

Harry smiled at the memory. He remembered how he sweet-talked Bussey and Miss Sharon into giving him a second chance. How he had learned a lesson. How he'd never sin again.

He remembered how he sweated the night Bussey caught him stealing, thinking about how to get out of that situation; and after they banished him from the cafeteria, how the girls on campus felt sorry for him. And they would feed him from the buffet line. And how they pawed over him, and how the staff felt sorry for him and did all they could to feed him, knowing he lived off campus and needed to eat. It was a sweet gig, he remembered; but he also remembered how his guilt-ridden conscience kept him from ever stealing again, and when he noticed David watching, he wiped the smile off his face and said. "What? So, you want to steal cheese again?"

"Something just as valuable. Gold."

That made Harry stop and turn his head. "Gold," he said as if anything that came after that was okay. "As in raw gold or gold bars?" Harry was thinking of the different options.

"Gold that the French left behind."

"Buried treasure. Right up our alley." He had no idea that the French were even involved with Vietnam, let alone anything about French gold. For all he knew, the Americans were up to their necks in government-toppling and communist-blocking. Politics was not his thing. Instead, he held up his hand and, directing the conversation, steered it to where it made sense he should listen. "Go on."

"Ideally, archaeologists go after ancient, buried gold."

"I'm feeling kind of old, David."

"There is a black market in Saigon," David said. "In Saigon, everything is game." Still, exuding confidence, he got up and paced the floor, ending by the window again. "We can do it. And the feds will pay for it."

Harry quieted down, meaning the conversation was over—for now. The last thing he needed was to involve the Feds. "How?"

"How many planes do you sell over there? Considering they don't last too long."

"Couple dozen a year. Not enough to have a surplus. And the last time I looked, the US government was not in the business of trading planes for gold."

David was unfazed. "I said, black market."

"What did you major in?"

"I told you I learned a lot over there."

Harry had no idea what this would involve. How would they even find the gold, and how would they afford to buy it? It seemed insurmountable. "What do you want from me? I don't even know what you're talking about."

"Planes for gold."

"This is a half-baked idea. What is the risk-reward ratio?"

"Money, my friend. Cash."

He knew exactly who they needed for the job. David stopped selling it. Harry was glad, too. To David, the lack of confrontation was the same as affirmation.

Ted, his uncle, was high up in the OSS during WWII, and Harry figured it wouldn't hurt to ask for his help. Harry remembered Ted saying once to his father, "It's easier to ask for forgiveness than for permission."

Ted, who made the final decisions in the business, happened to be in his office at the factory in Byberry Township where Harry had whetted his skills. "We don't sell weapons," he said.

"Weapons? No. We make planes, and there is a need for them. A premium need."

"The government already buys them from us."

But Ted, ever the adventurer, didn't prove the ally they needed. "You need someone with real connections, someone who knows the market. You need Franz Hageen."

Franz Hageen's family had owned the Bank du Luc, the third-largest bank in Bern, Switzerland, for over a hundred years, and Ted was sure he would help with his nephew's venture. "He owes me," Ted said with a victorious smile.

Harry remembered when Franz was an associate professor of business at UAC and a close family friend. He was between Ted's age and Harry's, and Harry knew him from childhood and all the times he had dined with them on holidays. The Thursdays had done business with the Bank du Luc since the First World War, and they had built a lucrative business together. Alfred and Harry were close to Franz in business and in life. After a few calls, Ted found that Franz was "working in Hong Kong."

Harry filled David in on the company business. "I forgot to mention, we also sell a two-man helicopter, which we subcontract with Hughes Helicopters to manufacture. TI-6 Rounder is a two-man craft that is light, fast, very maneuverable, and able to reach speeds of 150 miles per hour. But first, we need an old family friend, Franz Hageen."

David was surprised, "The professor from UAC?"

* * *

Two days later, Ted, Harry, and David were in the company warehouse in Jersey.

"We've made some minor changes to our planes and the TI-6 Rounder," Ted explained as they surveyed the floor. "They're prewired for radar."

"Those aren't radar mounts," Harry said. "I may not know much about guns, but those don't look like radar mounts."

"That's true, but with a few minor adjustments the wire mounts are interchangeable with other functioning hardware. Guns would be illegal," Ted said. "Our contract with the Feds expressly states that all aircraft we sell to them must be for non-combat use." He looked at Harry. "There is a section in the contract, a codicil if you will, which allows for supplementary modification in case of emergencies. How much of this is David's idea?"

"I approached Harry, and he took the bait."

"David the bait monger?"

David pretended offense.

"This is all hypothetical. Assuming we have to use Thursday Aeronautics to achieve our end game. What obstacles will we face?"

"You're smiling, nephew. You approve?"

Harry played devil's advocate and looked like an attorney searching for a response to his opponent's argument. He said, "Thursday Aeronautics doesn't make weapons."

"Never say never," David said. "Anyone can get a gun. They're lying all over the ground there."

Back in the office the supervisor, Johnny Bigelow, was busy with payroll. There was a lull in the conversation, and he looked at the men in his office and excused himself. He knew enough to understand what he was meant to hear and not hear. Ted poured a round of whiskey. "I can't, ethically or otherwise, knowingly sell any kind of weapons."

"Because we don't make them," Harry said. "Look, I'm covering my ass here. I don't like being unprepared." He lowered his voice to a whisper. "If," he said, "And that is a big one. If we need something to trade with, where do we get .50 caliber machine guns?"

"China."

The next day, Harry was on his way to Hong Kong while David made for Saigon.

Read more about the adventures of Harry Thursday
in *The Mask of Minos* and more.

———•❧ ABOUT THE AUTHOR ❧•———
ROBERT WALTON

Robert Walton is the author of the Harry Thursday Thriller series, including *Fatal Snow*, *The Mask of Minos*, *Wish to Die*, and *The Relentless Sun*. He began writing in 2014 and published his first novel, Fatal Snow, in 2015. He lives in New Cumberland, Pennsylvania, and continues to write novels and short stories.

The Spy

BY A.A. WEISS

A false Canadian passport, a mistranslated code phrase, a rush to board a railcar heading east—on the first mission of his career, Luke had been too stupid to know his life was in danger.

Perhaps it was the sense of calm that protected him—making free eye contact with the guards as he exited the Grand Kremlin Palace, saying *spaciba, udachee vam* in his butchered Russian, nodding respectfully. No foreign agent would flee the scene of a botched assassination with such *joie de vivre*.

Kiril Danilov, a warrant officer in the Red Army, was knifing his way into politics. He sipped vodka respectfully while moving from conversation to conversation, waiting for the attention of important men, and getting shut down at every turn. Two weeks before, within earshot of a hidden CIA microphone, Danilov had claimed he could expedite the "elimination of political resistance," and now Luke was shadowing to see if this man could follow through. But Luke needed just an hour to see this wasn't a major actor in the coming wave of Soviet global dominance. He was a background extra looking to audition for a larger role.

Once Danilov got frustrated enough, he'd start to drink more. And then, once he took his portions of toasting vodka in gulps instead of sips, Luke could engage him. If Luke managed to get a certain promise from Danilov, Luke's handler would provide clearance for further engagement.

So many steps involved to make a proper kill, thought Luke.

Leaving the reception hall, all guests funneled past security into the main gallery. Among the dignitaries and foreign visitors, according to

117

the handler, was a secondary asset. One of these other scholars or government officials was also collecting intelligence for the US government. Luke scanned the room to see if he could notice any telling features.

"Almost too boring," said a man at Luke's side. "Agriculture, labor—so many similar conversations. Makes you just want to read a novel."

From across the room, Luke watched as Danilov made his way to the periphery of a group of senior administration officials. Had he taken that last shot of vodka in one gulp, or in a more patient two? This intruding conversationalist wasn't helping Luke's focus.

"Boring, absolutely," said Luke, annoyed, yet proud to have remembered what he believed to be a Canadian inflection to his Russian. His cover was a visiting graduate student, in Moscow at the invitation of the agricultural university to share a McGill professor's research on altering vegetable DNA to better resist cold climates.

"Tolstoy. Dostoyevsky," said Luke. "Yes, I like books."

"Jack London for me," said the man. "You are Canadian, yes?"

"Yes, yes. Canadian. But I speak some Russian."

"I'm glad you understand my language. The French language too, I imagine, as a Canadian. Languages are good. I'm working on my English, but it's not quite there."

And then Luke looked at the man. The bald head. The birthmark. Luke didn't need his handler to confirm the identity. The bodyguards standing two feet back on either side were all the confirmation needed. Intel had put this man far away, in the north, inspecting the construction of a supposedly clandestine naval base.

"President Gorbachev," said Luke. "An honor."

The man received Luke's handshake with a smile. "Misha," he said.

Luke's cover name was *Georges*.

One of the bodyguards tapped the president on the shoulder, and Gorbachev put his hands in the air to communicate he was helpless to fight their wishes.

"Hopefully we'll find another moment to discuss literature."

And then he was gone, absorbed into the collection of officials who parted for his entrance to their private conversations.

Luke had lost Danilov.

With all attention on the president, Luke entered the bathroom and locked himself in a stall. On his Casio wristwatch, he messaged his handler.

Danilov inconclusive. Engagement interrupted. MG present.

The handler responded immediately.

Disengage Danilov. Confirm MG present.

Luke confirmed Gorbachev's attendance at the gala. The handler repeated his message.

Confirm MG present.

What's not to understand? thought Luke.

Confirmed. MG present.

The next message didn't come quickly, not like Luke thought it would. He flicked the Casio watch-face with his fingers, thinking it to be defective. *Casios now instead of Rolexes,* he thought. *From high class to a new age of useless technology.*
Finally, the handler reestablished communication.

Give toast. Single berth train awaits at 22hrs.

The train made sense to Luke. That was part of the original plan. But what was this about giving a toast? A final beep from the handler:

Confirmed. Give MG toast and proceed to train. Good luck.

There should have been no confusion on the first mission of a new operative. A case officer collected information. A handler processed intelligence into meaningful actions for the operative to execute. An operative, very simply, without deviation, did what he was told—assassinate, yes or no.

Give MG toast, Luke mused.

The briefing case officer had said Danilov was a clear danger. The handler now said to disengage Danilov and give a toast to President Gorbachev. On foot, the journey from gala to the train station would take forty-five minutes. Luke flipped the watch-face back into place to read the time—only fifty minutes before the train would depart Yaroslavsky station.

Back in the main gallery, one of the generals was speaking with his glass raised to President Gorbachev. There was a joke that made everyone laugh—something about Gorbachev outlawing alcohol in Russia—and then Gorbachev was again near enough for Luke to make eye contact. They didn't get to speak—but Luke removed a flute of champagne from a passing tray and held the thin glass in the air. Gorbachev did the same— *a pleasure to converse with you ever so briefly*, his look seemed to say—and then Luke headed for the exit.

After turning the corner, the Kremlin no longer in view, he walked with a gait just short of jogging. The time constraints and the dark night didn't allow him to properly check for someone following him, his path to the station a little more direct than his training had told him was prudent. He looked over his shoulder twice during the walk. He saw nothing. And this would haunt him later. Even looking back with the benefit of hindsight—he had seen nothing.

* * *

Only once sitting inside the private berth on the train did Luke appreciate the fight or flight chemicals coursing through his body. He was sweating, his pulse elevated.

The handler's message beeped just as Luke locked the berth's door.

Confirm mission.

Luke stared at the message. He hadn't killed anyone. What was there to confirm? He imagined the handler at a desk in Washington, filling out paperwork with a series of checks on a list. Target killed or disengaged? Exfiltration successful or compromised?

Luke whispered the message into the Casio's microphone.

Confirmed. Danilov disengaged. Train berth secured.

Luke inspected the berth. Two beds, one on each side, with a small table in between under the window. This premier cabin had a water closet with a toilet and a tiny sink he could use to wash his hair. He'd be in this cell of a room for two weeks.

A series of knocks pounded on the door. Passport control, Luke assumed. But instead of the uniformed man who'd inspected his ticket on the way inside the train, he was surprised to find a young woman.

"Why is my berth locked?" she shouted in Russian. "Why are you in my private berth?"

She paused her screaming to look at Luke's face. "You're American."

"Citizen of Canada," said Luke in Russian.

"Speak English," said the woman, also in English. "And show me your ticket."

Luke held out his ticket, but wouldn't allow her to pass as she pushed forward. She seemed surprised when he didn't step back. She held up her own ticket. "You see? Same berth. The criminals in charge have double-booked the expensive single cabin."

"You can't come in," said Luke.

His attention shifted to his wrist as the handler sent a message. He tilted the angle of the watch-face away from the woman's view.

MG? Confirm status.

Status? Still president of the Soviet Union, as far as Luke knew. Probably at home in pajamas reading a thick book.

"Come in and sit for tea, Ekaterina," said Luke. "We'll figure this out before departure."

"How did you know my name?" said the woman.

Luke pointed to the name on her ticket.

She nodded. "Show me yours, again."

"My name is Georges," said Luke. "How did you know I speak English?"

"An instant stereotype," she said. "Walking and talking. And you didn't say anything abusive when I knocked on your door with aggression. So, yes. American, I think."

"Canadian," said Luke.

"The same to me."

This isn't right, thought Luke.

The woman, Ekaterina, had spread her belongings over one of the beds in the time it took Luke to prepare two cups of tea.

The handler repeated the message.

MG? Confirm status.

Luke tried to think of a fancy way, a professional way, to say he had no clue.

"Excuse me," he said to Ekaterina. "Please drink the tea without me while I freshen up."

He stepped into the water closet and whispered into the Casio watch-face.

> *MG's presence did not complicate exfiltration of site. Cabin berth secured. Shadow activity suspected. Postpone delivery of next mission until threat confirmed and corrected.*

Luke felt stupid as soon as he sent the message. There was probably a single set of code words to communicate all of that. If the handler didn't know he was working with a rookie, then he certainly knew now.

The handler responded.

> *Mission failure confirmed by secondary asset. MG alive.*

Luke froze. Failure confirmed. Another message arrived from the handler.

The Spy

Secondary asset confirms shadow activity. Secure berth and reestablish communication 24 hours before arrival in Beijing.

Luke inhaled deeply, felt the pulse on his neck slow slightly—*I was supposed to kill Gorbachev*—then opened the door.

Luke's hands were both free to grab this intruder's wrists if she lunged at him, but her posture wasn't combative, but rather panicked. Ekaterina stood abruptly, saying nothing as she pushed past Luke and entered the water closet, where she spit her mouthful of tea into the tiny sink. Then she poured the rest of her cup down the drain.

"You're definitely not Russian." She returned to the table, inspected the place setting, unrolled a tiny spoon from inside a maroon napkin, and held it up in the air between them, as though prepared to teach him the word in Russian. She put a small amount of sugar on the end, less than a packet, and held the spoon in front of Luke's eyes.

"Civilized people don't require such sweetness from tea," said Ekaterina.

Luke didn't react. *Shadow activity confirmed.*

"Do you understand me? From now on, *I* make the tea."

Luke sat back. He understood.

She re-made the tea. They drank in silence while sitting opposite one another on separate beds, looking into each other's eyes—not for intimacy, but to see if something biological would betray their true motives.

Her shoes were flat, good for running, which didn't match her fine green dress.

"Were you at the gala?" asked Luke, finally.

"What gala?"

"Did you follow me from the presidential palace?"

Ekaterina smiled. "It seems I don't understand English very well."

Luke repeated the question in Russian.

"Oh," said Ekaterina. "Follow you? Ha. Do you think I'm a spy?"

"I've seen many movies with beautiful women doing such things, yes."

"You think I'm a spy and you think I'm beautiful. Must I accept your delusions in order to keep the compliment?"

Luke sipped his tea. "Forgive me, I'm nervous. I know Moscow can be a dangerous place. Many misconceptions circulate abroad, evidently."

Ekaterina laughed through her nose and had to wipe something from her face with the tea napkin. "New York City is dangerous, yes. Tell me, where is danger in Canada?"

Luke's mind, instinctively, went to polar bears, cutting oneself while ice-fishing, playing hockey with too much aggression.

"It's very safe—true. But all cities have their bad spots."

"And where is the most bad spot? I should like to visit one day and prefer to avoid feeling nervous like you do now."

"Start with Montreal. Do you speak French?"

"Do you? Say something. Say, *I am afraid of women and of Moscow*."

Luke put down his teacup. Ekaterina stretched her neck to see that he'd finished. She nodded, as though pleased.

"But you're very right," she said.

"About what?" asked Luke.

"Moscow has many bad spots."

* * *

For the next thirty years, Luke carried a secret.

Secret wasn't the right word—because no one ever asked. But if a colleague had ever questioned his patriotism, challenged his commitment to the unequivocal success of the American way—Luke *would* have lied.

As it had been on his first trip as a newly-minted assassin through the countryside, sharing the berth on the Trans-Siberian Railway with Ekaterina, as it was the day he retired, thirty successful years later, the sensibility was the same: Luke Lundy—Cold War assassin for the United States government—adored spending time in Russia.

Each time he touched Russian soil was like being an astronaut setting foot on another planet, slowly building up the courage to remove his helmet, fill his lungs with the unfamiliar blend of air, and discover there was more than enough oxygen mixed with all the other strange particles.

But he didn't know that about Russia, about himself, while on that first journey.

"You'll love the countryside," Ekaterina had said on their third day in the cabin. "If you don't, you're not human."

"You've been to Siberia?"

Ekaterina shook her head. "We can be human together."

"Why are you traveling there now?" asked Luke. "I'm traveling to Beijing to continue my goodwill tour on behalf of my university's agricultural department. I've told you—now it's your turn."

"A complete story," said Ekaterina. "Well-rehearsed and presented now three times in forced conversation. Your story hasn't changed one bit."

"You're a spy," said Luke.

Ekaterina smiled. After a moment she looked out the window. Luke watched as her pupils danced from side to side while they tried to focus on passing trees. She wasn't looking at him, and wouldn't for quite some time. He loosened his grip on the knife he concealed under the bedding on his side of the berth.

"Please tell me you're a spy," said Luke. "It will make such a great story when I get home. The Soviet Union. The Trans-Siberian railroad. A beautiful Russian spy, cornering me in my own berth."

She said nothing.

"You're a spy," said Luke, trying to appear calm. "I know you are."

She continued looking out the window. Her eyes danced.

"Your name is Lucas Xavier Lundy," she said at last. "You're a spy, too."

*   *   *

Years after the train ride with Ekaterina, at one of his five retirement debriefings, Luke was advised about needing company permission to write his memoirs.

"I met Gorbachev once," said Luke. "I went to one of his functions in Moscow. We talked briefly of literature."

"A cultured man."

"I liked Yeltsin better."

"You met Boris Yeltsin, too?"

Luke recalled the stern look on Yeltsin's face. He ordered the handlers and helpers to leave once he confirmed that Luke spoke Russian. "I don't think it's possible," Yeltsin had said. "What your president promises cannot be achieved. They've already dispersed."

"Barcelona, Budapest, and . . ."

Yeltsin leaned in.

". . . and closer to home, in Kazan."

Yeltsin groaned and smiled. "I knew he was close! You've discovered their locations. And the American government is willing to do me this favor? Okay, you have my permission. Eliminate my opposition. Be my guest. They'll be on to you and gone from each city by morning."

Luke placed three photographs on the table.

Three dead bodies, each in a different city: Barcelona, Budapest, Kazan.

The last photograph was Kiril Danilov.

As Yeltsin shuffled the photos in his hands, one, two, three, Luke noticed the left hand missing two fingers and thought this man would be a terrible card player.

"You have a new friend," said Yeltsin. "Tell that to your president."

"Would you be able to check in on a friend of *mine*?" Luke asked. "She's Russian."

Yeltsin began typing on his computer, pecking with fingers, and then motioned for Luke to come around the desk and finish the search.

"My secretary is quite good at typing."

Luke entered the name.

Yeltsin's bear-hand tugged at Luke's shoulder, turning the American's body away just as green script filled the black screen. "Even a friend must be protected from Russian state secrets." Yeltsin put on his reading glasses and motioned for Luke to retake his seat.

Yeltsin read her full name. Andreyvna—such a common patronymic. Ekaterina Andreyvna.

"KGB? Correct?"

Luke shifted in his chair. It was her.

"Killed in action while serving in the east. You were friends, not enemies? I'm sorry for your loss."

"Vladivostok?" asked Luke. "Is that where she died?"

Yeltsin politely refused to confirm or deny this state secret. "A hero to her country," he said. "Shall we honor her with a toast?"

Both men looked at the bottle within Yeltsin's reach on the desk, the alcohol brown and viscous, not clear vodka like Luke had assumed Russia always used to toast its dead heroes.

*   *   *

By the end of his career, nothing would scare Luke more than sleeping in the same bed two nights in a row. But on the train heading east, sharing a cabin with Ekaterina, he slept well, only jumping up when he opened his eyes, remembering he was sharing a cabin with a Russian agent. Ekaterina had covered Luke in a blanket while he slept.

"Morning chill," she said. "You were sneezing in your sleep."

"I'm fine. You also look cold. Are you well?"

Luke pulled the blanket back over his shoulders and accepted Ekaterina's cup of tea. He smelled it. He took a sip and kept it in his mouth, ready to reject it if anything tasted bitter or too sweet or peculiar. After the first sip, he gulped it down.

"I allowed the tea to cool before waking you," said Ekaterina. "Very civilized."

Luke didn't say anything. He just stared at his cup. To Ekaterina, he must have appeared like a little boy, chastised, ready for someone to relieve him of his guilt and say everything was okay.

"I am aware of your identity, mission, and further intentions," said Ekaterina.

Luke opened his mouth but said nothing.

Ekaterina took his empty cup, washed it in the water closet, and continued speaking after replacing it on the table for future use.

"You have committed no aggressions against the Soviet government, and so you are being permitted to continue to your next assignment. I am tasked with making sure you arrive to the Soviet boarder en route to your next post. China, yes? Beijing?"

Luke nodded. Admitting everything felt easier without words.

"We will have a lovely trip to China. Yes, you will go to China, and I will continue to Vladivostok. A beautiful city, I'm told."

"I've heard the same."

"That makes me happy. I'm glad you've heard good things about my country."

"And you'll have another mission once you arrive in Vladivostok? Nothing to do with me?"

"If I see you again, then something will be wrong. And then I must carry out this mission in a less than lovely fashion. But you will go to Beijing, yes? Excellent. But you must talk, eventually, yes? You must get over your fear of women. And besides, I'm told it's essential to learn about the enemy."

The train sped past a small lake. It was summer, and Luke could only imagine the water being too cold for swimming.

* * *

Soon, Luke would learn that Ekaterina had gained strength during her youth by carrying water from a well up three flights of stairs. She'd wanted to learn French. Her favorite food in the morning time was a bit of salted cheese wrapped in a thin crepe, drizzled with honey.

"Problem?" asked Ekaterina.

Luke looked up, realizing he'd been fiddling with his Casio watch in her view. Less than 500km away from the Chinese border, he still hadn't received follow-up instructions from his handler.

"New technology," he said. "Still figuring it out."

"You must wash," said Ekaterina. "You cannot enter the next train with a smell."

As they approached the border, the tone of the cabin grew quieter, more reserved.

Luke assumed his new career would be filled with such moments of alternating intimacy and professionalism.

"Your train is number 422," Ekaterina said. "I'll get in trouble if you miss it." Her tone indicated he shouldn't linger on the platform, as though there might be danger. "Good luck."

Luke said, "Good luck to you," in Russian, and once he stepped in the corridor, the door closed, and the lock slid into place.

Train 422 was easy to find.

His handler still hadn't checked in when the landscape urbanized, forest changing to cement squares. On the platform in Beijing, still without contact, he walked to the first rendezvous point. A man wearing a red cap, waiting by the far end of the platform, would mean the on-site team was prepared to receive him.

No man with a red cap appeared. Ten minutes passed. His watch buzzed, tickling the back of his wrist.

Proceed to rendezvous two. Leave suitcase in fourth bathroom stall.

Inside the bathroom, the fourth stall had an *out-of-order* sign taped to the door and opened to a hole in the floor. Luke pushed the suitcase inside. His cover identity contained in this bag—the life of Georges, Canadian scholar, his clothes and books, his toothbrush—would no longer be needed. His watch buzzed.

Proceed to rendezvous three.

Rendezvous three was a Kentucky Fried Chicken that had opened two years before, a thirty-minute walk from the Forbidden City.

Should I take a taxi? Luke wondered.

He felt pressure on his lower back as a hood went over his head, his arms pulled back and the weighted object—whatever it was—pushed deeply into his right kidney.

"Walk," said a voice in his ear.

It only took ten seconds to march him from the bathroom to the waiting van.

"Pay attention to my voice, and only answer me," said his interrogator.

A test, thought Luke. They'd practiced this activity in training. Your mind would answer the question you weren't supposed to if you had something to hide.

Three questions came simultaneously from three different voices inside the van.

"Are you a spy?"

"Who is your contact in the Soviet army?"

"Did you give the toast?"

Luke sifted through the voices, all men, twenty to forty years old, American accents. The interrogator, the one he was supposed to answer, was asking about the code phrase from his handler on the night of the gala.

Give MG toast.

"Don't hesitate," said a fourth person's voice—a woman. For a moment, Luke expected the hood to be removed and to see Ekaterina sitting before him.

The van turned a corner and Luke lost his balance. Two gentle hands placed on his shoulders kept him upright.

"I already know the answer," said the woman. "So, tell me what I know."

Luke sensed there were many ways to fail this test.

The woman removed his hood. Luke had never seen her before, nor had he ever encountered the man holding the gun, seated next to her. The other two men were in the front seats, one driving, one navigating with a folding map of Beijing's many rings.

"Give MG a toast," repeated the woman. "I know what it means. Tell me what it means. Tell me what I know."

Luke scanned the back of the van, briefly inspecting the door's lock to see if he'd have to pull up or over when escaping. A bicycle was in the way of that escape.

"Tell me what I know," repeated the woman.

Luke couldn't focus. How much could he lie before they put a bullet in his brain?

"Did you misinterpret the code phrase, or did you fail to follow orders?"

"I didn't know what to do," said Luke. "It made no sense. I followed the original orders and got on the train."

Luke held his breath.

"I know," whispered the woman, and then, turning to the others, "Engage Operation Daymoon."

The woman returned her focus to Luke. "Congratulations. You've passed your first mole hunt."

Luke managed to say, "Thank you," which made the woman laugh, but no one else.

"I placed you on the Moscow mission last minute without your handler's knowledge. If you'd understood that passcode, what to do with it, then you'd now be an accessory to an unsanctioned assassination. You were either a turned agent, or a stupid idiot."

Somebody tried to assassinate Gorbachev, thought Luke.

"I can fix stupid," said the woman. "I can't fix treason."

"Pretty easy with a secondary asset like that," said the driver over his shoulder.

"Yes, Ekaterina was helpful," said Luke, attempting to sound more comfortable in the group.

Everyone looked at him, even the driver in the rearview mirror.

"Gorbachev was the secondary asset," said the woman. "He reached out to us, suspected a member of his circle had linked up with one of ours. You just made a powerful friend."

She dumped a folder in Luke's lap.

Luke scanned the faces in the first five pages—local police reports of student agitators from Peking University that the American government wished to know better.

"Your cover is on page 87," said the woman. "Focus on that now."

"Am I still Canadian?" asked Luke.

As Luke pulled the bicycle from the van and began pedaling, a map of Beijing's inner ring unfolded in his mind. The Kentucky Fried Chicken, where he would meet the faces from those police reports, was three blocks away from his current location, in Qianmen, just on the other side of the large Tiananmen Square. His new name was Marc-André.

As he increased speed on the bicycle, his mind briefly wandered from his new targets back to Ekaterina. Many years later, he'd finally confirm that she died before reaching Vladivostok, her body discovered in the cabin they'd shared, the accumulated poison in her system finally taking effect. That first sip of his poorly-made tea had been enough, even when she'd poured the rest down the drain. Soldiers lined the large square in Beijing. Luke felt concealed among the many bicyclists on the road. His mind couldn't be elsewhere if he wished to survive. He'd remind himself of this fact every day for the rest of his life.

Tag along on Luke Lundy's next mission
in *THE APOLOGIST*.

————❧ ABOUT THE AUTHOR ❧————

A.A. WEISS

A.A. Weiss is the author of the novel *THE APOLOGIST* and the travel memoir *LENIN'S ASYLUM*. His essays and short stories have appeared in various journals and twice received special mention in the Pushcart Prize Anthology. He lives in Washington, DC.

Learn more at www.aaweiss.com.

The Fall of a Sparrow

BY J. M. WEST

There's a special providence in the fall of a sparrow*
—*William Shakespeare*

November 23, 2016, 9:00 A.M.

When the floorboards squeaked, Gloria Ingram lumbered to the back door. "I don't want what you're selling; You! Get off of my property!" she shrieked, waving a wooden spoon. Her neck and face flushed blood red. "You stole my husband. Don't ever come back, or I'll shoot you." She advanced, whacking the person on the arms, shoulders, and head.

"I'm delivering a package! Stop! That hurts!" The blows delivered hot pain. A hit to her temple caused dots to dance before her eyes. Backing away, the person bumped into the bicycle; the tin in the rear basket clinked.

Ingram kept up the assault. "No, I wouldn't shoot; you're not worth the gunpowder it'd take to blow your brains out! Don't ever come back here!"

Charcoal clouds hovered, threatening rain.

Holding the left arm up to shield her head, her right hand found a weapon; she must have pocketed it instead of tossing it back into the kitchen drawer. Opening it against her leg, she plunged it into her attacker, who dropped the spoon, and backed up against the screen.

"What've you done, you wicked bitch? Slipping down she yelled, "Help! I'm bleeding!"

The dark clouds burst; rain needled the alley.

* See also Matthew 10:29-3.

The cyclist climbed on the bike and pedaled away as thunder rumbled, sounding like God moving furniture, followed by gutters gushing water. Knocking on the neighbor's door, the bike rider said, "Call 911! Your neighbor just slumped down on her porch."

The elderly woman nodded.

Picking up speed, the bike skidded right onto Giant Lane and then into the parking lot. As rain let up, the rider pulled off the clear plastic poncho and draped it over the bike, locking it to the first pole. Snapping open the umbrella and dashing into the store, the rider slipped the burden into the trash. Hurrying down the kitchen utensils aisle, weaving between last-minute Thanksgiving shoppers, she found a digital thermometer and checked out. Once outside, she saw that her poncho was gone. She ran into the dollar store and found one, but the cap had a bill on it. "Maybe Dad won't notice." Suddenly the rain stopped, and a weak gauzy sun peeped out between charcoal clouds.

* * *

The dead woman glared with empty eyes. The November wind lifted her worn housedress, giving an eerie semblance of life. Her grey wavy hair hung limp. She'd slid down the porch's screen door, leaving a trail of blood. Her up-turned palms revealed a dusting of flour; her legs splayed out. A wooden spoon lay beside her. To her left, a wicker table separated two black chairs. To her right, a lone rocker tipped back and forth.

The black and whites out front blocked both ends of the street, lights twirling.

Carlisle Homicide Detective Erin McCoy stepped out of her husband's SUV and clipped her unruly auburn curls back. She reached for her cup of steaming mocha, sipping slowly. Her husband, Detective Christopher Snow, shut the driver's door, pocketing the fob. His eyes combed over the two-story clapboard house that cried for a paint job.

Erin smelled coppery, metallic blood and feces. "Augh!" She slid her detective kit out and groped for the mentholated goop for her nose and a piece of gum.

"You'll get used to the odor someday, Mac," her husband teased. Both tugged on the white coveralls, caps, and blue booties, as the police photographer, Jackie Andrews, snapped photos. Her black Afro pushed back her hood. "Haven't seen you two in a while."

"Yeah, we thought we could enjoy turkey dinner without interruptions this year," Erin replied.

"Let's wait for the ME." Snow scanned the alley. "Send some uniforms back here to tape off the crime scene," he ordered the officer on guard, who complied.

A shiny black Caddie slid into view and braked. Dr. Haili Chen pulled her medical examiner's bag from the vehicle.

"Speak of the devil," whispered Erin. They had tangled on McCoy's first case: a man had cheated his siblings out of their inheritance. When Erin had voiced her own opinion, Dr. Chen had snapped that her job was to determine the cause of death, not some rookie cop.

"Give me some room," Chen groused. Her black hair fell into a neat, slick bob that peaked at her chin. She suited up, tucked her hair daintily under the white cap, and mounted the steps.

A hunter-green Mustang sped up the alley and slid sideways to block it. Detective Zachery Fields hopped out of the car, his dash bubble strobing.

"Where's your partner?" asked Snow.

"Savage's on desk duty. Chief had a meeting in Harrisburg. I'll start interviewing people."

Snow said, "Talk to the neighbors on this block. Find out if anyone saw or heard anything." Raindrops dripped from the eaves of the houses.

McCoy reached for her cell and called Dispatch. "Sonja, send Shannon and her partners to assist with interviews. Yes, 117 Pomfret Street. Thanks."

12:00 P.M.

Next door, a window opened, and a neighbor called out. "Hi. The rain's making a racket. What's happened?" A woman with permed white hair and a friendly face waved at them.

"Did you see or hear anything out of the ordinary?" McCoy asked.

"No. Did Gloria black out again?" the woman asked. "I've been telling her to see a doctor, but no. Stubborn old broad won't."

135

"Too late for that," the ME mumbled.

"Did she live alone?" Snow asked.

"No. Two sons—the older one's in college. The second one, a senior in high school, plays basketball, so he won't be along 'til 7:00. She keeps things pretty close to her vest—or is it chest? I'm Violet Turner, by the way."

"Mind if I come in to ask a few questions?" Fields looked up at her.

"A good-looking young man like yourself? Come on in. Want some coffee and pumpkin pie?" The window closed; the back door opened. "Wipe your feet."

Snow turned to Dr. Chen. "Can you give us anything specific?"

"The woman's dead. The killer used her for a pin cushion. Cause of death is exsanguination—by stabbing; manner of death, homicide; liver temp tells me she's been dead about three hours."

"Did the weather affect the timing?" McCoy sipped her mocha.

"Yes and no. The body was protected by the covered roof and sides, which offsets the temperature a bit." Chen used a magnifying glass to catch fibers, find fingerprints or other evidence. She dropped the spoon into a clear evidence bag, sealed, and dated it. Bagged the victim's hands. "I'll know more when I get her on the table."

As if cued, the meat wagon pulled up the alley and beeped. The driver and an EMT unloaded a gurney from the van with a black body bag on top. They lifted and loaded the corpse aboard; the van disappeared down the alley.

"Autopsy?" Snow asked.

"Eight a.m. tomorrow." Dr. Chen climbed to her feet, her joints popping. She stretched her back and then removed her paper protective gear.

"Tomorrow's Thanksgiving," Mac interjected.

"Not mine." Chen paused. "All right—7:00 P.M. tonight." She climbed into her Caddie and sped off.

CBS and ABC vans approached, reporters jumping out before the vehicles stopped. *The Evening Sentinel* and *The Patriot* also sent people for the scoop of the day.

Snow said to the officers standing guard, "No one gets beyond the crime tape."

They nodded and turned to face the media onslaught.

"I'll get this neighbor," Mac said, indicating the one on the left.

"Come back after and help me inside," Snow said as he hurried into the victim's domicile.

McCoy jogged through a gap between houses and mounted the steps to the sagging house. A Styrofoam chest squatted in the corner of the stoop.

Lightning flashed its roots across the sky; thunder rumbled; rain drenched pedestrians.

Thundering cycles approached. The Three Musketeers cut their engines and kicked the stands down. Mahoney, Rivers, and Summers removed their helmets. Mahoney's honey hair tumbled down. Rivers flipped the hood of his CPD raingear up. Short and compact, he reminded Mac of Richard Hammond, one of the guys on *Grand Tour*. Summers sported blond hair and sea-blue eyes. Mac signaled up and down the street. They nodded: interviews.

1:00 P.M.

Knocking on the door, Mac stepped back, her shield open. After a few minutes, she knocked harder. The door inched open. A wisp of a woman looked her over, her eyes widening at the sight of the detective shield. A knitted cap covered her bare head. She wore an oversized sweatshirt, navy leggings, and Converse sneakers. "What? Does Carlisle have women cops? Come on in. You might drown out there. I'm defrosting my freezer." She pointed to the open freezer with towels and a dishpan collecting the melting frost. A tabby lounged in the front window.

"I'm Detective Erin McCoy. Yes, we have several women on the force. May I ask you a few questions about your next-door neighbor?"

"What happened?" She dried her hands on an old hand towel. "Come in. Sit." She pointed to a rocker by the window. "Water, tea, or coffee?"

"Water's fine, thanks. What's your name?"

"Lindy Stone." She handed Erin a bottle of water and then parked herself on a padded stool opposite Mac.

"Did you know Gloria Ingram?"

"Next door? I know her to say hello. I keep my distance because the woman's not friendly. She yells at Ginger. Yells at her kids and me! I may be old, but I'm not hers to command, and Ginger's a good mouser. But Gloria's mostly quiet, well, until her boys are home. Nice flower pin."

Lionel Howard, an FBI Special Agent, gave Mac the pin after she completed her training at Quantico. The daisy was recording their conversation.

"Kids?" Mac's eyebrows quirked up.

"Two boys. Don't remember their names, but the youngest is friendly enough."

"Is she married?"

"Oh, yes. Or was. Her husband comes around now and then. He doesn't live there anymore. They had a big row eight, ten years ago over the daughter, a tomboy; even at five, she climbed trees, played ball, or rode her bike. Gloria mistreated the girl, in my opinion."

"How so?" No one had mentioned a daughter. Mac made a note to talk to her.

"One time I watched from my upstairs window. Gloria gave the kid an order. If she didn't come right away, she'd whip her child with a switch. The five-year-old cried and tried to pull away. Gloria looked up; my phone at my ear, I wagged my finger at her like I was reporting her."

Do you know where the father—and I'm assuming the daughter—lives?

"Lands, no. We're not that neighborly. The woman's moody—too busy to chat. She makes desserts for the local restaurants. I've seen her carry pastries out to her car—works of art. All's I know." She stood abruptly. "I have to get back to my thawing. She slipped the sodden towels into the dishpan, then dumped ice into the sink. Stone picked up a hammer and chisel to dislodge the ice.

"And where were you this morning between 7:00 and 9:00 am?"

"You're kidding?" She noticed Mac's quirked eyebrows. "You're not. Making my filling." She pulled on the fridge door to show Mac. "See it's still warm."

"Yes, ma'am. Oh, one more question. You live alone?"

"Ah, my Al passed twenty years ago, just dropped over in the garden. And I lost my only son to Desert Storm. "Please excuse me. Can you see yourself out?"

Mac stood. She laid her card on the counter. "Please call if you think of anything else." Turning up her collar, she walked out into the oppressive grey day and returned to Ingram's house.

Since she didn't see Chris, she called at the foot of the stairs, "Hey, I'm here!" The kitchen startled her: state-of-the-art appliances, a farm sink, sleek granite countertops, and a Kitchen-Aid mixer. Snapping on gloves, Mac opened drawers and rifled through the contents. Moving to the island, she spied an open cookbook. *Why didn't the crime guys take this?* She checked the pantry, the cupboards, and the bookcase. Opening the door to the basement, Mac found keys hanging on a hook. She took them. The dining room yielded nothing.

The living room had heavy brocade curtains, now closed. Light filtered through the stained-glass transom above the front door. The plaid sofa and matching recliners stood empty. Rolling back the Oriental rug, Mac found nothing but dust.

Chris lumbered downstairs, stripping off his latex gloves.

"Find anything?" Erin wondered.

"Nada," her husband answered. "Let's go over the porch one more time." Rain pelted the roof again.

They would send cleaners out to remove the blood. Each detective stepped over the rusty puddle. They started at opposite ends and worked their way to the middle. "Nothing of substance here." Mac checked on either side of the wooden stairs. "I found the top of a brown barrette!" Mahoney arrived, followed by Rivers and Summers.

"Find out anything?" Snow asked.

"No, sir. A young couple living two houses down reported a person wearing a transparent rain poncho streaked by their house. They couldn't give a description; the person was wearing a helmet, jeans, and boots." Gabe offered. "The wife wasn't happy we woke their baby."

"Nothing from the people I talked to," Rivers said. "Other than their names and alibis.

"People are concerned for their safety," added Shannon. "Accident or suspicious death?"

"The woman was stabbed," Snow volunteered. "Finish interviewing people across the street. Mac and I will locate the spouse. We'll meet at the precinct for a 4:00 P.M. briefing."

"And she had a daughter," Mac added.

Zach entered, brushing raindrops off of his coat. "Ms. Turner knew the spouse's address. Ingram gave it to her for emergencies." He paused, smiling at his find.

"I'd call murder an emergency," Snow remarked. He reached for the sheet of paper.

"Yes, sir. It's 217 Front Street in Boiling Springs."

"Mahoney and Rivers, check all the cameras between here and the Farmer's Market on York Road and back to the MJ Mall. Summers, locate all the cameras at stores in town. We may catch our biker. If the stores have any records of our cyclist, get copies. Fields, check with all the restaurants the victim had listed in her appointment book. Back to the precinct at 4:00 P.M." Snow ordered.

* * *

The O'Neals' red brick house on Front Street faced the Children's Lake in Boiling Springs, its waters roiling in wind and a fresh onslaught of rain.

"Hey, Dad I'm home," Jay called while closing the front door. "My clothes are drenched. I'm going upstairs to change." She dumped her wet clothes in her hamper, pulled on a turtleneck and sweats and refreshed her make-up.

"I'm glad you're home, babe," Mr. Frank O'Neal said. "I could use some help here." His hands were mixing eggs, chopped onions, and celery into the bread crumbs.

Washing her hands, she asked, "What do you want me to do?"

"Would you make the pecan pie? Your Aunt Jill is making a pumpkin pie."

Jay preheated the oven, gathered the ingredients together, and then stretched the crust to fit the pie pan. The teen fluted the edges. Grabbing a mixing bowl from the cupboard, she selected a whisk from a drawer. Whipping everything together, she poured it into the crust and popped it in the oven. Next, Jay chose their best but wrinkled tablecloth and napkins from the linen closet. Into the dryer went the tablecloth with a damp dryer sheet to smooth out the wrinkles. "Is Ant coming?"

"I think so. Uncle Carlos and—"

"Aunt Jill are coming." Jay finished his sentence. "They're so excited Ant passed the bar exam and is working for a law firm in Hanover."

"I hear passing on the first attempt is quite an accomplishment." Frank dumped the stuffing into a plastic bag and put it in the fridge next to the fresh turkey. "Next, we need to put the sweet potato casserole together."

"'K. I can do that or set the table. Oh, I need to wrap Ant's present."

"Yes, please set the table. I'm still confused about the order of the silverware."

"Dad, we have flatware." She smiled and scampered out of the kitchen to get the tablecloth.

* * *

4:00 P.M.

At the briefing, the detectives settled themselves around the oblong table in the conference room after getting their coffee. Sonja had put a fresh pot on. Fields walked in with a tin of pumpkin cookies to pass around.

"Oh," Mac groaned. "Here we go with holiday sweets. Thanks, Zach."

"These have no calories," Zach returned.

"Alright, guys and gal, settle down. We have a homicide to solve. Time to put the evidence together. Let's just go around the table and report your findings."

"On Giant's tape, we found a bicycle chained to a pole. A transparent raincoat was draped over the bike. Someone wearing all black with a hoodie took the garment and ran out of the camera's range. Then a figure with an umbrella walked out of the store juggling its handle, the helmet, and a plastic bag." Shannon reported and nodded to Gabriel to continue.

"Wearing a transparent rain poncho, the bike rider looked around, unlocked the Schwinn, and cycles away. We've asked our computer guru to enlarge and refine the helmet for a brand name because the rain made everything fuzzy. This could be our killer."

"Good job. Stay on it. If we can get a still shot to pass around that neighborhood and the grocery store to ID, we'll have a suspect to interview."

"We have a photo of that person in the parking lot." Chase passed it around the table. "It's grainy, but we still can't ID him or her."

"Mac?" Snow asked.

"I found a hair barrette, though no hairs were attached. I sent it to the lab, and expect a report Friday, tomorrow being Thanksgiving. I also bagged the cookbook left open on the vic's kitchen island. We might glean something from the notes. And the neighbor next door had a beef with the deceased about child abuse. Dad and daughter live in Boiling Springs. I plan to interview them after our briefing. Then I'm going home for dinner and to see Ian."

Mac dialed Reese's number. "Find a judge who'll give us a warrant for 217 Front Street, Boiling Springs, to search the premises."

4:30 P.M.

Snow lifted the antique knocker. A three-speed Schwinn bike was chained to the porch rail. A man wearing a green knit shirt and navy jeans answered the door. He looked sixtyish with wavy black hair and blue eyes. Stocky but solidly built, he was wiping his hands on a dishtowel. "May I help—" he stopped at seeing their shields.

"May we come in?" Mac asked.

Looking confused, he stepped aside, gestured for them to enter, and motioned for them to sit down. They settled onto the saddle leather couch near the windows while O'Neal backed into a brown recliner. Mac could smell onions; her stomach rumbled. She'd skipped lunch.

"Are you Mr. Frank O'Neal?" Snow inquired.

"I am."

"Are you familiar with one Gloria Ingram?" Mac asked.

"Yes, she's my wife, but we've been separated for years. Is this about my sons? Has anything happened?"

Snow softened his tone. "No. This issue is not about your boys. We're sorry to inform you that your wife died today."

His eyes widened and filmed with tears. O'Neal buried his head in his hands, raking his fingers through his hair and shaking his head. "No, no. no. Can't be. I saw her a week ago. Was it a heart attack or stroke? She's been having migraines." His body shuddered. He fished a handkerchief from his back pocket, wiped his eyes, and blew his nose. "Why just this morning I—"

"Dad?" The perky teenager wore her onyx hair in a high ponytail with a brown barrette pinning back the short strands. She paused in the archway. Her ice-blue eyes locked on her dad. "I can't find the mix—" She stopped abruptly when she saw the detectives. Her head darted from her dad to the detectives and back like a bird sensing danger. Purple bruises were showing through her makeup.

O'Neal stopped and turned to his daughter. "Your mother's passed away today. Did you see her this morning? How did she seem? Did you deliver the sticky buns?"

She didn't blink an eye. "I tried to, but she wouldn't let me. Didn't want them, I guess. Yes, I saw her."

McCoy noticed that the teen didn't seem upset.

"Come here. What caused those bruise marks on your face? Why are you wearing make-up now? He stood to inspect her and pulled one sleeve up revealing deep purple bruises along her arm.

"I fell over my bike trying to get away from her." Her voice wavered, chin trembling.

"Joanna, what did you do?" her dad asked.

She lifted her chin; her lips compressed into a hard thin line.

"Was she alive when you left her?" Snow looked sternly at her.

"Yes."

"Stop right there. Don't say another word," her father ordered.

"Did you know our coroner said your mother was murdered?" Mac asked.

"She's no mother to me. My parents separated because of me, or she would've been arrested for child abuse."

Mac stood and pulled a zip tie out of her raincoat's pocket. She turned the girl around. "You are under arrest for your mother's murder.

Anything you say can and will be used against you in a court of law. You have the right to remain silent. You have a right to an attorney . . ."

"I think you're jumping the gun here. She's only fifteen. Where are you taking her?" O'Neal interrupted the Miranda rights. I want to take photos of her bruises!" His demeanor switched from grieving to protective.

The detective secured the teen's hands behind her with a zip tie.

"To the police precinct where she'll be processed and housed until she's arraigned," Snow informed him.

"We'll take photographs," Mac assured him.

"Do you have any concrete evidence—like a weapon? There's not a drop of blood on her." His voice thickened, and he stopped to clear his throat. "She's a minor; you can't question her without me."

"You can't do this!" Jay's lips trembled. "Can't I at least get my coat and purse?"

O'Neal hurried to the mud room for Jay's lined rain jacket and placed it over his daughter's shoulders. He hugged her.

"Back away sir," Snow ordered. O'Neal complied. "And no purse."

"I'll call Anthony right now. Until he arrives, do not say a word. Just be quiet." O'Neal repeated. "I'll follow in my car. Let me turn off the oven and get my coat." He put the pie on a rack. Just as he was shutting his front door, the cell phone in his pocket chirped. "Hello."

"Dad, What's going on? I can't get into the house. What's happened?"

Mac could hear the panic in the boy's voice.

"Ryan, just come here; we'll be at the police station. I'll explain everything when we get back."

Tears tracked the teen's cheeks as the detectives walked out and ushered her into the back of their vehicle.

Chris talked to Mac over the roof of the SUV. "Reese and I can attend the autopsy if you want to go home, or I can call Mom to tell her we'll be late.

"After we drop Miss O'Neal off, I want to stop at home for a bite to eat and see Ian." She peered at her watch. "We have time."

"I'll take care of the booking. Take my vehicle. Would you pick me up when you're done? See you at the autopsy."

* * *

7:00 P.M.

Arriving at the morgue, Snow and Mac saw the naked corpse on the stainless-steel table. Dr. Chen looked through her goggles at them. Gloved up. The X-rays were clipped to the whiteboard. "Let's begin." Her scalpel incised the Y cut. She talked into a mic. "The deceased has a puncture wound . . ." Chen continued her narration moving down the body but stopped abruptly and shut off the recording. She picked up a magnifying glass and leaned in closer. "Come here." She handed Mac the magnifier. "What do you see?"

Mac leaned in, holding her breath. "I'll be damned." She gave the glass to her husband.

"Two puncture wounds side by side," Snow commented. "What kind of weapon did the killer use?" Snow asked.

"Perhaps a screwdriver or a knitting needle. No, something thinner." Chen paused. "The first one wasn't lethal. The second one punctured the aorta. See the X-ray? She photographed the wound up close and then studied her tools. The coroner pushed up her goggles and reached for a probe, dousing it with alcohol. She inserted it into the first wound and marked the depth. "Three inches." She eased the probe into the second one. "Seven inches. So the second one was the fatal thrust."

Snow noted. "Just two wounds? If an enraged person did this, there'd be more. So two killers with different weapons?"

Mac pointed to a mass the size of a dime on the X-rays. "Is this a brain tumor?"

"Yes. The deceased had about a year to live. But that didn't factor in her death."

A thought niggled her brain. Mac said, "What about an ice pick?"
Snow added, "Or a meat thermometer?"
Mac peeled off the paper gear. "Thanks, Dr. Chen. Let's go. I'll drive."
Snow used his cell, "Reese, cordon off—" he looked at Mac.
"119 Pomfret Drive."
"You heard that? We need backup. Over and out." Snow thumbed end.

Mac said, "The neighbor had means, motive, and opportunity. She was defrosting her freezer with an ice pick. I didn't think about it then."

Arriving at the house, Mac braked and cut the engine. Reese climbed out of his Jeep. "I'm right behind you."

She led while Snow slipped around back. "Police! Open up!" Mac waited a second, and then Reese threw his weight against the door, which splintered and collapsed.

Lindy Stone stood in the middle of the kitchen. She dropped the suitcase but pointed an ice pick at Mac, fear in her eyes. She trembled but still held the weapon. "I'll kill you. Let me go."

Mac flipped the taser from her jeans pocket. "I can offer you better options. Drop the weapon."

Snow appeared and rushed behind the woman, twisting her arm until she dropped the ice pick. "You're under arrest for the murder of Gloria Ingram. Anything you say can and will be held against you . . ." he finished Mirandizing her. He anchored her arms behind with a zip tie.

Mac bagged and tagged the weapon. "I bet Luminol will show blood on this pick."

Her shoulders sagging, Stone said, "It's not fair that Gloria had a husband and three living, thriving kids, and mistreated the girl; but I have no husband now. My only son was killed in Iraq."

They stepped over the door, settled Stone in the back seat, and drove to the precinct.

Read along as Homicide Detectives Erin McCoy and Christopher Snow track down elusive and dangerous killers in their many adventures.

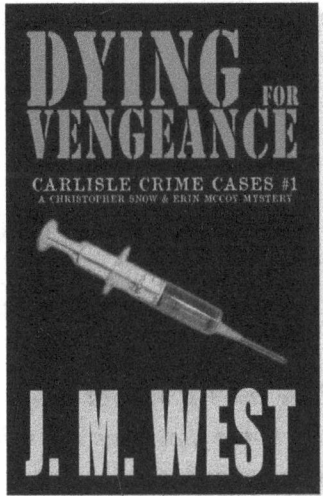 

ABOUT THE AUTHOR

J. M. WEST

Professor Emerita J. M. West's latest book, *Carlisle's Molly Pitcher* was released in October 2024. In *American Roulette*, she wrote the chapters about Leah McCall. Her first local history book, *Madam Bessie Jones, Her Life and Times,* won the Sunny award in 2021. West also penned the fact-based *Carlisle Crime Cases* featuring Homicide Detectives Christopher Snow and Erin McCoy.

The Good Senator

BY PAT LAMARCHE AND ROBERT BRADSHAW

Senator Hooper walked to his car, pulled the handle and swung the door wide. Inside, he shifted gears and put the car in reverse. Checking the rearview, he watched as his assistant pulled up sideways behind the hatchback. As she did, his phone pinged.

Want me to follow you, sir? There were some hot heads at that meeting tonight. I'd be happy to head home that way. I can jump on Route One after I watch you close your front door.

The senator smiled and waved. He tapped the callback button as the two spoke on the phone from 10 feet away. "No need, Stephanie. A lot of heat and no flame in that room. I've had constituents mad at me before and I will again."

Stephanie didn't sound convinced. "Seems different nowadays. In the past the angry folks have been those Greenpeace and CODEPINK types. They'd spout off about you being a planet killer or war monger. This time, the vitriol's coming from our side."

"Oh, they've gotten themselves all whipped up by that guy in the White House. They'll settle down. If they don't like me voting to protect the farmers by keeping workers in the country, they can always take it up at the ballot box."

In his side view mirror Hooper watched as his assistant fumbled with something in her front seat. The young woman popped something into her mouth.

"You still chewing that nicotine gum?" The senator smiled sympathetically.

148

"Yeah, it's my own fault. Every time I get stressed, I have a cigarette, and I have to start the whole process over again." Looking down at her hands then back to her boss's reflection in the side mirror she added, "I got to tell you, that's pretty often lately, sir. Me getting worked up, I mean." Popping a second square of gum into her mouth she added. "Need a piece?"

Hooper got out of his car, buttoning his overcoat against the biting Maine wind. He walked to her driver side window. She lowered it.

Hooper patted his assistant on the shoulder. "It's all going to be fine. I'm the most conservative member of the chamber—by all accounts. Once they realize we can't get those Washington County blueberries to the stores without foreign labor, they'll calm down."

Stephanie looked up at him and frowned. She didn't look convinced. "The guns."

The senator placed his hand on his hip, revealing his own Glock 19. Now, you know I've got an A+ rating from the NRA. I'm not telling a few fellas they can't carry at our meetings, just because they're getting hot under the collar. Getting angry over politics is the oldest trick in the book." He patted her shoulder again. "You run along home. If it makes you feel better, I'll text you when I'm in my house with the door locked and the alarm set."

The senator turned, walking back to his driver side door. Grabbing his phone from his overcoat pocket, he pressed the flashlight icon and peered into the long SUV. Calling over his shoulder he yelled, "See, no boogie men in the back seat!" Turning, he saw that his assistant had already gone.

* * *

Steven Bradley bounded up the stairs of 262 Chad Brown Lane. The sheriff's deputy on the porch moved to bar his entry. Steven flashed his ID. The officer murmured something unintelligible as he retreated to his post on the left side of the door. Pulling open the storm door— as he had at the Senator's house a thousand times before—the disaster response professional kicked the snow from his shoes and stepped across the threshold.

Scanning the front entry, the tall man took long hurried steps down the hall. He passed open doorways, glancing into the living room, dining room and kitchen before found his way back to the Hooper family den. At first glance, the pictures that peppered wall seemed to be of one face—with different hair and clothing. The Hooper genetics won every battle they fought. Each of Bob and Jan's kids—strike that—every Hooper relative, had the same crystal blue eyes, straight nose and rugged jaw. More than half the children's temperaments favored their mother, but when it came to looks, all the kids favored their father, the senior senator from Maine.

Outside, the sun had reflected bright sunshine into Steven's eyes. In the back of the house, tucked into the windowless den, he could barely make out a crumpled form on the couch. Pulling his sunglasses from his face, he waited for his eyes to adjust. The heavy breathing coming from the blanketed figure on the couch led his eyes to her form.

"Jan! There you are!"

The grieving woman pushed herself up from the couch.

"No, no, sit down." Steven rushed to her side.

"The deputies still here?" she asked.

"Yes, I expect they will be for a while. I'm surprised that's all you have."

Jan moved to the side of the couch, "Have a seat." Taking his hand and addressing his comment she added, "The staties were here. Told me not to touch anything. They said they'd be back after the forensic team made it to the county. We're about four hours from Augusta, you know."

Steven nodded. "Yeah, I got lucky. I had a conference in Boston. I hopped a puddle jumper from there to Bangor. Not too many folks in line when I got to the car rental counter. I think I got on the road less than 20 minutes from touch down."

Reaching out to take his hand, Jan sighed. "I can't thank you enough for dropping everything. I'm sure you're more than upset about Bobby. It's good of you to care about me."

"And the kids. How are they?" Looking around, he added, "For that matter, where are they?"

"The twins are upstairs. They're hurting pretty bad, but they have each other. When the staties asked us to not touch anything, they asked if they could stay in their room."

"Good idea." Steven patted her hand. "I'll go up and see them in a bit."

"Andrew and Chuck returned to college Monday. You know, winter break just ended. The other four are skiing with Jason's wife's family. I told them all to stay put. There's nothing they can do until the feds release Bobby's body."

A tear rolled down her cheek. "I expect they'll all get back here by the weekend."

Steven pulled off his parka and set it at the end of the couch. Settling back more comfortably, he wrapped his arm around his best friend's newly minted widow.

"Have they shared any details . . ."

As Jan shook her head from side to side, two plainclothes federal agents walked into the room.

"Mrs. Hooper, I'm special agent Frank Wills, this is special agent Emma Franz. We'd like to ask you a few questions." Turning his gaze to Steven, he added, "Sir, could you excuse us, please?

"Oh, of course." Steven rose to leave as Jan interrupted, "No. Please, can't he stay? Mr. Bradley is a dear, dear friend. There is nothing you have to say that he can't hear."

Settling back down, Steven said, "Good to meet you Agent Wills. And Agent Franz, well, I'd like to say it's nice to see you again."

Franz straightened her back and nodded. "Understood, Steven. Seems we've set a precedent for meeting at deadly serious moments." Turning to her partner, the FBI agent added, "Mr. Bradley and I worked together following a mass shooting at the Liberty Mall a few years back. We haven't seen each other since."

Agent Wills nodded, "Thanks for the background, Franz. That's the situation that got you the invite from the Bureau, isn't it?"

Franz nodded.

Glancing back and forth between the two, Wills asked, "No conflicts here?"

Franz shook her head. "None, sir. Just good to see him after all this time."

"Good." Crossing the room to address the victim's wife, the agent crouched down and looked into the woman's tear-streaked face. "Mrs. Hooper, I'm sorry for your loss but I have a few questions for you."

* * *

Steven waited at the end of the café counter for the drinks he'd ordered. "Bradley!" the barista shouted as Emma pulled the door open and walked inside.

"I'll grab a table," the agent called to her friend.

"Sure hope you still drink double espresso, 'cause that's what I got you." Steven smiled.

Emma stood as he set the drinks down. Wrapping her arms around him, she hugged the man who had debriefed her after the horrific shooting that nearly cost her everything. Stepping back from their embrace, she added, "Sorry if that was awkward. But I've owed you a hug ever since you helped me, my mom, and my kids recover from that awful mess."

"Yeah, well, now you're one of us. A responder after the fact. I have to admit, I wasn't sure you'd end up in law enforcement after all of that."

"Me either. But I think it's where I belong. Victims deserve to have somebody in our shoes who understands what they're going through. Even if we never tell them that we do."

"Fair enough." Steven gently stirred sugar into his cappuccino. "Speaking of telling victims what you know, what can you tell me?"

"Well, first of all . . ." Emma hesitated, seeming to choose her words carefully. "Steven, I trust you implicitly. You know how this works. You're in the business. Confidentiality matters. If I share what I can . . ." Emma's voice trailed off.

"I'll keep it to myself. Deal."

"Good, just had to say the implicit stuff out loud. I knew you wouldn't mind. Of course, there's one other thing about the details." Staring at her friend she added, "They may be tough to hear."

"It's okay. I guess you know that we stood up for each other at our weddings. Even though, I must admit, I was shocked when Bob agreed to be best man when I married Michael. He'd voted against gay marriage every time it came up in congress. But once the supreme court came down on the side of it—well, Bob loved the Constitution more than anything else that he used to call 'of this world' so he accepted it as the law of the land."

"He never ridiculed you? You know, for being gay?"

"Well, he didn't approve." Steven let out a sigh. "But he was kind to Michael. And at the end of the day, even though he felt that his religion condemned us, he simply voiced his concerns then accepted our lifestyle as protected under the Constitution."

"None of his business?" Emma asked.

Steven rocked his head. "Don't get me wrong. I still think he prayed every night that Michael and I would go straight. But at the end of the day, it was about my soul, not his." Chuckling he added, "And besides, he was loyal. Hell, I think if I told him I wanted to sell drugs to pay for medical bills like that *Breaking Bad* show, he'd have prayed for me, but he never would have turned me in."

"You think he might have looked the other way for some criminal enterprise or other?"

"Well, wait, Emma. Now you're putting words in my mouth." Steven pushed his chair back. "Besides, I came here to pump you for information. While I ponder that ethics question you just leveled at me, why don't you tell me what you know."

Emma sipped her coffee, cleared her throat and detailed what the FBI files contained, to that point. "Early this morning, about 3:30, the cleaning crew arrived at the Senator's downtown Houlton office building. The old J.M. Rice building. The Senator leased the entire top floor."

"I remember when he told me he was going to put a senate office in this itsy-bitsy town. I tried to tell him that senators' offices go in population centers. He laughed and asked me, 'You know I'm representing Maine, right? What population centers? Besides, people out in the willy wags need access more than the yuppies in Portland do.'"

"Willy wags?" Emma smiled.

"Yeah, and yuppies."

Emma continued. "The custodial crew went through their normal routine, emptying trash cans into large garbage bags." The agent pulled out her notebook and flipped to the third page. "A ten-year employee of the cleaning firm . . . brother-in-law of the owner . . . guy named Dan Cormier took two large garbage bags out back to drop them in the dumpster. That's when he saw the senator's body crumpled in a heap on the ground under his office window."

"Poor Bob." Steven put his head in his hands.

Emma continued her narration without interruption, "Finding what he thought was a weak pulse, Mr. Cormier dialed 911. I can email you a copy of the emergency transcript if you'd like."

"Sure, I'd appreciate that." Steven's words slipped out from behind his hands.

"An ambulance transported him to Houlton Regional Hospital. He never regained consciousness during transport. The emergency department reported him dead on arrival."

"Christ!" Steven leaned back, exposing weary eyes and clenched jaw. "How Russian Mafia this all sounds."

"It does at that. Tell me, Steven, did the senator piss off the Russians?"

"Piss off the Russians? I guess maybe when he voted aid to Ukraine. But 22 Republicans voted to send arms to help Ukraine. We don't have 22 U.S. Senators dead this morning, do we?"

"No." Emma spoke softly, "I know he's your friend, but we must explore every angle. At this point, it looks like a very Russian defenestration, which means one of two things."

"Either it was the Russians or someone who wants to make it look like the Russians."

Agent Franz nodded.

"Did you get anything from Jan today? Any idea of who might have wanted to kill her husband, my friend?"

"No. But while we wait for forensics to finish sweeping the crime scene and toxicology to come back, maybe you could talk to her."

Steven looked bewildered. "Me? Pump the widow of one of my best buds to see if she killed her husband? You want me to do that?"

Emma shrugged. "Or you could be helping us gather information on other culprits, while you help us rule her out. She has zero alibi and . . ." The young woman swallowed hard. "Seriously, she seemed to be holding back."

* * *

Steven scraped the food from the dishes into the garbage disposal. "You didn't eat much," he called over his shoulder.

Jan sat quietly at the table, staring at what was left of the red wine in her glass. "I'm happier to drink my dinner this evening. Thanks anyway."

"Okay. I understand my job tonight." Steven wiped his hands. He grabbed a bottle of claret from the wine rack and rejoined her at the table.

"Bob hated it when I drank. But he never forbade me. And I didn't do it often." Jan struggled to pull the corners of her lips up. Aside from the slightest twitch of her cheeks, no smile appeared. "I always did what I was told. No birth control . . ." She paused and let out a snort. "As you can tell from the enormous brood of ours who are now busy booking tickets to crisscross the nation so they can attend their father's funeral. No birth control and no booze!"

At that moment, she did smile. "Except for when I really wanted it. He'd just look at me disapprovingly and head off to bed, or back to his office. I used to wish he'd stay and have a drink with me." Jan sighed. "After a while, I was happy to see the back of him. So, I could enjoy a nice red or a martini in peace."

Refilling her glass and pouring a fresh one of his own, Steven spoke, "I got a call just as I left my motel room." Staring into his glass, then taking a sip without looking up he added, "The FBI called. They said you'd filed for divorce."

Jan jerked her head in his direction, "So what? Does this make me a suspect now?"

"You're the spouse, you're always a suspect."

"I'd already filed for divorce, why would I kill him?"

"Great question. I'm not accusing you. I'm just telling you that in most cases, it's the spouse. Bob being a senator complicates it, but it doesn't change human nature."

Steven leaned in, looking straight into Jan's face. "Here's my advice. Be transparent. Tell the truth. People with nothing to hide don't hide things." Steven paused and continued, "They tell me you have no alibi."

"I was here in my house. The twins were upstairs, but we didn't talk for hours. I can't believe I need an alibi. If I had known someone was going to kill my husband, I'd have made the children play Scrabble with me."

"You didn't log onto Netflix or anything? They can subpoena your viewing history and maybe clear you that way. You didn't email anyone?"

Tears welled in Jan's eyes. "Nope, read a good old-fashioned murder mystery. Agatha Christie! How ironic is that? If only I'd thought ahead, used an e-reader instead of a book made of paper and ink!"

"Look," Steven took her hands in his, "I'm not trying to get you all flustered. The sooner they can rule you out, the sooner they can find the killer."

Jan leapt to her feet. "Steven, I know you're doing your best. But I want you to go now. Please, it's time for you to leave. You can come back in the morning and deal with the media for us if you want to—but other than that, I'd like to be left alone."

Steven stood, walked down the hall and gathered his coat from the hook by the door. Jan followed him. "I'm sorry. I don't mean to be rude. It's been a long day. And look, you've been here for hours. We haven't seen the twins once. It's more than possible to be in this house and not see a couple of teenagers until they decide to see you!"

Steven leaned down and kissed Jan on the forehead. "I know, we've both lost a lot. Even if you wanted a divorce, this can't be easy."

Jan struggled to remain composed, "No. Not easy is an understatement. I never loved anyone more and I've never hated anyone more."

Her friend brushed a tear from her cheek. Jan turned away. "I promise you, if I ever throw someone out of a window, I'll make sure to have an airtight excuse for where I've been."

Steven turned her face back toward his. Staring into her eyes, he asked, "Jan, who told you that Bob went out a window?"

* * *

Steven climbed to the top floor of the J.M. Rice building and ducked under the yellow police tape that crossed the corridor to his left. Emma stood, arms folded, in front of an open office door. "Perfect timing," she called to him. "Forensics has finished in here. They're bypassing Augusta and sending everything to the Boston field office." Pushing open the door to Senator Hooper's office, she added, "I told them you wanted to look around—for old time's sake."

Steven nodded, "Well, that's not a lie. I will miss him, terribly."

Emma frowned, "I know. That pain of losing someone never goes away. It's the bitterness of them being ruthlessly taken from you that'll eat at you though, if you're not careful."

Having been on the ground as part of the disaster response for Flight 77 after the 911 terrorist attacks, Steven had spoken publicly about the corrosive quality of unsatisfied injustice.

Emma struggled to move beyond the tension, "Anyway, they said you couldn't do any harm. They've finished collecting evidence."

Steven picked up the framed photo from his best friend's wedding. His thirty-year-old self stared back at him. "Look at me in that fancy best man garb."

Emma leaned in, "Are those Captain Kirk sideburns?" She stifled her hilarity poorly.

Placing the picture back on the desk, Steven smiled. "Smarty pants! We all had them in those days."

"Just like you all said, 'Smarty pants,' too, I imagine."

Changing the subject back to the serious topic at hand, Steven asked, "Did the lab guys find anything here?"

"Not that they mentioned to me. Most of that stuff will come back to us in a report later this week." Emma paused and turned away.

"I sense a but . . ."

"We got the coroner's findings earlier today. We were told to look for nicotine gum. Here and at his home. Did the senator smoke?"

Steven raised his hand and cupped his chin. "We all did back in college. But no, I don't think he has in decades. Why, did he have nicotine in his system?"

"Yeah, and a sedative. Not enough to knock him out, but enough to make him pliable and easier to shove out a window." Emma swallowed hard, "I'm trusting you, here, Steven. This is for you and no one else—because of what we've been through back at Liberty Mall."

"I appreciate your faith in me. I won't betray that, I promise."

"He had some temporary dental work. You know, those emergency crowns are porous as hell. It's why they feel so funny in your mouth. Some gum fetched up in there and it contained residue of nicotine and Buspirone—that's an anti-anxiety med that can make a patient lose their balance. You know, get nice and woozy with difficulty walking."

Steven walked to the office door and looked down the hall. Turning back, he signaled Emma to follow. He tried the door across the way. It wasn't locked. "Did they look in here?"

Emma stammered, "I, I think so. Why? What office is this?"

"This is his assistant's office. The few times I've met her over the last three years, she popped that nicotine gum like it was candy."

* * *

Steven drove down Route One as it wound through pine groves and around granite outcroppings, most of the rugged terrain softened by the freshly fallen snow. He slowed as he approached a turnoff flanked by a set of cabin roads. He stopped long enough to read the names painted or duct taped to the sides of mailboxes—each perched atop a few long wooden logs. "Michaux—there it is. Stephanie's married name."

The speaker on the phone came to life with Emma's voice. "I'm still not sure you should be venturing down there by yourself. What if Ms. Michaux's home? What if she's not alone?"

"We went over this, Emma. She knows me. I'm hoping she'll just chat with me. No worries, I'm no hero. You're still parked at the Dysart's convenience stop, yes?"

"Roger that," Agent Franz responded.

"Good. If I smell a rat, you'll be the first to know. You call for back up and get your butt down here. If anything goes awry, I expect you to come save me."

The unconvinced agent responded flatly, "Roger that."

Steven turned down the camp road indicated by the arrow above Stephanie's mailbox. Gravel mixed with snow crunched beneath the weight of the car as he gently depressed the accelerator. "I see the cul-de-sac. That's her house at the far end. Most of the places out here are summer camps. Hers is the only home with lights on."

Emma's voice came back, "Exercise caution, Bradley." The formal nature of her response implied a heightened concern for safety that Steven already felt.

"Yeah, I'm nervous too." Pulling up to the edge of the drive, Steven related the scene. "Her car's in the driveway. That's odd. What Mainer has a perfectly good garage and doesn't use it in winter?"

"Someone who loves their snow mobiles more than their Toyota." Franz answered, adding, almost clinically, "What else do you see?"

"The front door; it's open about nine inches. It's weird, though. I don't see any footprints in the snow. Who opens the door if no one has knocked?"

"Someone who wants to be found. Steven, I don't like this. I'm on my way."

The disaster response professional mimicked his friend, "Roger that. I think you better hurry." Killing the call and popping the cell phone into his pocket, he spoke to no one, "But I'm going inside. She could be hurt."

* * *

Pushing the door open, Steven tapped the snow from his shoes, muttering to himself under his breath. "Michael, I know you won't like this. But I must see if this woman is hurt." Glancing around the foyer, the disaster response professional turned amateur investigator noticed an eclectic mix of trophy heads lining the walls alongside three gun cabinets. Further away, one of the cupboards had a door hanging open with a key nestled in the lock. Peering into the case, he eyed empty pegs that looked like they might have held an automatic pistol.

Sirens began to wail in the distance. "That'll be the cavalry. One thing for sure—from here and from that business at the Liberty Mall—whenever I'm in trouble, I hope Agent Franz is around."

Steven reached inside the cabinet. His right hand stopped millimeters from a revolver. "No," he told himself. "The last thing you want is a few sheriff's deputies storming this place and shooting you because you're wielding a firearm."

Tip-toeing toward the back of the hall, Steven noticed blood coming from under a door. Pressing an ear against the wood, he grabbed the handle. It turned easily in his hand. As he pulled the door toward him, he felt a significant weight forcing it open. A hand still clutching a Glock spilled out into the hall followed by an upper body that slumped over the forearm.

Bright pink nail polish shone on the hand. "Goddamn it, Stephanie. What did you do?"

* * *

"You heading back to DC?" Emma asked.

"Yeah, later today. Michael's pretty spooked by all this and I only told him half the story. I'm saving the gory parts for when I get home."

"I'll be here another day or so." Agent Franz didn't wait for Steven to ask her what was next. "I have a few more interviews to conduct before I leave for home. Do you need a ride?"

"Nah. I still have the rental. Besides, I promised Jan that I'd help her with the media."

"She's fortunate that you're here."

"Yeah. I don't mind. It's what I do." Fiddling with the tag on the rental key fob he added, "I guess it took her totally by surprise. Stephanie being involved with that radical militia group. The suicide note said that when she gave her boyfriend the code to the Senator's safe, she never dreamt Bob'd return to the office that night after she left him in the parking lot. Or that they'd kill him."

"Yeah. We got her cell log. A burner phone texted her that they were on their way. Told her to get the heck out of there. What is it that she called herself, again?" Emma asked.

"An unwitting pawn."

"Do you believe that?" The young FBI agent asked. "Do you believe that she didn't know they'd kill the senator over his votes on immigration?"

"And make it look like the Russians did it, you mean?" Steven dragged his hand through his hair. "I don't know. They say love is blind." Walking toward his rental car, he turned and stared at Emma. "I think this is going to have a chilling effect on every other U.S. Senator in DC." Rocking his head, Steven added, "The way the president gives out pardons, I don't think anyone's even going to make a half-hearted look for the killer."

Emma leaned over and opened the car door for her friend. "I will."

Learn about the mass shooting that started it all.

—⊛ ABOUT THE AUTHORS ⊛—

PAT LaMARCHE AND ROBERT THOMAS BRADSHAW

LaMarche and Bradshaw received critical acclaim as they collaborated with eight other authors on a spine-tingling mass murder mystery, *American Roulette*.

Pat LaMarche is an award-winning broadcaster and journalist with extensive experience reporting on poverty and homelessness—in both the US and around the world.

Robert Thomas Bradshaw has dedicated his career to tackling challenging and complex topics by making them approachable and relatable to diverse audiences.

An Elemental Decision

BY CLAUDE BERUBE

Port St. George, Maine

Water

The boats started getting underway at four a.m. In the cove, you could hear the lobstermen and their sternmen drive their pickups on the dirt road to the north to the co-op. There they walked down to a dock and their dinghies before motoring a few dozen yards to their respective boats—*Grayshade, Beastly Bruin, Adroit, Lizzie Leigh,* and *Maine-stay*, among others. Connor Stark knew them or their families, as he had spent most of the past twenty-two summers of his life here with his cousins who owned two boats.

Some of the tourists who summered here were always awoken by the morning preparations, but he didn't sleep much these days. He had forgotten what it meant to sleep through the night. From then through the blue hour before dawn, he tried to distract himself by reading a book, usually a tome on ancient history, though he had delved into other periods or genres. Today he was perusing Kipling's works. When the sun rose behind him and the villages, he sat on the deck with a fresh cup of black coffee.

A mussel cracked and opened against the wooden pier after being dropped from thirty feet above by a seagull, who proceeded to pounce on it, pecking and gulping its fresh catch. The dock was littered with dozens of shells by now, as seagulls dined freely on what passing tourists would pay a small ransom for.

The water was still in the early morning. At low tide, most of the cove's bed was exposed, showing at least two hundred years of rope, wood, and metal—the tools of sailors—decaying. At high tide, you could jump off the docks and swim—if some of the boats didn't need the docks for repairs or picking up refurbished lobster pots.

He stroked his new beard, the product of months of travel in Europe, including a few visiting some ancestral sites in Scotland. He had barely propped his bare feet against the rails of the deck overlooking Johnson Cove. With his cousin out at sea as third mate on a merchant ship, his uncle offered Stark her room as he continued his recovery—his shame, his exile. He had his family home here and the old home in New Hampshire that went back nearly two hundred and fifty years when his ancestor, a Revolutionary War general, built it. But he felt like a man without a home, without a country, and he was without a job.

The phone rang in the kitchen. It was now six a.m. sharp. His Uncle John was out on his boat for the day. The other family boat was at the property's pier below. The boat was in the name of his two cousins—Jaime, who was serving on the merchant ship, and her brother Carey, who was out for a week off the Grand Banks on a larger fishing vessel. His uncle encouraged him to take the boat out. It would do him good, he had said. His uncle was never wrong.

The phone kept ringing. With no one else at home, Stark made his way inside and picked up the handset.

"Johnson house."

"You ought to try these new phones you can carry. It'd be much easier to reach you."

The voice of Bill Maddox, his oldest college friend and roommate, lightened the heaviness of the morning, as each morning had become.

"Never."

"I have an idea," Maddox said quickly.

"When has that ever been a good thing?"

"Listen, the only good idea you had was when you introduced me to Susan."

"No, that was a bad idea. She was a hard-working engineering major and clearly too good for you. I feel sorry for her," he kidded. He knew the two would be a good match. Maddox had built up his father's construction company from a statewide enterprise to ventures across the country and the world.

"I want you to work for me," Maddox said.

"No."

"You haven't heard the offer."

"I had a job. I don't want another."

"I need you. I need someone I can trust," Maddox offered.

Stark paused for several seconds.

"Okay, what is it?"

"I need a Director of Security. I'm not subcontracting anymore. I want the whole operation in-house. Remember that opportunity in Yemen. We got the job. We're building the oil rigs. But I need security given everything in that part of the world. You've been there."

"No."

"You can't say no."

"I just did."

"I'd tell you it pays well—which it does—but I know that doesn't matter," Maddox admitted.

"You know me well."

"Would you at least consider a temporary position, just to start it up? Seriously, this is important to me."

Maddox had appealed to the one tug that might work—loyalty to a friend.

"I'll think about it. Love to Suze, Bill," he said as the two ended the call.

He took the remainder of coffee from the pot and poured it into a thermos, then made a sandwich, and packed a bag for water and an extra set of clothes for the day. He headed to the pier and started the engine on the *Rubicon*. She coughed and sputtered, then purred as she relaxed. He loosened the lines from the pier's cleats, carefully jumped in, put the boat in reverse and pulled in the lines. A dog barked at one of the houses on Blum Road, just above the lobsterman's co-op, bringing him back to the present.

Rubicon gently glided past the co-op as he waved back at one of the men working topside, then through the empty dinghies tied to the greater

harbor's moorings hoping for the safe return of their masters. A few minutes later, he was in the main channel that emptied into the bay and the
Atlantic ocean. The lighthouse was off to his port. A couple of tourists were
there taking photos of what they thought an iconic image—a lone lobster
boat on its way to haul up traps. Except he wasn't a lobsterman, there were
no traps for him, but those in his past. He pulled down his cap to avoid
being captured on film. At the end of the rocks was someone in a kilt—the
Piper of Port St. George, who he had heard about from other lobstermen.

As he entered deeper waters, the morning ferry to Monhegan Island
passed him with a load of cargo. It was past tourist season, otherwise
the ferry would be crowded. The vessel cut through the channel as lobster buoys bobbed around its wake. The old—former?—surface warfare
officer in him could not help but think of dangers and threats on the
water. What if, he wondered, an enemy used explosive-filled buoys that
would wrap around a hull? Even putting a few small holes in a navy
ship would be a challenge for damage control teams. The danger would
be exponentially worse for a commercial ship without steel plating. He
shook his head at the implausibility and returned to the calmness of the
local waters.

He turned on the VHF marine radio to Channel 16 and depressed
the transmit button.

"*Mis-Chief, Mis-Chief, Mis-Chief.* This is *Rubicon*, over."

A few seconds later came the reply: "*Rubicon*, this is *Mis-Chief.* Go
to Channel 72."

"Channel 72. Copy. Out."

After he switched channels, the booming voice of his uncle came over
the receiver.

"You made it out?"

"Don't worry, Uncle John. I'll fill her up like I found her. Just wanted
to let you know I was taking her out for a few hours. Thinking of going
to Monhegan."

"You been to Benny's lately?" his Uncle Mike asked.

"No, haven't been there in years, why?"

"You might want to go out and take a last look around. It went up
for sale. Good place to go and think for a bit."

"Thanks, Uncle John. Will do. Going back to 16, out."

Uncle John was never wrong . . .

Earth

Benny's Island was difficult to reach in high sea states but today had been a breeze. Less than thirty minutes from Port St. George, it lay to the southeast, off the beaten track or channel to Monhegan Island. The 200-acre island had its own sheltered cove on the north side which had a natural rock barrier, hiding the structures on the southern part of its small range and out of view of any tourists. No one had a reason to come to Benny's Island, as it had been abandoned several years before. He tied the boat up to the rusted cleats on the old granite stone quay, turned off the engine, grabbed his backpack and hiked to the top of the rocks. From here he looked down on the complex of granite stone buildings that had since the mid-19th century been a monastery—St. Francois-sur-la-Mer. St. Francis on the Ocean. It should have been called St. Francis on the Rock. It had been a Benedictine order, hence the locals called it Benny's Island. The eastern and western ends of this oblong island still had red spruce and balsam fir trees. Between them was the old farm and a series of smaller granite structures for storage and work like a blacksmith shop.

Steps had been carved scores of years ago from the top of the ridge down to the main entrance, though they were now covered with lichen from lack of use. The complex still seemed pristine, a testament to the care the monks took in building to last, like the fifteen-hundred-year-old order had been. There was no reason to visit here now, even curiosity-seekers were encouraged by the locals to stay away. It was not unheard of for lobster boats to approach ships and bump them away. In 1931 during a major storm, a fishing vessel foundered nearby. The crew was saved but three monks lost their lives in the process. From then on, the island was protected.

History had always had paladins—those committed to protecting others.

The monks had a life of *ora et labora*—prayer and work. During his recent travels through Europe, he had seen other old island monasteries, like Mont Saint-Michel in Normandy, and Iona Abbey on Scotland's

Isle of Mull. But none had the memories of St. Francois. The monastery of a hundred monks had always had a close relationship with the local economy. Monks cultivated seaweed as fertilizer for Maine farmers, fished and salted cod, and produced cod liver oil, or smoked herring. But they were most noted for their boat-building skills like *Peapods*, the double-ended workboat, and *Whitehalls*, a sleek, fast-rowed boat. It had, in fact, been *Whitehalls* that the monks used to save the crew of that 1931 vessel among others.

The entrance was an unlocked wrought-iron gate, ten feet high. Just above the arch was an embedded bronze medallion, two feet in diameter, that had long ago acquired a greenish patina due to oxidation. In the four quadrants of the cross were the letters CSPB—*Crux Sancti Padre Benedictus*, the Cross of St. Benedict. On the horizontal cross were the letters NDSMD. From what the monks had told, it was the Latin for "Let not the Dragon be my guide."

He opened the creaky gate to the ten-foot-wide corridor. He entered the first door to the right, the chapel where monks had gathered several times a day and night. Though raised as a Presbyterian, he had long ago become agnostic. His only guide in his life was duty to his country, a duty that no longer existed.

On the east side of the corridor were the large refectory where they all ate together and the kitchen behind it. Further on, the great room that served both as a library and a communal area. Beyond the chapel was the open cloister, with a covered walkway on three sides for contemplation. On the south end were guest rooms—a Benedictine tradition. The final corridor led to two wings of rooms for the use of the monks, several of whom had come from local towns and villages.

They had had stability, a purpose, and teamwork. Those had been lost to him. This had been a place for those men for so long, but they were now gone. The last monk had passed away a few years ago in a hospital. To show their appreciation for the monastery, Uncle John led a procession of forty lobster boats and ground-fishing vessels. His boat carried the monk's remains to the island one last time and buried him on the island's cemetery along with all his brothers, forever in the ground and stone, in their belief to rise again from it on the last day.

The island deserved to be alive and not simply a testament to the dead. It had been grounded in its faith and work. What a tragedy, he thought, if it was purchased and developed without that long-time community in mind. But what purpose could it serve now.

Wind

He returned to the cloister and walked the stone-floors where perhaps five hundred men over the course of the monastery's life had trod, slowly pacing in prayer, meditation, and reflection. The first two concepts were foreign to him, but he had had too much of the third in the past year. He walked toward the stone benches that overlooked the water, and took a slow, deep breath of the sea air, that he was raised with, and had made his all-too-brief career. A few lobster boats were in the distance. The distinctive red hull of his Uncle John's was among them. A sailboat made its way south, likely before the winter gales set in. She was on a beam's reach. The wind had picked up since earlier that morning, ideal to sail the simple elegance that had been sailing vessels since the first made their ways on the oceans. A large fishing trawler that he didn't recognize made its way toward Port St. George, reminding him of J. M. W. Turner's famous 1839 painting, "The Fighting Temeraire," contrasting the beauty of a classical fighting ship to the new steam-powered ships, the "sea monsters" described by a Secretary of the Navy.

He unfastened his backpack and opened the book on Kipling where he had left off in the middle of "McAndrew's Hymn."

> *The winds are calling, calling me to go*
> *Across the world that's full of life and woe.*

He stopped after those two lines, chuckled and returned the book to the backpack, reflecting on the words that had haunted him.

"You are hereby found guilty on all charges. Does the defendant have any words before the court considers its sentence?"

He stood before the judge, attired in his service dress blues for the last time.

"Your honor, I took the actions that I believed necessary. Under the same circumstances, I would do so again." He took a deep breath and very slowly exhaled, barely perceptible even to his defense counsel, a young Lieutenant junior grade on her first case. He readied for the sentencing of jail and a dishonorable discharge. Only a half dozen people were in the court, including the judge and the lawyers. It had been closed due to the nature of the incident. No press or other witnesses were allowed to be present. A petty officer entered the courtroom and handed an envelope to the judge, a navy captain, who opened it. She sat back, looked at the defendant, then straightened her back.

"Time served. The defendant shall receive a general discharge immediately following this proceeding. The petty officer will escort the defendant for out-processing. Court-adjourned."

All his lawyer could whisper was, "Wow. That is NOT what I was expecting."

That was it for him. Not a dishonorable discharge, no additional time in the brig. How had this happened? He was ready to face the consequences, but this? This wasn't possible. With that his Navy career was over. His service on ships, including command of a Cyclone-class coastal patrol boat and an experimental ship in preparation for command of a destroyer, was in the past. All that he had learned and experienced could never be applied to a future command, for the Navy or for the country. Gone was serving a cause "greater than yourself."

Humans had freedom of choice, perhaps its greatest attribute. But it did not have freedom from consequences for those choices. He accepted both maxims. He had made his choice in Canada. He knew there would be consequences.

He had been selected for a one-year assignment to Senator Padraic O'Rourke's staff as a military legislative assistant. In the months that followed, he accidentally identified a terrorist group seeking Quebec's separation from Canada. He had reported it to his chain of command, all of whom dismissed him. When people close to him were killed, he again was ignored. He found only empty bluster. The easy thing for him to do was nothing, let wrongs go unaccountable, let justice be quietly blown away by political winds.

He took another path knowing well what would happen. On an airport tarmac in Quebec, justice was served, but laws had been violated and those in high positions threatened with exposure.

He didn't know how exactly how long he sat on the bench at the edge of the cloister, looking to the west, replaying again and again those events, but the sun was about to touch the horizon. All the lobster boats had disappeared; they usually made it back by early afternoon. He had seen the process enough to envision it. One after another the boats would pull alongside the dock, some proving their boat's—and their own—skills as they made the last-minute pivot, gunning the engines for just a moment. As each boat unloaded their day's yield from the traps, the captains and sternmen would trade friendly insults with the workers in the co-op helping them, or sharing coastal news, or complaining about the latest political candidates whose ads flooded the airwaves as the lobsterman tried only to listen to music while they provided bounty for the restaurants near and far. Uncle John would be there by now, tying up his own boat and checking into the house before he and many of the rest headed to the pub.

He checked his watch. The tide wouldn't be high enough to return to the family's pier in the cove. He'd head directly to the town's marina and tie up for a few hours until he could coordinate with his uncle. He took a last look around the monastery. There was so much history here, he thought. And maybe a lot of opportunity, for the right person and the right reason.

Fire

The lights of Port St. George welcomed him back as the boat made its way to the marina, the sun's last flicker of the day having gone out. One of the vessels moored in the harbor was the trawler he'd seen earlier that day, and it was flying a white, red and blue flag. Russian.

He pulled into one of the many unoccupied slips. The walk to the house would only take ten minutes. He realized he hadn't eaten his sandwich or even had breakfast. He heard music and voices at the pub. He had only been back in Port St. George a few days and hadn't yet gone in. With all his time at sea in the Navy or his one shore assignment, he hadn't been to the pub since his college days. Shortly after his last time there, his cousin Jaime mentioned there were new owners, a family from Scotland.

170

"They made a lot of changes. You should go next time you're back there," she wrote him when she was in her second class year at the Academy. "I think you'd like it."

The noise grew louder from the pub as he approached the deck. It was more than music and voices. People were yelling. A woman could be heard screaming. He was about to charge in to the pub when a man larger than he burst through the screen door, back first, and tumbled feet over head. The man was mumbling something unintelligible before the Russian language became apparent as another man, also clearly Russian from his shouting, emerged from the pub trying to regain his balance. A tall woman in her mid-thirties chased after him, her long flaming-red ponytail whipping around. She was holding a long stick in both hands with the precision of an athlete. He tried to remember why it was familiar. At first it looked like a field hockey stick but then realized he had seen it the previous month in Scotland. It was a shinty, used in the Gaelic game of the same name.

The second Russian got his footing back and was about to charge her when she swung the shinty and cracked his kneecap, taking him down. She placed a boot on his chest and pushed him back.

"You think you can drink for free all afternoon, then start a fight here? Both of you get back on that rusty ship of yours, and tell your captain to pay your bills and not let you into this town again, or I will sink that crappy trawler me-self. Ye understand? Yeah, ye understand English just fine when you want a drink. Ye understand now. Get out." She went back in to cheers.

The two Russians picked themselves up slowly and made their way back to their ship as his uncle exited the pub.

"Glad you didn't miss the entertainment," he said, slightly swaying.

"Not all of it. Who was that?"

"That," his uncle said patting him on the shoulder, "is Maggie. She owns the place."

"How did the boys do?" he asked about the other lobstermen in the pub.

"They watched. Maggie doesn't need help. You going in?"

"Yeah, just a bite to eat and maybe one drink. I won't be long. See you back at the house."

He walked in as another man was trying to assess the damage to the door. Probably one of the owners, as Stark didn't recognize him. A few of the booths were occupied, but since no one was at the bar he grabbed a seat at the end near the wall. The woman with red hair was washing her hands and talking to herself before looking up in the mirror behind the bar and noticing her new customer. She dried her hands and walked over to him.

"What'll ye have?"

"Whisky," he answered.

"EY or Y? And so ye know, the answer is only Y." He understood. It was the difference between what was made in Scotland—whisky—and anywhere else—whiskey."

"Talisker. Neat."

She nodded in approval, grabbing a bottle off the top shelf.

He ate, had a drink, and then another. The bar emptied early at this time of year. She finally asked, "you Jaime's cousin?"

"Yeah, how'd you know?"

She pointed at a couple of photos at the end of the bar among all those of family members past and present who served in the military. Next to Jaime Johnson's midshipmen photo was one of him back when he was a lieutenant.

"Tough to tell at first behind all that hair on ye face," she said as she took a drink for herself as the last customer left.

"I'm Connor. Connor Stark," he said extending his hand.

"Maggie," she replied accepting the handshake.

"I just got back from a trip to Scotland. I loved it. Where are you from?"

"The Highlands. Nothing like here. Near where I grew up the summer is red and purple from the blooming heather. In old stories, they call it the 'fire upon the hills.' We heard that a lot growing up—the 'heather on fire.'"

"Why are you here?" he asked. "I mean why did you come here to Port St. George?"

"It's a long story, but it seemed the right place to be. Why are you here?"

"It's a long story, but I don't know where the right place is."

"What are ye lookin' for, Connor Stark?"

"I don't know anymore," he answered quietly.

"Sometimes the right place is just where ye are."

They shared a few drinks and some stories about the village. She excused herself as she started to clean up. He offered to help as he cleaned off one of the tables.

Sometimes the right place is just where you are.

Connor Stark's mind was here in the pub, but also on Benny's Island, a place of privacy, easily secured, and with some investments able to house and train scores of people. Even room for a command center. With some work . . .

"I need a phone," he called to her, and she pointed to one next to the register.

"Hello?"

"Bill, it's Connor. That job. I'd like to take it."

"What?"

"Yeah, but I have ideas and they're non-negotiable."

"What exactly?"

"There's a facility here I want to buy—I want you to buy. And rebuild. As a base of operations, no matter what we do in the world. It's here in Port St. George. And I want this venture to have a name."

"Go ahead."

Stark paused glancing over at Maggie who smiled at him.

"Highland Maritime Defense."

"An Elemental Decision" precedes the first novel
of the Connor Stark thrillers, *Pariah*.
Books 2 and 3 are *Privateer* and *The Philippine Pact*.

—•⊙ ABOUT THE AUTHOR ⊙•—
CLAUDE BERUBE

Claude Berube, PhD, is a retired Commander who taught at the
US Naval Academy for twenty years and worked on Capitol Hill. In
addition to naval history books, he writes the Connor Stark novels.

HISTORICAL MYSTERY

A Thoreauly Hawthorne Mystery

BY KATE DIKE BLAIR

"Of all modes of death, methinks drowning is the ugliest." My older brother Nathaniel Hawthorne, shaking with cold and grief, swiped at his sleeve with an already sodden kerchief in an unsuccessful attempt to protect the Old Manse's parlor sofa from a dribble of muddy water, as he described to me his disturbing discovery of a woman's corpse in the nearby Concord River.

Nath and his wife Sophia had rented the Old Manse, as Nath dubbed it, directly after their marriage. The 18th century house had some notoriety for its close proximity to Concord's North Bridge and the vantage point from which the Emerson family had witnessed the start of the American Revolution. Nath enjoyed working in what had once been the reverend Emerson's study and had already written several short stories appropriately titled *Mosses from an Old Manse*. And Sophia, in a fit of new-married bliss, had carved with her engagement ring, into an upstairs window-pane, a poem celebrating their love.

But they were also in trouble with their landlord Waldo Emerson, the reverend's grandson, for punching a ventilation hole in the kitchen, so Nath was in no hurry to bring more vengeance down upon his head. However, comforting him after a failed rescue attempt took precedence over protecting the furniture. And since Sophia had ridden yesterday's stage to Boston to visit her sister Elizabeth's West Street bookshop, it was up to me to distract him with logic.

"Do you think she took her own life? Something, or someone, drove her past her breaking point and she threw herself into the water?" Oddly, I shivered as if that someone had walked across my own grave. I threw another log on the fire, and then paced about the cluttered room, my long skirts tucked into my waistband for ease of movement, my cap askew as I sought to find the reason behind such an eminently unreasonable act.

Nath wrapped a blanket from the sofa around his lanky form. "She was fully dressed when we found her in the muck by the bridge. My oar connected with her body and friend Channing jumped into the water to determine if she might still be alive. Sadly, she was the very image of death agony." He paused and shut his eyes to protect himself from that horrific spectacle. "We pulled her into the boat, and her bodice came unbuttoned to reveal a scarlet 'A' emblazoned upon her skin, as if she had been branded and then thrown into the river in some ironic antidote."

"An A? Let's see, Abigail, Amelia, Annette . . ." I counted the names on the fingers of one hand while imagining their personages on the other.

Nath's blue eyes rolled. "Louisa, it stands for adultery, you goose! Her name was Martha, and she lived on the 'other side of town,' if you understand my meaning." He raised one eyebrow, intimating the less fortunate housing in West Concord. "Have you not read the Puritan's screed about punishing a woman who sleeps with another's husband?" He strode to the book shelf, his grief momentarily forgotten, mumbling to himself as he ran his index finger along the spines, finally yanking out a dog-eared history which he tossed to me. He leaned against the paneled wall, arms folded beneath the blanket, brow furrowed, daring me to find the chapter to which he alluded.

"Fine" I muttered, annoyed at being given a task not immediately in league with the drowned woman's fate. But indeed, there in a marked passage was the information about the Puritan's punishment of an adulterer. A scarlet letter A was to be sewn onto her dress, as if that would keep her from any other untoward associations. But an A sewn upon a dress was very different from an A branded upon flesh. Someone was sending a brutal message of revenge.

"Told you so. I've been doing research for a new story." Nath flopped upon the sofa and flung off the blanket, his horror at the drowned woman's fate forgotten in his triumph over his younger sister.

"Will you be part of the murder investigation?" I knew that Nath had a relationship with many of Concord's selectmen, having met a fair number over pints in Wright's Tavern.

He spread his hands as if to state the obvious. "Of course. I was a member of the rescue party. And the Concord citizenry loves the articles I write about their exploits. But I am not sure I want to delve into the crime too deeply, it troubles me so."

"Perhaps we should make a field trip to the tavern to take comfort in your friends. I promise to protect you if the subject matter veers too much toward the macabre. And a pint might do you some good." I banked the fire, let down my skirts and tidied my hair in anticipation of a walk into Concord. But I paused as a deeper thought surfaced. A drowning was one thing; a branded victim was another. "Who would be making the determination of death? In Salem I know it to be the coroner, but Concord is a smaller town."

"Are you saying we have not the same legal necessities here in this provincial community as in our city of origin?" He shrugged in dismissal. "At least in fair Concord witches were not burned and land stolen. Or have you forgotten our ancestor?"

Nath was of course referring to Magistrate John Hathorne, who had presided over the Salem witch trials. When Nath added a 'w' to his own nom de plume after his first publication, my mother, sister, and I all added it as well, so as to be connected to the famous, not the infamous, Hawthorne.

"Maybe one of your townie friends has heard some news." I threw a shawl over my shoulders to ward off the autumn chill. Nath flung on a threadbare coat and balanced a beaver hat upon his curls, and we stepped out onto the long drive leading from the Old Manse onto the road to Concord, woodsmoke scenting the air and the bordering trees aglow in orange, red, and yellow on this chilly October afternoon.

"Nathaniel Hawthorne, how wonderful to see you out and about," cried a familiar voice. Margaret Fuller, a disciple and house guest of Waldo Emerson's, a dear friend of my brother's, and a mentor to me, ran to catch up, skirts flying and hair askew. A tropical flower bounced about above her ear, and Nath reached over to rescue it before it dropped in the mud.

"Margaret, we are making our way to Wright's Tavern for a pint and a revelation. Do you wish to join or do your feminist philosophies forbid such pleasures?" After his experience at the supposedly utopian Brook Farm, Nath had no patience for temperance, which he lumped in with all suspicious forms of higher consciousnesses. He tucked the flower back behind her ear, his hand briefly cupping her cheek.

She blushed and lowered her gaze. "I would beg to join, as Lydian is in bed with toothache." She met his eyes again in concern. "Besides, I hear that you were part of the attempted rescue mission at the river, and there is bound to be more information spread as lips are lubricated."

"Perfect. Join us then, for six ears are better than four for memory." Nath strode forth, his long legs making short work of the trip into town, while tiny Margaret flailed in his wake, and I dropped back to keep her company.

"This horrific event has almost done me in," panted Margaret. "Drowning is a recurrent nightmare of mine, as if my subconscious were sending me a warning. But even worse, I hear that the young woman had been cruelly branded upon the chest." She shook her head in disbelief and asked rhetorically, "Why do women love bad men?"

"Indeed. And Nath is hoping that someone at the Tavern might have an idea of the perpetrator. Or at the very least, might know who has been having inappropriate relations with whom." I turned away so that Margaret might not see my own guilty blush. After all, I had been enjoying dalliances with my married uncle John for several years now. If whoever had branded Martha knew of my relationship with John, I must escape in a stagecoach to Salem forthwith.

Wright's Tavern squatted on a knoll in the center of town, its red clapboards and black trim echoing the surrounding scarlet maples. Generations of drinkers had refreshed themselves under its steep-pitched roof, including the notorious British General Pitcairn himself after the battle at the bridge. I hoped I would not take his place at the bar.

Nath ushered us into the gloom and tossed his hat upon a far table beneath a soot-stained muslin-curtained window. The fug of wool and unwashed bodies enhanced the haze of cigar and wood smoke. A frazzled bar maid limped over with a pitcher of ale and three tumblers, and we made ourselves as comfortable as we might, given the many curious eyes that followed our progress. Margaret drew the most attention, with her flopping flower, trim figure, and lovely, lively face, but Nath had enough of a checkered reputation to put those who were less than angelic at ease. Several raised their tankards toward him in greeting.

He surveyed the crowded room, and focused on one stooped, bearded young man gazing into his ale as if the entire natural world swirled in its depths. Nath placed a calming hand upon his friend's shoulder and respectfully interrupted his revery. "Henry Thoreau. I am so very sorry to hear about your brother."

Henry took his time looking up, and when he did, tears sparkled in his deep blue eyes. He nodded, as if speaking would be too difficult. Nath gestured toward an empty chair at our table, and Henry slid into it. Margaret gave his shoulders an affectionate little hug, I enveloped his two cold hands in both my own, and he slowly returned to the land of the living.

"We have some questions about the drowning victim, but perhaps her fate will be too much a reminder of John's tragedy for you to consider." Margaret rubbed Henry's back in calming circles, her voice quiet and kind. John Thoreau had died from lock-jaw contracted from a putrid cut, and Henry had held his dear brother's body as it spasmed and shook in the end stages of that dreaded disease. We were not the only friends to hope for a miracle cure or preventative potion to protect us all from such a miserable end.

But Henry nodded his acceptance of an inquiry, so Margaret continued. "We know you have an ear to the ground through your school and other enterprises. Perhaps you might have heard some . . ." She paused, searching for a less pejorative word than gossip. "Perhaps you have heard some rumors regarding her last few days."

Henry cleared his throat and then pronounced one word: "Loveless."

Margaret glanced at Nath and me. We both shook our heads in confusion. The word could have several meanings, none of them hopeful for the unfortunate Martha. "She was not loved?" Margaret asked gently, ceasing her rubbing and turning Henry toward her to catch his expression.

"No. Mr. Loveless. He is the villain. No one knows his first name, but Martha was afraid of him. She said he threatened her, after her suitor's wife found out about their secret affair. And he has a brother, too, in Salem, who subscribes to the same evil activity." Henry paused, stuck in a painful memory of his own, but then cleared his throat and continued, "Loveless has disappeared. Gone back to Salem, apparently." Henry again stared down into his drink, refusing to look at any of us, as if the reminder of this villain had returned him to his depths of despair. We all stayed in respectful silence, hoping another memory of Loveless might surface.

"I know the blackguard." A tall, bearded man, dressed more formally than most of the gathering, stood and approached our table. "Sorry to eavesdrop, but I am the Salem coroner, come to Concord to examine the body and determine the cause of death. Loveless's name, which we assume to be a nom de guerre, has been implicated in Salem in regard to two young ladies' suspicious deaths. We are not sure whether or not he is the instigator, or if other perpetrators are hiring him to do their dirty work, or why he might have branched out into Concord."

"Loveless. What a perfect alias for a lady killer." Nath took out a piece of stationery and a pencil nub from an inside coat pocket and began taking notes. "And your name, sir?"

"Dr. Charles T. Jackson, at your service. And you are?"

"Nathaniel Hawthorne, author and interested citizen. And these are my compatriots. Please tell us more about this Loveless character."

"He appears to make his living as a rented assassin, as there are no known connections between himself and his victims. This is the third young woman to be drowned, the other two in Salem harbor. His calling card is the letter "A" branded upon their breasts. I am distressed to say that, according to my findings, they are still alive for this torture but he subsequently strangles them before throwing them into the water."

Nath winced, Henry's hands trembled, and Margaret stood up and paced around the table, her white face a testament to her disturbance.

Again, I had the oddest sensation of familiarity. Then, a shiver of recognition as an old memory surfaced: *Clarissa*! Samuel Richardson's epistolary novel of a century past, about an unfortunate woman who is abused and raped because she will not succumb to the dastardly antagonist's advances. But was not that villain a Robert Lovelace, pronounced "Loveless" as a clue to his true self? Perhaps anyone cursed with such an evil homophone must follow its implications, and correcting the spelling might point a finger toward the true perpetrator.

"Have you looked for a Robert L-o-v-e-l-a-c-e, pronounced Loveless?" I asked, expecting Margaret to laugh at my literary reference. But she stopped her pacing and nodded thoughtfully, the flower bobbing in agreement.

Dr. Jackson's expression changed from frustrated to intrigued. He bowed to us, popped his stovepipe hat upon his head, turned on his heel and exited Wright's Tavern with alacrity. We watched from the window as he swung himself into a carriage and pointed the driver toward Salem.

"Can a medical examiner arrest a criminal?" Nath mused, thinking as always about his next plot twist.

"I don't believe so, but he can certainly pass the knowledge on to his colleagues in the constabulary. Louisa, you may have solved a mystery! Today a reader, tomorrow a leader!" Margaret stood on her chair and addressed the crowd. "Let us raise our glasses to education for all!" Led by an enthusiastic Henry, a weak cheer emanated from the almost entirely male audience, yet the bar maid caught my eye and winked.

Our group was quiet on the walk home in the autumn twilight. Henry, after hugs all around, headed to his mother's home for his nightly dinner. Margaret turned in at Emerson's Bush House to sit once again at the feet of her master. And Sophia greeted us at the front door of the Old Manse, her face alight at her husband's fond smile.

I made myself scarce until dinner time, sitting alone in my upstairs bedroom, gazing out the window at the famous bridge over the idyllic Concord River, recalling our own momentous day and my possible role in the catching of a killer.

The household was awakened early the next morning by a vigorous knocking upon the front door. "Mr. Hawthorne! Mr. Hawthorne! I have news!" shouted a deep voice. I hurried down the stairs from my aerie, hair still loose, to aid in whatever mystery might be unfolding. Sophia, untying her apron as she ran in from the kitchen, pulled open the door to find Dr. Jackson, stove pipe hat pushed back upon his brow, cravat askew, leaning against the door frame, panting, as if he had run all the way from Salem.

"I must speak with your husband. We are anxious to have this information disseminated in whichever periodical he is published."

Sophia ushered Dr. Jackson into the office, where Nath, after a hasty grooming, sat ready, pencil in hand, to record Dr. Jackson's statement for the *Concord Freeman*.

"Miss Hawthorne, you were absolutely correct about the spelling of the villain's name," began the coroner. "He is indeed Robert Lovelace and well known to the criminal elements of Salem with whom we have an understanding. He was found quite content in his bolt-hole near the harbor, and is in custody, waiting for the Salem sheriff to bring him in for questioning. But do not fear: he will hang for his crimes."

Nath paused in his writing, pencil hovering above the sheet of stationery. "Henry spoke of Lovelace's brother. Any news on his whereabouts or whether he has the same cruel inclinations?"

"Indeed he does. His Christian name is Horace, and the Salem constabulary are searching for him, but have been unsuccessful so far. We will keep you apprised of the situation." He stood and gathered his gloves and hat. "Now I must take my leave, as your place of birth has an unfortunate degree of deaths to be examined. Be grateful for your new bucolic haven."

Nath stood and the two men shook hands in solemn agreement of the subject's gravity. Sophia showed the doctor to his carriage and then returned to the kitchen, but I could not accompany her, for that strange feeling of dread had resurfaced. Something inspired me to walk along the Concord's bank and mount the celebrated bridge, and as I stood at the top of the arch and gazed into the depths below, the lapping waves seemed to drum out a warning upon the pilings. I resolved to be vigilant in my adventures with John. Mr. Horace Lovelace, or whoever might avail themselves of his services, could shoulder the roles of judge, jury, and executioner, decree our love unpardonable, and take their revenge.

Historical Notes: *Nathaniel and Sophia Hawthorne rented The Old Manse in Concord after their marriage in 1842. Nathaniel and his friend Ellery Channing recovered the drowned body of Martha Hunt, determined to be a suicide. The first line of this story is a quote from his description of that incident. Louisa and Nathaniel Hawthorne were born and grew up in Salem, but Nathaniel added a W to his name to differentiate himself from Salem Magistrate John Hathorne, and his family followed suit. Louisa drowned in the* Henry Clay *Steamboat disaster in 1852, and a family friend brought the news to Nathaniel several mornings later. Margaret Fuller drowned in a shipwreck off the coast of Fire Island in 1850. In his era, Henry David Thoreau's last name was pronounced to rhyme with "thorough". His brother John Thoreau died of tetanus from an infected cut in 1842. The Wright Tavern was visited by Major Pitcairn on April 19, 1775. The Old Manse was the vantage point from which the Emerson family watched the fight on the North Bridge on that day.*

Literary Notes: *In Hawthorne's novel* The Blithedale Romance, *reflecting his experiences at the utopian colony Brook Farm, main character Zenobia, based on Margaret Fuller, wears a tropical flower behind her ear. Zenobia also drowns. Hawthorne's novel* The Scarlet Letter, *published in 1850, features a scarlet "A" sown onto the bodice of a woman who committed adultery. Robert Lovelace was indeed the villain in* Clarissa; or, the History of a Young Lady, *by Samuel Richardson.*

Follow Nathaniel Hawthorne as he
solves the murder of his sister.

—◦ ABOUT THE AUTHOR ◦—
KATE DIKE BLAIR

Kate Dike Blair is a direct descendant of several of the principal characters in her historical novel, *The Hawthorne Inheritance*. She earned her Diploma in Theater Arts from the Wykeham Rise School for Girls, her Bachelor of Arts from Boston University, her Certificate of Medical Assisting from the Bryman School of Boston, and her union cards from the Screen Actors Guild and the American Federation of Television and Radio Artists. Since retiring from her medical consulting business Health Research Associates, she divides her time between writing novels and memoirs and acting on stage and screen. She resides with her family in Wayland, Massachusetts.

Portents

BY GINNY FITE

Before a storm, leaves turn their silvery underside to the sky to catch the raindrops. Mom delivered this information with the simplicity of fact, and being young, I believed her. One thing portends another, she meant to say, even if the announcement is only a breeze. She knew what was coming and was teaching me to watch for signs. I wish I had heeded her warning.

I'm sure she was trying to tell me the one important thing I needed to know about life in general, or about the world, or what kind of woman I would be when I grew up, but she died when I was seventeen, and I never learned it.

If I had known what she meant, if I had understood the signs sooner, that might have simplified my life. But for the longest time I ignored what the world was telling me. I was never good at obeying my better angels. As you know, our demons—in their bowler hats, cravats, and carrying canes—are more intriguing. Their antics capture our imagination as they caper down the lane, dancing and clicking their heels as if to say, "This way is freedom and all that you desire."

It was my demons you saw and why you waited for me to make a mistake. Your certainty that I would stumble was why I resented you. Maybe all sisters align themselves this way without discussion or explanation. We are required to be each other's opposite. Not that it matters now.

After Mom told me about leaves and rain, I did watch the world for portents, although I didn't grasp their meanings. Without understanding,

I told myself I shouldn't be hasty about doing anything. My method for reading the signs was similar to decoding a cryptic Magic 8 Ball message, "Cannot predict now." More guess work than insight.

You said I was content to lie back and let life roll over me. It wasn't that. It's that there was so much life, taking it in occupied all my time. I had to mull each new idea, put it on like a new coat and walk around in it. I couldn't, like you, glance at something and jump to a conclusion— on or off, right or wrong, yes or no, stay or go.

The world isn't binary, contrary to what software coders tell us. Binary is as complicated as a machine can get. Humans, and quantum computers I suppose, can entertain multitudes, but as far as I can see, there's always one more bit of information that might change how we view the universe.

You were always way ahead of me as if you knew where you were going. In one of my earliest memories, we are walking through a wood, the leafy branches of a thousand trees reaching to the sky far above my head. Mom had taken us on a picnic, and you suggested running away. Maybe I was four. I would have gone anywhere with you at that age. Sunlight filtered through the leaves, littering the ground with white puzzle pieces I tried to pick up. You, an imperious eight, turned and beckoned to me, yelling, "Come on, hurry up." Or maybe I dreamed that.

How odd, then, that I got here first, and I'm the one who has to tell you what's coming. And to hurry up.

I should have told you what happened the day I talked to our neighbor, though telling you sooner wouldn't have made any difference in the end. She was a widow, like us but all alone, and her dog had died. It was clear she needed human contact, so I reached over the fence to touch her cheek. We weren't wearing masks. I knew the minute my fingers touched her hot skin that breaking our no contact rule would change everything, but I didn't stop. Perhaps I was defying you. If so, I'm sorry for that.

After that, I didn't have enough breath to tell you everything I wanted to say, so I'll tell you while you sleep.

All the signs say they're coming for us. The government wants to lock you away because you cared for me as I was dying. They'll call it quarantine and take our children and separate them. You can't let that happen. Wake up. Get moving.

A long road stretches out ahead. Light blinks off the silver thread of a necklace that rides the pulse in your neck. You drive with both hands on the wheel, eyes focused straight ahead. In the locket is a photo of me and another of Ted, the husband you cherished. We're already dead, and you're taking us with you in your dash across the country.

In flight you're beautiful—long dark hair in a ponytail, chin resolute, dark eyes intent on seeing what no one else can. I remember from childhood the indigo shadows beneath your eyes—how you were always calculating our escape in your sleep. Since Ted died, you haven't looked in a mirror. When you get dressed, you avert your eyes as if to see yourself would open the hasty stitches on your grief.

Remember how one morning, we woke up to see a white Mercedes parked in the lane, still wet from the drenching rain. A spray of petals from the bough of blazing pink crepe myrtle that hung above the driveway had glazed the car making it look as if it had been to a wedding.

The car was Mom's surprise birthday present from Dad, and made me wonder if we were rich and did that make us different? Should I walk with my shoulders back and my chin raised as if I carried a book on my head? Could I ignore people when they called my name? I liked the idea and tried it on for a few days. My attitude infuriated you, and that amused me.

I was seven then and didn't know that being suddenly rich is something to be careful with, to not take for granted, because in no time, we could be un-rich and living in the back seat of that car. During the rich time, I had my own room and my own bed and when I look back, I see that having my own bed was the greatest luxury. You make strange noises in your sleep, as if you're running away from someone and can't get your breath.

You were cautious with our sudden wealth—your room neat, with everything in its place so you could find it at a moment's notice. It's like you knew we'd have to move in a hurry. You knew from your dreams, although you didn't know you knew; you were always getting ready to flee. Your go bag with stuff you couldn't bear to be without waited on the closet floor. You said you'd tell me when it was time.

Now it's my turn to know, and I'm yelling as loud as I can, "It's time. Hurry up! Let's go."

It's not like it was easy for me to leave. I was in love with the place where we lived, the physical space, the geology, the air, the colors. The first time I crossed the bridge over the Potomac River to visit you in your new house and saw the mountains surrounding Harpers Ferry, I knew I'd come home. You felt that way too, though we never spoke about it. With all our differences, we had that in common.

Had I been good with words, this experience of coming home to a place I'd never been would still have been hard to explain. I hadn't known the area existed. We weren't from there. The farthest thing from. Mom used to say she'd never seen a cow until she moved to Howard County, and Maryland was the farthest south she ever wanted to go.

Home, oddly, had to do with the combination of mountains and rivers, how the water was the color of the sky, and how the color changed constantly. Home had to do with apples, how every fall the air was ripe with them and in summer the pervasive aroma was peaches as if this valley was the real Eden, before all our mistakes began.

If we had talked about it, you would have said the mountains triggered an unconscious collective memory, an image stored in our genes that reminded us of who we were, the patch of earth we came from. Who knows if that's true? You have such strange theories, and you're so sure you're right, but I love the idea of being connected to the land, of being from somewhere that I carry with me like a handful of dirt in my pocket. My roots are in this earth—dust and water, bone, and blood—for a thousand lifetimes, as you would say.

Every Saturday morning for that first year, I stood in the middle of the pedestrian footpath on the bridge that spanned the Shenandoah River looking east toward the river's confluence with the Potomac. Slate colored water rushed beneath me, and I waited for the sun to emerge from behind the mountain to the east. A halo of sunlight crested the ridge, gilding everything, and in an instant, I was kissed by light. My pores opened; my heart expanded as if my brain were swamped by dopamine.

I was the aperture, the channel through which light poured, the paper on which it printed itself. The photographs I took were as much about me as they were of the sunrise and clouds, mountains, and rivers. I couldn't explain that to you either. I was still developing my theory of why this spot called to me.

And then came the day I arrived on the bridge and someone else was there at my spot. I stopped in my tracks. A man in his early thirties with short hair, dressed in jeans, a white t-shirt and one of those khaki vests with all the pockets, was standing there looking out over the river. He hadn't shaved for a few days, but his clothes were clean. He had a camera slung over his neck and had set up a tripod onto which he was fixing another.

He wasn't dangerous, but he was in my spot, readying himself to take the photograph I was meant to take. I thought of various tactics I might use to get him to move off the bridge, to take his pictures from another spot, to just leave the area so I could have my moment. One moment in an entire week was all I asked of the universe, one moment, and here was someone who was going to steal it from me.

I cleared my throat and said good morning. Feeling outrageously brave, I told him he'd found the best spot for a photograph in all of Jefferson County. He turned and looked at me. The corners of his eyes crinkled when he smiled. His teeth were white and straight. When he resumed setting his f-stop and shutter speed, I had the feeling he thought all the awkwardness between strangers had been handled.

"I found this spot a few years ago," he said as he fiddled with knobs and peered through the viewer. "I've been out of the country for a while, in Afghanistan and Iraq, and this is the first place I wanted to be when I got back."

I asked if he was from here and waited, my skin prickling.

He smiled again and light crossed his face, like the sun rising. "Born and bred," he said, and asked about me.

I wanted to say yes, I am from here, I'm from this place. I wanted to assert my rights, but I couldn't. I wanted to tell him to go away, but that wouldn't be fair. He was on the bridge for the same reason I was. He was capturing a portrait of home, of the place that healed him, the place he had yearned for, that made him feel whole. I couldn't deprive him of that. I couldn't make him move off.

Feeling robbed, I stood mutely watching him prepare for his shot. Each time he moved I felt the hairs on his arm brush against mine though he was several feet away. When he was set, he stood behind his camera waiting for the sunrise, quiet, without fidgeting or hurrying. He knew how to wait. I wanted to hate him, but I didn't.

191

The sun rose, gold sliding over the water and the tips of tree branches, gilding the underside of white clouds, embracing them with its warmth. And then a blush of pink suffused the sky. I took my photo and looked at him.

He was transfixed, tears stealing down his cheeks. He didn't wipe them away. His bottom lip trembled. His shutter whirred, shot after shot after shot, a waterfall of light.

I waited. It seemed wrong to leave him when he was vulnerable. Wrong to speak. Here was someone I understood. He was somehow my responsibility. I had to protect him until the moment passed and he had collected himself and could deal with the world again.

"I'm very glad to be home," he whispered. "I wasn't sure I'd ever see this again."

He began packing up his gear. From a crouch, his hands still settling the cameras in the bag, he looked up at me and asked if I would like to get a cup of coffee. I said yes right away as if I were the kind of person who decided quickly, and this had always been our plan.

It was the beginning of my deciding everything immediately. I didn't need to know another thing. This was Nate, who already knew that it didn't matter if I couldn't instantly say what I meant, who understood timing and how I needed to wait to know what's right.

After that, it was simple algebra. If this was his home, and it was my real home, then he was my home, and I was his. I was always coming here no matter what, and when I leave you, I'm going where Nate is, where I'll be home forever.

Meanwhile, do what you were always supposed to do. You have to leave the place we love. I'm yelling as loud as I can. Get the kids to safety.

Before, a sound on the stairs, a glimpse of a shirt from the corner of your eye, a touch in the night, a voice in your ear was enough to rouse you. Listen now: some realizations can come too late. Someone is following you. I can see her. She's all in orange, dayglo, like an emergency beacon on the highway. You're the emergency she's chasing. She's bearing down now, she's close. Can you hear me? Do you understand?

Keep moving, being elusive is working. Get away, as fast as you can and hide where no one can see you. Keep going. They're coming for you.

I don't know if you can hear me, but I'll stay with you as long as I can. Listen to the children. They're clearer than you are. They see things you don't see.

"Aren't children wonderful?" you murmur in your sleep.

I'm in love with my children. It's no secret. They are my soulmates, and Nate's immortality, and as long as they're alive, I live in them. I never expected to leave my daughters in your care. You must be more than enough, sister; you must be everything. You must get them to our sanctuary.

How odd that my vision of your destination is the bathroom in Aunt Dee's house. I remember how the frosted windows let in pale natural light. Black and white hexagonal ceramic tiles with thin gray grout between them swirl across the floor. A white pedestal sink with two faucets stands solid against an acid green wall. There's a mirror above the sink. In the reflection, I see a girl, your Amina, hacking off her braid.

I hear the soft plink of the dripping faucet, the knocks and thumps of a steam radiator coming to life, the rattle of wind on the windowpanes. The air is chilly by the windows, the rose-scented soap is slippery in her hands, the woven towel rough. She scoops a handful of cool water and slurps it from her palm.

I must have been twelve, and you were sixteen when we stayed with Aunt Dee the summer our parents divorced. Away from the drama, Mom said as if pain were as contagious as chicken pox. Although she was just getting the hassle of us out of the way, she might have been right about that. Children catch their parents' emotional chills.

You blushed to your roots at something new every day and giggled. How I loved to laugh with you. Laughter was a freedom we didn't have at home. Dee taught us we could be any way we wanted to be, that we were allowed to be happy too. We could bend the world to our will, at least to a certain degree.

We needed to be on our own to learn that. We needed time to watch, to turn over in our minds what we'd seen, to explore our own feelings about it without being told what to think. Being at Dee's gave us permission to be ourselves. I claimed that treasure though you were unsure of its value. You were still measuring yourself against Mom's standards.

Children are their own kind of thing, a perfection of being. We were wonderful just as we were. Never mind what Mom said, or anyone else. Never mind improving us. When I look at Mira and Pam, I see you at that age, and you're already flawless. That was all you ever needed to be.

When our father died, his clothes filled half of a small closet and two drawers of a tall bureau. He had a separate drawer for his cotton handkerchiefs which were cleaned and ironed along with his work shirts at the Chinese laundry. There was another separate small drawer for his socks.

His clothes, chess set, a football he taught us to throw and catch, a few great books, and records of *Tosca, La Boheme, Carmen,* and *The Pearl Fisher* were the sum total of his possessions. The rest belonged to his wife, our stepmother. She made that clear. Whatever of his possessions we were given was by her largess.

You made faces behind her back. "Our memories," you said to comfort me, "belong to us. We get to keep them."

Memories are sticky, but they change. Is that because when we change, we see them from another perspective? Turn slightly to the left or right and a face looks different, colors alter, the event changes. Death changes memories. We grieve for what could have been but never was and never will be. We grieve for the loss of hope, the absence of a future.

We grieved for our mother when she died, though she could be cruel. She could destroy a year of our lives with a single word. You used to close your eyes and tilt your chin toward the ceiling as if a different view of the world would stop the hurt.

Words are the things that stay with you 'til you die, the statements you're always refuting in your head, the attacks against which years later you finally think up the right rebuttal. Mom called you a coward because you wouldn't do what she wanted. She said you were poison when you opposed her, and that you were too dependent on other people and would never amount to anything, that you would never matter.

She was wrong. You're my hero, Sister, the strongest person I know. You will do what you are supposed to do. The virus squad is coming, and worse. The journey is perilous, but you will save our children, whatever it takes. I can't ask more of you. Now, get on the road.

Follow Caro into more dark thrills.

—⁌ ABOUT THE AUTHOR ⁍—
GINNY FITE

Ginny Fite is the author of *SANCTUARY*, the grueling journey of *The Road* meets the shifting perspectives of *Station Eleven* in a dystopian speculative fiction about a family that survives their worst fears as the known world and their certainty about who they are disintegrate during a thousand-mile race to safety.

To Catch a Witch

BY NANCY KILGORE

Isobel Gowdie
Auldearn, Scotland, 1662

I scattered crumbs for the chickens and watched the children.

Maria, bright of eye and browned by the sun and weather, her dress half on and half off, a torn and ragged thing, sat on the ground. She threw sticks into a circle she had inscribed in the sand. She was seven. The two little ones, five and three, sat watching with full attention, as Robert, who was also seven and lived across the farmtown yard, stood behind the circle chewing seaweed.

The day was windy and raw, and the bairns shivered in the gusts of cold air; but they were used to the cold, so none of them thought to run into their homes. Robert chewed and watched as Maria led the game with her stick.

I knelt down beside them. "Can I play, too, Maria?"

"Aw, you a big person," Maria huffed. She was losing control of her game, and the princess was not pleased.

I took another stick and made it hop, hop, hop and dance around the circle. "Now catch me if you can," I said in a low spooky voice.

Maria seized her stick and chased mine, and soon William was chasing, too. We were all laughing.

When Hugh Gilbert my husband came across the open yard, he stopped and glared.

Maria saw his face, jumped up, and ran away toward the sea, her blonde hair wisping every which way in the wind. She was so fast; we hardly saw her before she reached the top of the dune and scooted over it.

Hugh shouted at me. "What have ye thought, lass, to waste yer time playing? What of the teazing and carding, what of the cow with the lame foot? What of the washing that sits in the house?" His face became a fiery frown as he walked up to me. The other children scattered, Robert running after Maria and the two little ones to chase the chickens by the hut.

I stood up and faced him squarely, hands on hips. "I'll play when I like, and I'll go with the fairies when you don't like."

He scowled and raised his fist. "And ye'll do your work or feel the fist."

I stepped back to avoid the blow. To divert his attention, I asked, "Ye'll go to market now for the beef?"

"Aye." He hesitated, fist in the air, then lowered it and walked toward the cattle yard behind the hut.

I bent low and entered the hut, heading straight across the room to my kist, where I stored the herbs and potions. I opened it, rummaging through until I found what I was looking for.

When Hugh came back, leading the cow, I was ready. He stopped and let me approach. I took the feather, sheer gray tinged with blue—a swallow's feather, it had to be—and attached it to the head of the beast with a piece of yarn. The delicate feather was barely visible against the brown of the cow's coat. And now I recited in a singsong voice:

> "*I put out this beef in the devil's name,*
> *that mickle silver and good price come hame.*"

And again:

> "*I put out this beef in the devil's name,*
> *that mickle silver and good price come hame.*"

And then again, as it had to be thrice for the charm to work.

Some charms called on the Holy Trinity, some on the saints, and others the fairies. This one needed the help of the devil.

And though my husband disapproved—he was always lecturing me, thinking he be like the minister, Mister Harry, no doubt—he allowed it, because he knew the magic worked.

He strode off with the cow, confident that now he would get a good sale.

I went into the house, banked the fire, and gathered the clothes for washing. I stepped out and started to walk to the river, but now I heard the sound of hoofbeats. I stopped and looked. Over the dyke came three horsemen.

Who could this be? There was a stirring in my heart, and I heard a faint voice. It must have been my mother, whispering or calling in the wind, but the words I did not know. Something cold and fearsome came into me, and I was sore affrighted.

The three horsemen came. Three solemn faces: one red and puffy, yellow hair fuzzed around pale cold eyes; one black-haired with unsure expression; and lastly, the sheriff, tall, mickle red-haired Sir Hugh Campbell. All were fierce-dressed in plaids with scabbards. They stopped and dismounted, never taking their eyes off me.

"Mistress Gowdie, you must come with us," said Sir Hugh.

"And why must I?" I tried for my voice of power, but only a feeble sound came out. I knew the answer.

"I arrest you in the name of the king. You are charged with the crime of witchcraft."

I looked around and around. Was there anywhere to run, to hide? My Maria with big eyes was peeking from around the corner. Nowhere— but I dropped my bundle and bolted. I ran toward the sea. Up and to the top of the dune, with hoofbeats close behind . . . and then a rope around me. The yellow-haired one jumped down, grabbed me in a rough manner, and tied my hands together. He remounted, holding the end of the rope. I was forced to walk behind, half-dragged down the side of the dune and across the yard. We left the farmtown and continued in procession toward Auldearn, where Isobel Gowdie would be on display, led to the tollbooth.

Read more about Isobel Gowdie, a cunning woman
and magic practitioner in 17th century Scotland
in the novel *BITTER MAGIC*.

— ABOUT THE AUTHOR —
NANCY KILGORE

Nancy Hayes Kilgore is the author of four novels: *PENNSYLVANIA LOVE SONG* (Sunbury Press, 2025), *BITTER MAGIC* (Milford House Press, 2021), *WILD MOUNTAIN* (Brown Posey Press, 2017), and *SEA LEVEL* (RCWMS, 2011). She is a winner of the Vermont Writers Prize and a ForeWord Reviews Book of the Year award. A former parish pastor, a psychotherapist, and a writing coach, Nancy leads workshops on creative writing and spirituality. She is a native of Pennsylvania and lives in Vermont.

A Man In a Hurry

BY J. R. LINDERMUTH

I'm the third of my family to serve as sheriff here in Arahpot, Jordan County, Pennsylvania, and one thing folks know about me is I don't shirk my duty, especially not when it comes to women and kids. I just wasn't prepared for what awaited me this day.

It was one of those quiet mornings, not even the fleas stirring on the jailhouse dog. I was in my office nursing a cup of coffee and contemplating taking the day off for a little fishing when the telephone rang. I'm still not used to the blamed thing and probably still wouldn't have it if my sweetheart Lydia Longlow hadn't talked me into having it installed. So, it probably took longer for me to answer than it should have.

"Sheriff Tilghman?" a female voice squawked in my ear.

"Yes. Who's this?"

"You gotta get over here right away."

"Who is this? I gotta get where?"

After a hiss of expelled air, the voice bellowed again. "It's Maggie Snyder, that's who. You gotta drop everything else and get on over here."

"Now calm down, Maggie, and tell me what you're blatherin' about. Where must I come, and why?"

"It's little Charlie Purcell," she told me. "He's been missin' since early this morning."

It took no more than that to get me on my feet and moving. I've known Ralph Purcell all his life. He's a good young fellow and a hard worker. His wife Irene is just about the sweetest thing you'd ever want to meet. And three-year-old Charlie, their first and only child, is their pride and joy. A smart, handsome little tyke, the sun rises and sets on him in that household.

Well, sir, when I reached their place Irene was in such a state she could barely talk. But Maggie Snyder was present and steamed up to tell me exactly where my duty lay. That woman has been the bane of my existence since I took this job. A nosey neighbor, an unprincipled gossip, and a harridan who's driven off at least two men who thought they might tame her with marriage. Lydia keeps telling me I should be patient with the old woman, but she doesn't have to deal with her as often as I do.

"Now stop shouting, Maggie, and tell me what happened so I can figure out what needs to be done."

With her hands planted on her bony hips, Maggie advanced on me like a hen protecting her chicks. "I'm telling you what you go to do, Tilghman. You gotta get after them."

"I'd be glad to do that if you'll simmer down long enough to tell me who you're talking about. Take a breath, woman, step back, and start at the beginning. I can't do nothing unless I know what's been done."

Maggie hissed and hemmed a couple of seconds longer, her eyes scouring me and her lips twisting like she had something sour in her mouth. Then, stepping over to where Irene stood, she threw an arm across the girl's shoulders and told me what had happened. "Ralph was off to work. Irene put Charlie out in the front yard with a few of his favorite toys and came back inside to do up the breakfast dishes. She was only gone a little while and when she went outside again Charlie was gone. She summoned me, we checked the other neighbors, and then I called you."

"Gone? And you think . . ."

"I don't think. I know. The boy's been kidnapped."

"Who . . ."

"I'm getting' to that if you'll give me a chance, Tilghman." She advanced on me again, those nasty eyes of hers blazing. "Luther Gilger was sittin' on his porch. He can't see the front of Irene's house from his. But he told me a team came slowly past his house just as he came out. Then, just a short time later, that same team came by again, the driver whippin' up his horses as they went flyin' off in the direction of Masonville."

"So you think . . ."

"That driver snatched up Charlie and carried him off for God knows what purpose."

"Did Mr. Gilger see the boy in the wagon?"

"No. But that must be what happened. Why else would the driver go tearin' off like he did?"

The thought of it put a stone in my stomach and my mouth went dry.

"Why are you standing here, Tilghman?" Maggie barked. "Round up a posse and get after them."

The woman was right. That's what had to be done. I gathered up my deputy Cyrus Gutshall and I'm proud to say we rounded up a posse as quick as we did, most of the men being off to work. As I said, Ralph is a good boy and well-liked. His neighbors were glad to drop what they were doing and join in the search. Before long, we had a half-dozen men on horseback and some others willing to pursue the team on foot.

We riders set off at a gallop, pausing at every little patch along the way just long enough to inquire if anyone had seen the rig in question. The heat of the day came up and we went on, scouring the country-side for miles around. At every place, we heard the same refrain. A team passed, the driver whipping his horses and driving them at a furious pace. And it was always the same—the wagon went by too fast for anyone to tell if a child had been aboard.

It was frustrating, but we went on. The men and horses were bone-weary. Yet, how could we quit when a woman waited to learn the fate of her child?

Another eighteen miles and my horse threw a shoe. I drew up and dismounted. The others pulled up beside me, gazing down, questioning without words what should they do. "Somebody loan me a horse," I said.

Dusk was descending.

"The horses is all worn out, Sheriff," Luther Gilger's son Ed said. "Maybe we ought to give it up." Several of the others bobbed their heads, muttering in agreement.

"We can't do that," another voice rang out. I looked up and saw A. J. Kissinger wheel his big buckskin around as he could confront the others. All of them, especially Ed Gilger, hung their heads in shame. I don't particularly like Kissinger. He's a brusque, arrogant man who always has to be right. But this time I had to agree with him.

"He's right, men," I chimed in. "Ralph and Irene are depending on us to find their baby. Now, who's gonna give me a horse?"

Before anyone could reply, we heard the rattle of trace, the creak of wheels, and the snort of horses coming down the road toward us. It was too dark to identify them right away, but we could make out a group of riders escorting a wagon out of the gloaming. "That you, Sheriff?" a voice called out.

"Aye. Who's there?"

They advanced and I discerned it was another group who'd split off earlier from our posse when we came to a forking of the road.

"Who's that with you?" I asked, walking over to join them and gazing up at the driver. He sat hunched over on his seat. The man was pale and dust-covered. He had a rag wrapped around one hand. There was a bruise on his cheek, and he appeared to be nursing a split lip.

"Maybe a kidnapper," one of the men said.

"That right, mister?"

His eyes flashed in a bit of light as he swiveled them to meet my stare. "I haint no kidnapper. I haint done nothin'."

"He's got blood on his clothes," another of his captors told me.

"Sunbitch," Kissinger growled, urging the buckskin up closer. "You kilt that child."

"I haint never. I never seen no child. You got the wrong man."

"Then where'd the blood come from?"

He spun around to face me, holding up the hand with the rag. "Told them. I cut myself in my camp this morning. I was choppin' wood, the ax hit a knot and bunged me. Hurt like a bugger. Thought I might of lost a thumb."

"And did you?"

"Nah. But it were a bad cut. Took forever to stop the bleeding."

"So if you didn't steal no child and didn't do nothing bad why were you in such an all-fired hurry to get away?" Kissinger asked.

It was a question I would have asked, and it irritated me to have the man butt in. "I was told you turned around in front of the Purcell house and drove fast in the opposite direction. Sounds suspicious to me. Where were you going? What was your big hurry to get away from the scene of the crime?"

"I don't even know where that place is. I suddenly felt poorly. Thought maybe my cut got infected. I just wanted to go home."

"And where is that?"

"Next county over." He jerked his head at the riders circling his wagon. "Been there by now if'n they hadn't stopped me."

Kissinger leaned forward in his saddle, seized the fellow by an arm, and threw him off the seat. "You're a damned liar," he said.

The man thudded to the ground between us, groaned, and rolled over with his hands raised before him. "Please. Don't hurt me no more. I haint done nothin'."

"Then you better quick tell us what you done with that baby," Kissinger blurted.

"Told you, I haint done nothin'," the man said, rising to his knees and struggling to stand. He peered from Kissinger to me, then back again as though struggling to determine which of us posed the most danger to him. His body shook like a man taken with the cold, though it was a warm evening.

A tree limb cracked back in the bush and startled several of the horses. One of them snapped at Kissinger's mount, which bucked and swung around. The suspect took advantage of the opportunity and bolted between the horses, heading for the woods. "Hold on, you. Stop!" I shouted.

A ball whistled past my ear, and I felt its wind before hearing the sound. It struck the man. He gave a little moan, pitching forward on his face in the brush.

Brandishing the revolver I hadn't even known he carried, Kissinger urged his mount forward. I followed on shaking legs and bent beside the victim. There was nothing more he would tell us, and I didn't even know the poor fellow's name. I glowered up at Kissinger, who sat astride his horse like the hero of the moment. "What did you do that for?"

He shrugged. "You rather he got away?"

I rose and seized his bridle. The horse snorted, trying to shake its head. "He wouldn't have got far. Give me that damned gun."

"What for? You gonna arrest me? On what charge?"

"We'll see if the magistrate will accept manslaughter for starters."

Kissinger stared at me for a long moment, and I thought he might resist. Then he relented and handed over the weapon. "I was just tryin' to help," he said.

"If he knew anything about the child, he'll not tell us now."

I had the boys load the stranger's body into the back of his wagon, and we started our slow way back to town. I dreaded the fact there was naught I could tell Charlie's folks and I felt sick about the fate of the man Kissinger had killed. He didn't deserve to die like that even if he'd taken the child. If he had a family, they would need to be notified. That was never a task I cherished but it had to be done, and it was my responsibility.

It was full dark by the time I stepped up on the porch of the Purcell home. My deputy Cyrus volunteered to take the body to Follmer's funeral parlor. I'd asked those of the posse who could to join me in the morning for another search. I was considering just where to look as I knocked on the door.

The door popped open, and I staggered back in shock. There before me stood Ralph, cradling little Charlie in his arms.

Ralph grinned, stepped aside, and beckoned for me to come on in the house. "Sorry to be such a bother, Sheriff," he said. "Had you out there roamin' around all day and there was no need. Charlie was found right after you left. Little scamp was over in Luther Gilger's barn playin' with some newborn kittens. Don't that beat all?"

Follow the further adventures of Syl and his friends
in *The Bartered Body*.

───◦❧ ABOUT THE AUTHOR ❧◦───

J. R. LINDERMUTH

A retired newspaper editor, J. R. Lindermuth is now librarian of his
county historical society where he assists patrons with research and
genealogy. He writes the Sheriff Tilghman historical crime series.
He has published other novels and two regional histories. His short
stories and articles have appeared in a variety of magazines. He is a
member of International Thriller Writers and is a past vice president
of the Short Mystery Fiction Society.

Stealing First

BY J.B. MANHEIM

"I have seventy-five," sang the auctioneer, a somewhat dowdy fellow named Henry Benedict. "Do I hear eighty?"

One of the three bidders still in the running, a man in his thirties whom Henry did not recall having seen before, raised his paddle.

"The gentleman to my left bids eighty thousand dollars. Do I hear ninety?"

The auction room at Benedict Estate Sales was old and musty, more often the venue for disposing of ancient china and silver services, Depression glass pieces, mixed pottery, antique farm implements, and art of the dogs-playing-poker variety. But every so often a local collector passed away, and the heirs, if there were any, felt more comfortable dealing with a local estate bundler than with one of the outside firms. Henry's long-standing arrangements—he preferred to call them associations—with the local attorneys who handled most of the estates and trusts in the area often reinforced that comfort level. That was precisely how the lot currently on the dais came in.

On the small stage beside the auctioneer was a display of ten baseball bats, all quite old. What set them apart was the fact that each one was autographed by its original owner, and each owner had been one of the first ten men, pitchers excluded, who had been inducted into the Base-ball Hall of Fame—each one of them by 1939 when the Hall first opened its doors. Every one of those names was a household word in its day, and some remained so even now. Ty Cobb, Babe Ruth, Honus Wagner,

Nap Lajoie, Tris Speaker, Cap Anson, Eddie Collins, Buck Ewing, Lou Gehrig, Willie Keeler. Henry had done his best to advertise the sale, and obviously there were a couple of heavy hitters among the bidders. But he was simply not set up for all the rich buyers and fancy advertising that the big auction houses offered, and he knew in his heart of hearts that this pile of wood was worth far more than he was likely to bring in. Still, the twenty percent commission on a number like those he was now hearing . . . well, that would make his year.

The bidding reached a hundred and twenty thousand dollars before the pace slowed to a crawl. Henry did his best to bleed out one more set of offers, but none was forthcoming.

"Going once at one hundred twenty thousand . . . Going twice at one twenty . . . Fair warning . . ." He threw that last one in because he'd heard it at some of the high-end auctions he'd attended, and it seemed to add a bit of appropriate class to this particular sale. Then he dropped the gavel. "Sold to the man on my left, paddle number eighty-four, for one hundred twenty thousand dollars."

The room exploded in applause, which the buyer acknowledged with a modest smile and a nod. As Henry's assistant collected and removed the bats and prepared for the next item in the sale, an old butter churn, the buyer stood and worked his way to the outside of his row, then turned toward the table where the auction clerk waited to accept his payment and conclude the sale. He opened the small briefcase he'd been carrying and took out an envelope that contained several cashier's checks drawn on a Michigan bank. He pulled out two checks in the amount of fifty thousand dollars, and two more, each in the amount of twenty thousand dollars, endorsed them, and placed them on the table. That left him four thousand dollars short of what he owed once the buyer's premium was included in the tab, so he reached into the briefcase and produced another, larger envelope, from which he drew out a stack of hundred-dollar bills. He counted off forty of these, which he added to the pile of paper on the table. He pushed the checks and bills across to the clerk, who had been watching this process with interest verging on awe. This sort of thing just didn't happen at Benedict, at least not in the years she had been working there. By the time she had confirmed the count,

Henry's assistant had arrived with the prize of the day, which he had partially wrapped with craft paper to keep the bats together for transport, while being careful to leave enough of each one visible to allow the buyer to confirm his purchase. He also handed the buyer a sheaf of papers representing the provenance of each bat.

The auction was still going strong when the buyer accepted his receipt, the authentication file, and his purchase, closed and grasped his briefcase, and left the building.

* * *

The number that had come up on his cell phone as it rang was not a familiar one, but Adam was used to receiving calls from strangers, so he didn't hesitate to answer.

"Hello," he said, sliding the green icon to the right. "This is Adam."

"Mr. Wallace," said a male voice on the other end of the connection. "My name is Trace Strong. I got your number from your publisher. I hope you don't mind. Thank you for taking my call."

"Sure," replied Adam. "What can I do for you?" He was half expecting a solicitation for something—a new credit card, an extended warranty on his car, or perhaps a charity he'd never heard of. What he heard, though, was something a bit different.

"Mr. Wallace, I have a business proposition for you, a writing project I am hoping to interest you in. I'm not sure where you are located, but I'd really like a chance to come visit with you and see if I can interest you in what I want to propose. Would that be possible?"

Half of life, thought Adam, is timing, and Strong's was pretty good. Adam was, in fact, between projects at the moment, and you just never knew how or when something good would come along.

"Can you tell me something about your project?" he said to the phone.

"I'd rather do that in person," came Strong's reply. "But I am not making a random request. I've read all three of your recent books, the ones about the various baseball mysteries. Now, I don't have a mystery, or even a quest, but my project does have to do with some of the same baseball history you've been writing about the last few years. I really do think, or at least I really hope, that I can capture your interest."

Now, two weeks later, Strong sat across from Adam in the living room of the farmhouse he shared with his wife, Liz, and their young son, Hef, in upstate New York just a couple of miles south of Cooperstown. The farm had come down through Liz's family along with a landscaping business in town. And as the couple had discovered inadvertently a few years back when they had met as Adam was working on solving his first baseball-related mystery, along with that legacy had come responsibility for guarding access to a secret archive filled with baseball's deepest and darkest secrets, entrusted to the family four generations earlier by a small band of men devoted to protecting the reputation of the game.

"A couple of months ago," his visitor was saying, "my dad passed away. He had a long fight with cancer, so it was a blessing in its way. Anyway, as you probably know, when that happens, the family members left behind have to sort through the dead person's belongings. And since I was his only child, that's all fallen mainly onto me. So, I've been going through a lot of boxes full of old keepsakes—photos, graduation programs, and so forth. And I came across one thing that really set my head spinning. I'd forgotten all about it, but when I found it again in one of those boxes, well, a flood of memories came rushing in. And that's sort of what I'm here to talk with you about.

"I know you've been writing about baseball for the last few years. Have you ever heard of something called the Baseball Grand Tour?"

"You mean the thing where people drive around the country and try to visit every big-league ballpark?"

"That's the one."

"I know some people do that. But I've never really thought about it very much. Never saw the appeal. Why do you ask?"

"Well, when I was a kid—I don't know, maybe eight or ten when we started—my dad and my Uncle Jasper started taking me with them. And we'd drive around the country, maybe two or three cities each summer, and we'd go visit the ballparks. That was back in the '70s. I'm sure we never got to anywhere near all of them, and I don't remember them ever talking about trying to do that, but we did visit a lot of parks. I remember the trips really well. Uncle Jasper had this black '61 Ford Falcon van—those were the ones they started calling the Econoline a year or two later. He put a big engine in it and fixed it up real nice. Fancy red leather interior. And he and my dad would load up the back end, and we'd pile in and off we'd go on these road trips.

"For Dad and my uncle, those were actually working trips. They had a business making and selling Halloween costumes. And it was a pretty seasonal business, as you can imagine. Every fall and winter, they'd spend time designing and manufacturing the next year's line of costumes. Then they'd travel around in the summer with samples and take orders for the coming October. Mostly around the Midwest, but they'd branch out to the east some years as well. You'd think with all the small shops and one-off places they sold to, that'd be a pretty marginal living, but they must have had a real knack for it. We weren't what you'd call rich by any means, but we lived well enough. Jasper had a heart attack and died a few years ago.

"What I had forgotten, until I came across it in that box, was that during all those years I had kept a kind of journal of our ballpark visits. Not a lot to it, really, as I discovered paging back through the thing, but still, a nice little find that set me into a bit of a reverie. I never had the time to do anything like that with my boys when they were growing up. They're both off in college now. Don't get me wrong. I went to my share of plays and concerts and ballgames and the like. But we never did anything on the scale of that tour of the ballparks, anything they can look back on someday like I'm doing.

"Well, sooner or later, I expect there'll be some grandkids. Chances are I'll be too old to take them on a trek around the ballparks or the National Parks or whatever they're interested in—to make any sort of Grand Tour. So, I was thinking that it might be nice if they had the chance to read about mine—about their granddad's great adventure. I don't think they'd get much out of that kid's journal that I kept. But something more formal and more polished, some kind of private book or some such that tells the story of those trips, would be a nice family heirloom that I could leave for them.

"Problem is, I don't have either the time or the skill to produce such a book. And that's why I wanted to talk to you. I can pay you reasonably well to . . . I guess, do some sort of oral history interview to help me pull up some details from those old memories, maybe read the journal, do some other research on the parks to fill the thing out, then write it all up. Tell the story. I'm not talking a big book, but I'd like a nice one that we could publish just for the family. And I really think you're the guy to write it."

"Well," said Adam, his mind trying to work the problem in real time, "it's certainly different from anything else I've written . . . Don't get me wrong. I think it's a beautiful thing you're trying to do. But I've never really done much writing of memoirs, which is really what you're talking about here, let alone memoirs of a young boy.

"On the other hand," said Adam, his voice drifting away as his thoughts tossed back and forth. "Listen, Trace, tell you what. If it's okay with you, I'd like to take a few days to think about this, and about what a project of that sort that might look like. How I'd go about it, how much time it might take, what the product might look like. Maybe until early next week? Honestly, I don't know where I'll come down on it. Would that be okay with you?"

* * *

Randy and Jasper Strong had been manufacturing semi-disposable kids' costuming and flogging it to bottom-feeding retailers around the Midwest for a decade before they hit upon that one great idea, the one they'd been searching for all along. But eventually it came to them. And the more they thought about it, the better it looked.

"We know these towns like the backs of our hands," Randy said to his brother one day in 1969 or 1970. "We know these people, and they know us. We're already driving hundreds of miles and hitting all of these cities. It's just who we are, who they know us to be. 'Oh, yeah. The costume guys. Sure, we see them all the time, every summer around now.' Hell, Jasper, we're practically family for some of those people. And now, well, Trace is getting to be old enough where we could just bring him along and spend some time with him at this ballpark or that. It's a perfect cover."

"You're right. We could really get to know those ballparks, see how things really work there. And we could have a great time with Trace while we do it. Let him see some of the country. But do you think he's old enough to stay by himself in one of those motel rooms for maybe a night or two in each city?"

"Jasper," Randy replied, laughing even as he was scowling at his brother. "You are such a damned bachelor! But to your point, yeah. If we can find a place with a couple of pinball machines, hell, he'd probably be *happier* if we just went off for a few hours and left him on his own."

* * *

"You visited these ballparks, what, about fifty years ago?" Adam began. "And you saw them from the perspective of a kid. And the rest of the trip—the long drives on two-lane highways, the local greasy spoons and fast-food joints and hotels or wherever it was you stayed, and the roadside attractions if you stopped for any of those. But today it's all different. The parks are different, probably very different, but so is everything else about the trips. Interstates running everywhere, national hotel chains on the highways, and McDonalds on every corner. If you were to make that trip today, it wouldn't be the same experience. But I can make that trip, or at least revisit the part of the so-called Grand Tour you actually covered back then. And I have a little boy who's into baseball—I mean, he's growing up in Cooperstown, for goodness sake—and has the sort of unique vantage point on the game that you get from living here. He's a little younger than you were back in the day, but he's getting to an age where he might appreciate and remember the trip, or at least where it would be worth trying.

"So, here's what I propose. Rather than doing the limited personal and private memoir you were thinking of, let me write a real road book. Let me take your experience and mine it for everything I can, just like you suggested, but let me also take the same journey with my son half a century later and compare the two. It would give you the legacy stories you want for your family, and it would give me a chance to create a legacy for my own boy. Plus, I think we could have a book that was about a great deal more than just baseball and ballparks—maybe about how the game and the country have changed together over all that time. What do you think?"

Trace paused for a moment, then replied. "Wow. Adam, I'm blown away. That's a fantastic idea. I would never have thought of that, but I really like it."

* * *

Truth be told, Adam wasn't getting much he could use from the scribbled notes in Trace's old journal. The ramblings of a ten- or eleven-year-old boy told him more about ballpark food, mainly hot dogs, and players' names, than about the various trips the trio took, the stadiums, or the other sights and sounds of their great adventure. The only really useful information for the purpose at hand was the travel itinerary. Trace had been diligent in recording dates, the cities visited, and the matchups he saw on the field.

- Friday, May 21, 1971; New York at Cleveland
- Tuesday, May 25, 1971; Cincinnati at Pittsburgh
- Friday, May 28, 1971; Houston at Cincinnati
- Friday, May 19, 1972; Mets at Philadelphia
- Tuesday, May 23, 1972; Cleveland at New York Yankees
- Friday, May 26, 1972; Milwaukee at Boston
- Friday, June 2, 1972; Oakland at Baltimore
- Tuesday, June 6, 1972; California at Detroit
- Tuesday, May 29, 1973; Cincinnati at St. Louis
- Friday, June 1, 1973; Atlanta at Chicago Cubs
- Monday, June 18, 1973; Boston at Milwaukee [2 the next day]
- Thursday, June 21, 1973; California at Minnesota

It was easy enough to find box scores and writeups of the games themselves and even reports of the daily weather for each date, but this still left Adam with a quandary: how to add context to fill out the story. For that, he simply expanded his reading of the local newspapers from the time of each visit, looking at the days just before and just after each game that Trace had attended.

* * *

While Adam was busily at work on the book project and preparing for his own road trip, Trace returned to his home in Grand Rapids, Michigan, and as time permitted, continued digging through the old boxes his father had left behind. It was two or three weeks later, when he came to the bottom of the next to last box, that he saw the small cardboard envelope, one similar to the type that banks give their customers to store a safety deposit box key. But rather than one of the local banks, this one advertised a self-storage company two towns over. When he opened the clasp and turned it over, out fell, not a key, but a piece of paper, on which someone—presumably his father—had written the number 674 in large print, and beneath it, in smaller print, what appeared to be a four-digit combination.

This is strange, he thought. *No telling how long it's been here. Or why. Guess I'll check it out when I have a chance.*

* * *

Adam liked to do things systematically, so he started with the Cleveland game in May 1971 and looked at the local papers from the 19th to the 24th. Nothing particularly remarkable, he decided. Just the usual run of robberies, traffic accidents, a couple of murders. Life in the big city in the '70s. The only oddity was that one of the robberies actually happened at the ballpark. Somebody had broken into the ticket office on the 22nd and made off with the night's receipts. But he remembered that old ballpark—the Mistake By The Lake people used to call it. It was in a really bad part of town and that was probably a common occurrence. On to Pittsburgh.

* * *

"Liz," Adam said over dinner that evening, "do you remember a couple of years ago when we were down in the archive? Back before we knew what it was and why it was there, and that we weren't supposed to be poking around in it?" Liz had come across a set of keys and a logbook her late father had kept in the recesses of a drawer in his office desk, and the couple had spent weeks searching for the matching door, which they later found completely by accident. The door led to a tunnel, and the tunnel to a secret trove of documents and artifacts. It was only later that they were informed of the true nature of the secret her family had guarded for so long and admonished for having violated a cardinal rule when they entered the archive itself.

"Yes. How could I forget?" she replied.

"And do you remember that one of the files down there had a bunch of newspaper clippings and, I think, maybe a detective's report or two about a string of robberies at the ballparks back fifty or sixty years ago. They never figured out who the robbers were, and they covered it all up so nobody would see just how vulnerable they were? Bought some time, I think, to beef up their safes or their security or whatever they did. And then it stopped?"

"I remember something like that, but just vaguely."

"Well, I have a coincidence for you. I'm doing this memoir project for Trace Strong, right? From these trips to ballparks he used to take with his dad and his uncle back in the early '70s. And from what he's told me, they would all go to a game at the local ballpark one night, and his uncle would go off and wander around the stadium, stretch his legs or what-ever. Then the next night or two, the adults would park him in a bowling alley or a motel room and disappear for a few hours. He assumed they were visiting customers and selling costumes, which was the business purpose of all these trips, or maybe at some bar having a drink. They'd roll in late at night, then move on to the next city the next day—three or four or five cities each year."

"Sounds very exciting," Liz deadpanned.

"Well, for a young kid, it would have been exactly that. But here's the thing. I started reading the local newspapers for each of these little junkets and I stumbled across something kind of interesting. There were twelve stops on the Great Strong Mystery Tour over three years; and at eight of them, a day or two after Trace, his dad, and his uncle attended a ballgame, someone broke into the same ballpark and stole the receipts from one or two games, whatever was on hand. They seemed to know exactly where to look, almost as if they had cased the place and figured out its routines. The papers didn't have much detail, and it almost seemed like they were playing it down, but that would have been thousands of dollars each time, so a pretty big deal. And we can't be sure the same wasn't also true in the cities that had no news reports at all.

"I'll tell you. I would love to go back down into the archive and check out that file. I'd almost bet these things match up."

"Adam, don't even think about that!" Liz exclaimed. "You *know* we can't do that."

"Yeah, of course I know. I'm just saying. But here's the real dilemma. If what I suspect is true, what do I tell Trace?"

* * *

Speaking of Trace, curiosity had finally worked its will, and he had just arrived at the office of the storage-locker company, where he was explaining to the clerk who he was and how he had found this locker number and combination.

"This happens sometimes," said the clerk, who had worked in the same job for several years. "Let me look up this locker number on the computer."

After some rapid keystrokes and a muttered, "hmmm," he turned back to Trace. "Can I see some ID please?"

Trace removed his driver's license from his wallet and handed it to the clerk.

"You're in luck, Mister, ah, Strong. The box is in the name of Raymond T. Cobb. I don't know if that was your father's name, but whoever this Cobb fellow is, or was, he did list you as a co-lessee of the locker. So, you can just go ahead and have a look. You said you have a combination to the lock. If that works, you're in. But if not, we'll have to get the manager down here to figure out if you have the right to cut the lock. Above my pay grade.

"Take the elevator there to the third floor and follow the signs for Corridor 6. The rest should be easy."

Trace followed the clerk's directions, turning left as directed when the elevator reached the third floor. Toward the far end of the corridor, he found the locker he was looking for, number 674, which was, as expected, secured with a heavy-duty combination lock. It had been years since he had worked one of these, but he remembered the basics. Right three times past zero, stopping at the first number, and so forth. Reaching the fourth and last number on his father's note, Trace held his breath and pulled downward on the lock. It gave way. He pulled up the garage-style door of the locker and, noticing a switch on the left-side wall, turned on the interior lights.

What he saw left him speechless. The locker was lined with shelves, and every shelf was filled with . . . was he seeing this correctly? . . . autographed baseballs in plastic cubes, seemingly rare baseball cards in graded cases, baseball jerseys signed by . . . really? In the very middle was a barrel filled with what looked like antique bats. What was all this? Where did it come from? Trace was . . . confused would be an understatement. There weren't enough Halloween costumes in the world to pay for all of this stuff. How did . . .

Just then his cell phone rang.

* * *

"Trace? Hey. Adam Wallace here."

"Adam! How are you? I was just . . ."

Adam interrupted his client in mid-sentence. "Trace," he began, "I've been doing some research for the book and, well, I don't know how to tell you this, but . . ."

You can follow the adventures of Adam Wallace, the villainous Commissioner of Baseball, young night-school-trained attorney Andy Dennum, and their fellow cast members from the first book of the series (2023), *This Never Happened: The Mystery Behind the Death of Christy Mathewson*, to the very last (2025), *Field of Schemes*.

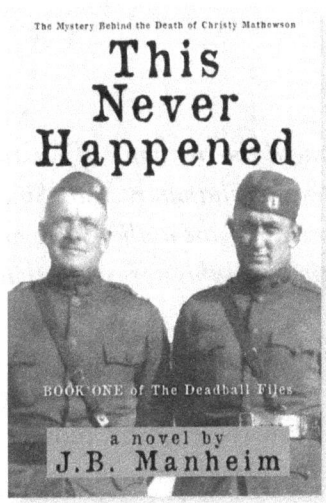 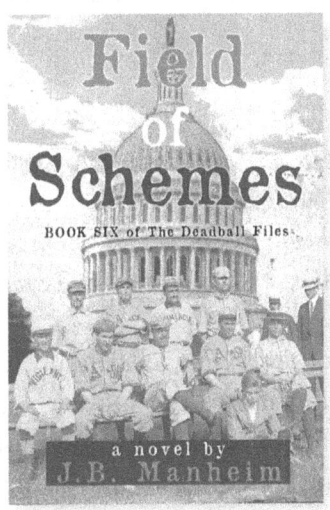

ABOUT THE AUTHOR
J.B. MANHEIM

J.B. Manheim is author of the award-winning Milford House series, *The Deadball Files*, a collection of present-day mysteries and legal thrillers grounded in the events and personalities of baseball in the early years of the twentieth century. Manheim was founding director of the School of Media & Public Affairs at The George Washington University. He is a past chair of the political communication section of the American Political Science Association and was 1995 Professor the Year for the District of Columbia.

Teeth the Color of Lightning

BY ADAM SMITH

AUTHOR NOTE: The Americans changed the city name of Charles Town, South Carolina, to Charleston after the Revolutionary War. Since today's readers know this historical gem as Charleston, the author chose to use that name. Also, the Wacataw Indians mentioned in this story are fictional.

This morning, Colonel Balfour, Commandant of Charleston, directed me to investigate the murder of five black men. They were among twenty-one black artisans to vanish from the city this month: six free men and fifteen runaways—carpenters, blacksmiths, masons, a tailor, and an estate cook.

"Charlotte," Colonel Balfour said, his arched eyebrows framing his sympathetic expression, "Winslow is one of them."

Winslow Welby, a carpenter and free man, was my friend. I had recommended Balfour hire him two weeks ago.

"One of the dead?" I asked, dreading the answer.

He shook his head. "The missing. He disappeared a week ago. Find him. Find all of them."

Children had discovered the five bodies while playing in the marshes of Cummings Creek. The British Army asked locals to identify the dead, stored in a morgue tent near their barracks off Boundary Street. Without ventilation, the fumes in the tent hung as thick and hostile as gunpowder smoke. My assistant, Heathcliff—a young British subject a few years my junior—and I examined the wounds. The men had been stabbed repeatedly in the back, and the abrasions around their wrists and ankles were telltale injuries from iron shackles. The killers had removed the restraints, but deep furrows suggested the men had been running to escape their captors, who had knifed their slower prey rather than risk drawing attention with gunfire.

The British had promised slaves their freedom when the Yankees eventually lost the war, leading thousands to flee both rebel and loyalist plantations. This exodus was further hastened by British seizures of rebel plantations, prompting more runaways to seek refuge in Charleston and nearby camps. We suspected an angry plantation owner, or a gang of them, having lost everything, was retaliating by kidnapping the most valued black workers and killing them. The victims' identical deaths and their similar professions warranted that likelihood.

The missing men, including the murder victims, lived on either George Street or Anson Street, a neighborhood of black artisans. We decided to surveil that neighborhood. I told my driver to position the covered carriage so my side faced George Street and Heathcliff's overlooked Anson Street. An hour or so into our vigil, Heathcliff tapped my arm.

"Look at that grimy boy," he said, pointing out his window. "He's just standing there."

A barefoot urchin stood behind a sycamore tree in an undeveloped lot, spying on residents. He never played with other children who wandered the street. Eventually, he pulled something from his pocket, looked around, and left. We followed on foot. On Broad Street, he spotted us and took off, snaking through the crowd so expertly that we had to race to keep up. I lagged slightly because of my dress and heeled mules, but Heathcliff's footing was nimble. When the boy darted under a horse, scampered through an open doorway, and dashed across a foyer toward a flight of stairs, Heathcliff wasn't far behind.

The second floor housed one of Charleston's more upscale taverns. The Crow's Nest overlooked the Exchange and Custom House on East Bay Street and the bustling docks on the Cooper River. The main room had two long tables and five smaller ones. Neither the urchin nor Heathcliff was in this crowded hall of men and drifting pipe smoke. I stepped into the neighboring room. No patrons occupied this smaller space, but the urchin stood in a shadowy corner, staring at me. Then, as if by sorcery, the boy rose off the floor.

It wasn't sorcery, of course. Heathcliff had bunched the lad's hair in his fist. The boy squealed, his hands clawing at Heathcliff's grip behind his head. I patted the air, instructing Heathcliff to lower him. Instead, Heathcliff hurled the child onto the floor with enough brutality to vibrate my feet.

Violence for Heathcliff was as effortless and natural as coughing. I preferred to handle the child with kindness. I squatted and cupped the boy's cheek in my palm, but he tried to bite my thumb. Heathcliff planted his boot on the urchin's chest, and the boy's squirming arms and legs reminded me of an insect panicking in the darkening shadow of a crushing heel. I frisked his pants pockets and pulled out a folded note. I showed Heathcliff: "75 more to Mary Stone."

"Seventy-five what?" Heathcliff said. "Spanish dollars?"

Of course, Heathcliff focused on the money.

"Who's Mary Stone?" I asked the boy.

He shoved Heathcliff's heel, and Heathcliff, flailing his arms for balance, fell on his derriere. The boy crawled frantically away, sprang to his feet, and flew out the door. The floorboards carried the beat of his feet on the stairs. We returned to the main room.

"He was here to meet someone," I told Heathcliff. "Stand by the exit, and don't let anyone leave."

I approached the service counter, where a man stood before a wall of neatly organized pewter mugs. He held a used white clay pipe, carefully snapping off as little of the slobbered mouthpiece as possible. The shorter the stem, the less he could charge for its rental—a perfect instance of men's lips ruining the value of something.

"Pardon me," I said. "Can I use a quill and paper, please?"

I told him I was a royal inspector for the Board of Police, speaking loudly so everyone would hear.

"I don't have any," he said.

"Are you the owner?"

He nodded.

"Those perfect rows of mugs," I said, "and that meticulously snapped pipe stem tell me you keep thorough inventory and sales records. Should I have my friend Byron Bêche, the royal tax assessor, inspect your ledgers?"

He hurried through an open door next to him and returned with paper, an ink well, and a quill. And a smile. I went from table to table and gathered the names of twenty-three men, including the streets each lived on, except for one fellow. He refused to comply. He eyed my bosom and grinned—an obscene facial relief sculpted by lewd thoughts.

I took my Order of Compliance from the satchel I wore around my waist. As a royal inspector, I had special powers, including this official decree issued by Colonel Balfour: it stated that anyone not cooperating with my investigations risked execution. The Order was a persuasive tool, especially since men tended to dismiss me because of my sex and age. I was only 21.

As the man leaned in to read, Heathcliff stepped away from the door and joined me.

"I'm a private banker," the man told Heathcliff. "I don't answer to a woman. Well, not one I'm not married to!" He guffawed.

Men at his table joined his merriment.

"The Provost Dungeon is filled with rebel traitors," Heathcliff told the man. "I'd wager everything I own that a private banker like you would last about two minutes in there."

"My name's Samuel Tiller," the man said, raising his chin. He shifted his gaze to me. "Why do you have a French accent if you're a royal inspector?"

"Because I'm from Québec City," I said. "Now it's your turn. Where do you live?"

"Watch what you say, Tiller," a man said. "She's half Wacataw. She'll take your scalp!"

Abrupt laughter shocked the still air, and fists banged the tabletops. Samuel Tiller chuckled as he raised his mug to his puckered lips. Heathcliff stepped closer to him.

"Everyone knows I live on Meeting Street," Samuel Tiller said, winking at Heathcliff.

I wrote that down.

"Who was that boy?" I asked Samuel Tiller.

He shook his head, frowning. "What boy?"

Heathcliff addressed the room. "Did anyone recognize that boy?"

No one spoke.

I turned and asked the crowd, "Who's Mary Stone?"

Pursed lips and raised eyebrows contorted most faces, but no one answered. The men started talking with each other, sipping mugs, sucking pipes, and blowing out tobacco clouds.

I pointed my chin at Heathcliff. "Let's go." Our feet drummed the stairs out of sync, mine tapping the steps much faster than his plod. When he finally stepped onto Broad Street, I said, "I bet Byron will know."

"Know what?" Heathcliff said gruffly. "Who this slut Mary Stone is?" He was losing patience with the investigation, despite knowing Winslow's disappearance was personal to me. He'd rather have been turning a profit somewhere in the city. Money was all Heathcliff thought about. "Why don't we cross-reference the names on that list you just wrote, with our little secret?" He lowered his head, smiling, and shadows filled his eye sockets. "You know, the Book of Sins."

The "Book of Sins" was his nickname for a valuable secret we shared: I owned a blackmail diary that once belonged to the most corrupt businessman in Charleston. It listed the crimes, indiscretions, and perversions of numerous folks in South Carolina, including British Army officers, tavern proprietors, artisans, sea captains, plantation owners—and me. That businessman, having opened my private letters to my husband, had copied my desires and conjugal fantasies. I obtained the diary two months ago, in March 1781, after someone tortured the cad to death.

We used it once to enrich ourselves.

I hid the diary from Heathcliff because he would otherwise abuse it.

"Never mind that," I said curtly. "I've got to find Winslow." I hurried ahead of him.

Byron Bêche wasn't just a royal tax assessor. He was also a port inspector. He prided himself on knowing everyone in Charleston. We entered the Exchange and Custom House, where he kept an office. He sat behind his desk, spreading his arms as we stepped inside.

"Charlotte," he said. "What a pleasure to see you."

He didn't acknowledge Heathcliff. He knew better.

"Likewise," I said, sitting in one of two upholstered armchairs opposite his desk. Heathcliff didn't sit. "I'm looking for a plantation owner named Mary Stone. I suspect she's a rebel widow." I explained our investigation. "I think she's getting revenge for losing her plantation."

"I haven't seen the recent roster of sequestered plantations," Byron said, glancing at Heathcliff, "but I did inspect a merchant ship named *Mary Stone*. It's carrying indigo, rice, and turpentine to Barbados. I told the captain he should store the turpentine on a lower deck because if any spilled during a storm, it would spoil the entire inventory. He has everything crammed in the upper hold."

"Did you check the lower deck?" Heathcliff asked.

"Of course. It was empty."

"Wouldn't that make the ship top-heavy?" I asked.

"I asked that, too." Byron shrugged. "The captain said he's got field stones for ballast."

"Who owns the *Mary Stone*?" I said.

"Samuel Tiller. He owns three merchant ships and two privateers."

Heathcliff poked my shoulder. "That's the sot from the tavern."

I held the list aloft, to show Heathcliff that Tiller lived on Meeting Street.

"Has the *Mary Stone* sailed?" I asked.

Byron shook his head, pointing his thumb out the window behind him. "It's anchored on the other side of the Cooper by the prison ships."

"Why so far away?"

"I haven't the foggiest."

"When was this?"

"When was what?"

"Your inspection."

"Two weeks ago." Byron raised a finger. "Why do I get the feeling you're interrogating me?"

"Maybe I am." I blew Byron a kiss. "Could Tiller have stocked the lower deck with illicit cargo over the last two weeks?"

"Sure." Byron frowned, tilting his head to the side. "But if he got caught, Balfour would seize everything he owns. Look, the captain told me he's got everything on the upper hold for easy offloading."

I thanked Byron, and we left.

"So the note means to add 75 men to the Mary Stone," Heathcliff said. "Tiller's going to sell them in Barbados."

"And he anchored the Mary Stone near the prison ships so no one will pay attention if they scream for help, thinking they're rebels."

"We should hurry," Heathcliff said, rushing me across East Bay Street toward The Crow's Nest.

Suddenly, Heathcliff was interested in our investigation.

Tiller wasn't at The Crow's Nest. On Meeting Street, we asked people where Samuel Tiller lived. A middle-aged woman pointed to a wide three-story house with piazzas on each floor. The urchin boy was sitting on the first-floor piazza steps.

"Who's that boy?" I asked her.

"Phillip Tiller," she said. "But he's not really a Tiller."

"What do you mean?"

"He's Samuel's stepson. Phillip's mother died giving birth to Samuel's child five years ago. The baby died, too. But don't feel sorry for Samuel Tiller. He's a disgrace to God, you ask me."

"Why do you say that?"

"That boy. He treats him worse than a stray dog. He never taught him how to read or write, and never takes him to church. Look at the rags he wears. And Samuel's rich."

"Did he ever remarry?" Heathcliff asked, scheming. "Any other children?"

"That's his only heir," the woman said, glancing at Phillip. "Samuel's sister died of smallpox."

"And he deliberately turned that boy into an illiterate wretch?" Heathcliff asked, grinning. He seemed to relish the idea.

The woman nodded, horror bleaching her face as she beheld Heathcliff's dark eyes glowing with delight. I thanked the woman, and she strutted away faster than the strolling pace she had a moment ago.

"That boy couldn't tell you what that note said any more than a carrier pigeon could tell you its message," I told Heathcliff. "Tiller's using him."

Heathcliff took off running. Phillip spotted him and bolted. This time, Heathcliff had a head start. Heathcliff dragged the kicking youngster to me.

"Calm down, Phillip," I said. "I'm not going to hurt you."

"Let me go," he shouted.

"I know your father's been kidnapping black men," I told him.

The boy's struggle to wiggle out of Heathcliff's grip affirmed my suspicion.

"Stop," I said. "You're not in any trouble. I need your help. My friend is missing. He's got dark black skin—darker than most—with high cheekbones and beautiful teeth the color of lightning. He's tall, too, and stands out in a crowd. Did Samuel kidnap him?"

"Teeth the color of lightning," the boy repeated, smiling, remembering.

I smiled, too. "Did Samuel take him?"

He nodded. He pursed his lips, looking at my feet. "He was here to build bookshelves or something in the study, but then some men took him away."

"Is that why you were spying on Anson Street?" I said. "To help your father kidnap—"

"I wasn't spying," he shouted. "I was supposed to give that note to a man. But he never showed up."

"What man?"

"A white man with a red handkerchief hanging out his right pocket."

"What's he do?"

"How do I know?"

"He got a name?"

"Are you stupid? I just said I don't know him."

Heathcliff chuckled, amused that the boy questioned my intellect.

"Is your father home now?" I asked.

He shook his head. "He's going to beat me when he finds out you took that note." Phillip tried to shrug Heathcliff's hands off his shoulders. Heathcliff let go of him. He didn't run. "I overheard him tell his clerk he goes to the runaways' camp outside the city gates, beyond the army tents, and tricks them by offering them work. But I don't know where he keeps them all."

I thanked Phillip, and he moseyed back to the steps.

"No ship can transport passengers—white, black, or Indian—" I told Heathcliff, "who aren't already part of a ship's crew, without permission from Colonel Balfour. I'll have the Royal Navy board that ship and I'll seize it if they're there."

"Damn the Royal Navy," Heathcliff said. His dark eyes narrowed. "I'll take control of that ship. With this war restricting sea travel, a boat-load of artisans must fetch a king's ransom in Barbados."

I swooned, swept by a sudden wave of anger. "You know Winslow personally, Heathcliff. How can you condemn our friend to a life of misery?"

He looked at me as if I had spat in his face, growling, "His misery is nothing compared to mine. Besides, they're mostly runaways. They deserve their fate."

Heathcliff genuinely didn't care about anyone. He only cared about getting rich. I also wanted to build my wealth, and we used each other to make that happen. Heathcliff's fanatical greed made him a cunning ally, and I valued him because he'd do whatever I asked. But he also did whatever he wanted. At times, dealing with him was like swimming near a waterfall. If I got too close, I wasn't coming back.

"What if I free Winslow?" Heathcliff said. "I'll drop him off some-where on the way."

"He'll tell Balfour. They'll come after you."

"No, he won't tell Balfour anything because he knows you work closely with me. He'd have to betray you. Then you'd have to tell Balfour about me. Then I'd have to tell him about you—but we'd never do that to each other, would we, my sweet?"

Criminal culpability was our bond of loyalty. Heathcliff and I had used that blackmail ledger, our Book of Sins, and my weight as a royal inspector, to blackmail and bankrupt an affluent Charlestonian for sell-ing munitions to rebels. He was a horrible man who worked boys from his orphanages to death scrubbing the hulls of ships, even in winter. The difference between Heathcliff and me was that I refused to harm innocent people. Was he as immoral as the scoundrel we blackmailed?

"I won't do that to those men," I said.

The muscles along Heathcliff's jaw bulged as greed churned his thoughts. He smiled suddenly, having schemed something new. He asked Phillip to join us. Heathcliff squatted and gently held Phillip's hands in his. The most charming fake smile brightened Heathcliff's handsome face.

"I'm sorry for hurting you earlier," Heathcliff said. "Allow me to make amends. Join me for a hearty meal at my favorite tavern."

The boy nodded eagerly, and Heathcliff picked him up. Heathcliff never went to taverns. He didn't imbibe, and he hated to be in the company of others while they ate.

"What are you up to?" I asked.

"We're going to The City Tavern." He leaned in, whispering. "But first, we'll see my estate lawyer. A carrier pigeon with an immense inheritance needs a guardian who can read."

Heathcliff practically skipped along Meeting Street, his boots scraping the dirt with the methodic rhythm of a gravedigger's shovel.

I spoke with a Royal Navy lieutenant at the Exchange and Custom House, requesting a longboat and soldiers sail me across the Cooper River to seize the *Mary Stone*. The officer understood my urgency but said he couldn't possibly organize a ship and soldiers in such short order. He promised to have them by tomorrow morning. Without evidence, I couldn't arrest Tiller. That night, I kept waking up, haunted by the image of Winslow trapped in that ship's dank, dark hold while Tiller—and I—slept in cushioned beds.

In the morning, I went directly to the Exchange and Custom House.

"Charlotte," Byron Bêche said, striding across the lobby. "Why did you send Heathcliff with a crew of thugs and that filthy Tiller boy to inspect the *Mary Stone*?"

"What are you talking about?"

"Heathcliff came back after you left yesterday. He said you told him to inspect the *Mary Stone*. I told him I could save him the trip and show you my itemized list. The bastard told me to shove it up my arse."

I scurried down the back steps to the pier and boarded the closest ship, asking the boatswain for a looking glass. I climbed a high coil of thick rope on the deck and peered through the narrow tube. The *Mary Stone* was gone.

A crowd gathered on the neighboring pier. Someone said soldiers had tried to rouse a sleeping drunk, but the man was dead. I slogged toward them. Two soldiers dragged the body from an embankment onto the dock, and his broken neck allowed his head to loll in every direction. It was Samuel Tiller.

The carrier pigeon's guardian was killing more than two birds with one stone—the bastard was slaughtering the entire flock: Heathcliff would inherit everything Tiller owned, including the *Mary Stone*.

Something jutted from Tiller's mouth. A soldier tugged out what appeared to be a large chicken's foot with a note wound around the ankle bone like a carrier pigeon. He unfurled the scroll.

"What's it say?" a woman shouted.

The soldier wrinkled his nose. "You will find teeth the color of lightning in Savannah."

Charlotte and her ruthless ally Heathcliff investigate
more murders in *The Journey of the Snake*, where she finds
controlling Heathcliff's greed a challenge that
could cost her her life.

⎯⎯❧ ABOUT THE AUTHOR ☙⎯⎯
ADAM SMITH

Adam Smith is an award-winning author and a graduate cum laude
of the University of Arizona. Born and raised in New England, he
lives on Cape Cod. He's an accomplished chef and avid runner. He
regards being handpicked by Dennis Lehane for his novel-writing
workshop at Writers In Paradise as a prized writing honor.

GREAT NEWS FOR BOOK CLUBS

Selected Sunbury Press authors will discuss their books virtually with your group FOR FREE! Plus, you can qualify for a special book club discount.

BOOK CLUB DISCOUNT

Receive a 20% discount when you order 5 or more copies of a single participating title through the Sunbury Press website.

Enter code "BOOKCLUB2025" when checking out to apply the discount.

AUTHOR PARTICIPATION

Many of our authors are available to participate in your book club meeting when you order 5 or more copies of one of their books from Sunbury Press. They will answer questions and/or make a short presentation. Contact the authors through their websites.

BOOK CLUB QUESTIONS

There are book club discussion questions for each book in our program to enliven your book club meeting and foster meaningful conversations. You will find these questions on the participating authors' websites.

HOW TO GET STARTED . . .

Simply place your order using the Sunbury Press Books shopping cart. Purchase at least five copies for the book you wish to discuss with your club. Be sure to enter the discount code. This will trigger an email back to you to make arrangements with the author.

Note: Orders over $100 AFTER discount qualify for FREE SHIPPING.